W9-BNP-623

PRAISE FOR AZTEC RAGE

"*Aztec Rage* is the most extraordinary historical novel to appear in years. It will leave you dazed, shaken, delighted, and moved."

—Douglas Preston, *New York Times* bestselling author of *TyrannosaurCanyon*

"*Aztec Rage* is a major epic, a grand literary canvas of thrills and chills, fire and passion. Even if you think you know Mexico, you will never again look at Mexico the same way. You will look on the Mexican people with new eyes as well, and you will be changed. The final chapter will move you to tears—'I am *Mejicano!*' will ring in your ears forever."

—Kathleen O'Neal Gear and W. Michael Gear, award-winning, *USA Today* bestselling authors of *People of the Moon*

"Big, bold, and bawdy, *Aztec Rage* is a rip-snorting swashbuckler. . . . It's fiction of the grand tradition."

—Stephen Coonts, *New York Times* bestselling author of *Liars and Thieves*

"This is a book that will change your ideas about Mexican history and the whole history of the Americas. It resonates with original research and vivid drama."

—Thomas Fleming, *New York Times* bestselling author of *Liberty! The American Revolution*

"*Aztec Rage* is an extraordinary novel for the accuracy of its history, the vivid voice of its narrator, its sense of drama and joy, and its explication of love and hate, told by a picaresque hero who is as fast with a woman as with his sword. Backdrop for action and adventure is the Mexican Revolution sparked by Father Hidalgo's *grito*—the cry of revolt that engulfs Mexico, and in time South and Central America, and squashes the Spanish empire. Amply anchored in world history and always fun, *Aztec Rage* is a splendid read."

—David Nevin, *New York Times* bestselling author of *Dream West*

FORGE BOOKS BY GARY JENNINGS

Aztec

Journeyer

Spangle

Aztec Autumn

Aztec Blood

Aztec Rage
(with Robert Gleason and Junius Podrug)

Aztec Fire
(with Robert Gleason and Junius Podrug)

Apocalypse 2012
(with Robert Gleason and Junius Podrug)

The 2012 Codex
(with Robert Gleason and Junius Podrug)

Aztec Revenge
(with Junius Podrug)

Visit Gary Jennings at www.garyjennings.net.

• GARY JENNINGS' •

JUNIUS PODRUG

A TOM DOHERTY ASSOCIATES BOOK
NEW YORK

AZTEC REVENGE

A Forge Book
Published by Tom Doherty Associates, LLC
175 Fifth Avenue
New York, NY 10010

www.tor-forge.com

Forge® is a registered trademark of Tom Doherty Associates, LLC.

ISBN 978-0-7653-5626-0

Forge books may be purchased for educational, business, or promotional use. For information on bulk purchases, please contact Macmillan Corporate and Premium Sales Department at 1-800-221-7945, extension 5442, or write specialmarkets@macmillan.com.

First Edition: October 2012
First Mass Market Edition: September 2013

Printed in the United States of America

0 9 8 7 6 5 4 3 2 1

For Hilde, who climbed out of the window;
Carol, who has a heart as big as her native planet Mars;
and Bob, who always has a friend's back covered,
including mine.
Also for Joyce Servis, who kept the memory of Gary alive.

ACKNOWLEDGMENTS

The staff at Tor/Forge have always been champions when it comes to publishing. This time, Whitney Ross deserves special recognition. Deserving special recognition also are the readers who make writing and publishing books a still-living trade.

I was born to hang.

—Juan the Lépero

PART 1

VALLEY OF MEXICO, NEW SPAIN

A.D. 1569

Men are not hanged for stealing horses, but that horses may not be stolen.

—George Savile,
Marquess of Halifax, *Reflections*

ONE

AYYO! ON A horse with a noose around my neck, my hands tied behind my back, and the steed about to be whipped out from under me, I could already feel el diablo's hot claws gripping my ankles tightly, ready to pull me down after the rope strangled me.

I held my legs tight against each side of the stallion's flank, a signal that he would recognize as a command not to bolt. He and I had been through a lot together. We knew each other well—or so I hoped.

The coarse rope—tied to a thick branch overhead that had been chosen to bear my weight without breaking—was biting into my neck, the slipknot choking me, threatening to crush my windpipe and cut off my breathing each time the nervous horse moved.

My wrists were raw from trying to pull and twist my hands out of the bindings. I didn't care if blood ran freely from them so long as it helped get my hands loose, but the hacienda owners—the hacendados—who had captured me had had their vaqueros tie the cords too tight.

As a man of many professions that brought me into close contact with the king's constables—horse thief, bandido, and impersonator of a wealthy caballero, to name a few of my trades—I knew only too well what would happen when my captors swatted the horse's rump with a quirt and caused the spirited stallion to bolt out from under me.

I would be left hanging—literally—but it would not kill me. Not quickly, at least. Dying would take an excruciating amount of time because of the short fall off of the horse. That is what hanging is all about, amigos—the length of the fall before the loop tightens around a person's neck.

Being lynched in the forest by vigilantes meant I would be pulled off the horse as he surged forward and drop only a couple of feet. That would leave me dangling at the end of the rope to slowly suffocate.

Unfortunately, since I am young and strong, it will take perhaps half an hour or more for that coarse rope around my neck to squeeze the life out of me, as I twisted, kicked, and jerked, my face bloated and red, blood foaming out of my mouth, my eyes bulging from their sockets.

Ayyo! Perhaps I should have been a priest instead of a bad man, but that was not the path that the Fates—those three remorseless old crones who decide our destinies—had set me upon. Had they a bit of mercy in their immortal souls they would have seen to it that I fell into the clutches of constables rather than arrogant Spanish horse owners who were only too ready to throw a rope over a branch rather than take the time and effort of getting the authorities involved.

The Spanish viceroy had had gallows erected in the Zócalo, the main square in Mexico City, as a reminder to the indios that he was in control of the colony. The gallows were built high so that when the trapdoor opened beneath the prisoner's feet, he fell far enough for the fall to snap his neck—if the noose was tied and the knot placed correctly, of course. And if the prisoner's family crossed the hangman's palm with a coin or two, a sack of sand was tied to the prisoner's feet to increase the chances of his neck breaking.

The hanged man was still strangled by the rope, but a broken neck caused a much quicker loss of consciousness and death.

Such were the dark thoughts that were going through my head as the Spaniards discussed my fate—not whether I would be hanged, of course, but how quickly it would occur. One of them actually wanted to get a priest to give me last rites—bless that man's pious soul!—but I could tell that his argument about it being the Christian thing to do was not setting well with the others who wanted a taste of blood—*my blood*.

The man who favored a priest even wanted to know my name, and I made up one because my true name, Juan the Lépero, would have hurried the hanging even more because léperos were street trash considered worse than lice and accursed by God.

The proof to me that those hags called the Fates had gotten an iron grip on my cojones and squeezed tight had to do with the strange twist about the mare—I was being hanged for stealing, but I had actually not stolen her. The Spaniards refused to believe that the mare was simply following me because she enjoyed the tune I was humming.

I didn't blame the hacendados—I wouldn't have believed the story myself if I were them—but it happened to be the truth, in a manner of speaking. I *was* humming a tune and the mare *did* follow me.

There were other times when I hummed that same tune and horses followed me. Sí, I do not deny it—I am a horse thief and I am able to make a sound that soothes horses and attracts them to me. Except this time I hadn't intended to steal the horse, at least that was not what I had set out to do. Acting from habit, I was just practicing the method I had used many times in the past with horses.

So I suppose one could say that in the eyes of Señora Justice, I was not being hanged for stealing this mare, but for the many other horses I had stolen in the past—but she is blind, no?

Truthfully, I don't wish to be hanged, period. However, I will admit that if anyone deserved to swing on the rope for horse stealing, it would be me.

But now was not the time, because forty-eight years after the defeat of the Aztecs and conquest by the Spanish of the One-World, I was on a mission to unravel a puzzle and solve a mystery about the finest horses of the colony.

Horses are, of course, *everything* in the colony. That is why I was being hanged so quickly.

Had I stolen the wife or daughter of a hacendado, my sentencing to death would have taken much longer. But to steal a horse—that was a mortal sin above the murder of a human being.

Many thoughts go through a man's mind when he is about to be hanged as a horse thief. Could I have run faster to escape? Chosen a different horse to steal? Shouted my innocence louder?

Did you expect me to be remorseful about my choice of occupation? Perhaps wish that I had been a priest smelling of wine and righteousness instead? Or a merchant with my heart pumping and my hands sweaty, counting my coins?

If you thought those trades were open to one who carries the blood taint of mixed indio and Spanish blood, you have been eating some of those mushrooms that indio healers use to open their minds so they might speak to the gods.

No, I was a horse thief—born to hang.

TWO

WORSE THAN BEING an ordinary horse thief, I was a very disgusting lépero, the worst kind of street trash who ever ventured even into the occupation of a bandido. Yet I had also been a gentleman and caballero of New Spain who was entertained with the best of society—at the viceroy's palace no less!

New Spain, of course, is the most important colony of our esteemed majesty, Philip II in Madrid, also called Philip the Prudent, who rules the largest and most powerful empire in the world.

As for me who was called a *hijo de una puta* at birth because my mother was a whore and my father nameless, I had hobnobbed with the king's nobles and bishops who rule this colonial gem in his royal name.

I was dressed now as a vaquero, but just hours earlier I wore the fine clothes of a gentleman and men put the respectful title of Don before my name—a name I had borrowed, of course.

Eh, if only those society matrons who had paraded their unmarried daughters before me could see me now—on a horse, with a rope around my neck, my hands tied behind me, the flame in my life's candle flickering and ready to fade.

That I had managed in my short life to survive in the worlds of half-breed lépero street trash, bandidos, horse thieves, and that of the highest gentility in the colony's glorious capital was an amazement even to me.

Left with my thoughts while the men argued about whether I would get absolution rather than going to hell without my earthly sins pardoned, my deepest regrets were that I would never again get to mount a horse or a woman. Ayyo! Thinking about it some more, I realized it wasn't just the horses and women—I was too young to die! No doubt that was the same wail of all who lie at death's door.

"The murderer of that cotton merchant received last rites and absolution," my advocate for a priest said.

"But this is a *horse* thief!" the man with the ready quirt spat.

I couldn't tell if only one of them wanted to wait to whip the horse out from under me until after a priest had prepared my soul for its tortuous journey or if the other men were more anxious to have me swinging at the end of the rope.

At the moment I cared less about the journey of my soul, which I know will be a sharp drop off a steep cliff and into the fires in the bowels of hell, than getting my corporeal body away from these vigilantes.

My mount shifted his weight nervously as the hanging enthusiast who voiced the loudest about sending me to el diablo without absolution from a priest yelled again that he didn't give a damn what the others say—I was a *horse* thief.

As my bad luck would have it, he was right—there was nothing worse than calling a man a horse thief. Being a murderous bandido, a defiler of women, or a rustler of cattle did little to raise a man's blood when compared to stealing his caballo, his most prized possession.

Horses were so important in New Spain that Spanish gentlemen were called caballeros—horsemen, just as our French enemies called themselves cavaliers in their strange tongue.

All the great conquerors rode horses into battle, from Alexander the Great to the Great Khan of the Mongols, not to mention all the great heroes of lore and history.

Even the conqueror-adventurer Hernán Cortés had horses that played an important role in the battles he fought, though he had only fourteen of them and fewer than six hundred Spanish soldiers when he began his conquest of the One-World's twenty-five million indios and defeated the Aztecs.

Even though Cortés had such a small number of horses when he first engaged the Aztecs in battle, the powerful warhorses could run faster than the wind and had powerful hooves that could trample a man to death. The Aztecs had never seen a horse before and often ran in terror at the sight of them. Cortés used the few horses to extreme advantage, charging into indio battle lines like a giant club, knocking aside common warriors so he could get to indio leaders and kill them to throw their soldiers into panic and confusion.

There were no horses, mules, donkeys, or any other beasts of burden in the One-World before the arrival of the Spanish conquistadors. Even today, nearly fifty years after the conquest, there were many thousands of horses in New Spain, but only a handful of indios owned one, and those horses were of poor quality.

No Spanish gentleman was without a horse, though the four-hoofed beasts and their stepbrothers, mules, were of importance far beyond just being used to carry a man—the food from farms that fed cities arrived mostly on horse-drawn carts and the backs of mules, while merchandise and people moved great distances by the power of the beasts of burden.

My horse started to shift its hooves nervously again. I pressed my legs against its flanks and hummed the gentle tune that always calmed the beasts.

Hopefully, the Spaniards—who were still arguing about whether my departure was to be blessed by a priest—weren't going to spook the horse with their loud voices and leave me dangling. If I had just a few short moments left of life, a few breaths, a sigh, I wanted all of them.

Had I only Spanish blood in me, or was even a full-blooded indio, there would have been no argument—a priest for certain would mumble a few words before the horse was swatted out from under me. But being of mixed blood, I was fortunate to have even one man argue in favor of a priest.

Not that the Spanish reserve their sharp spurs just for half-bloods. There are less of my breed—a mating of Spanish and indio blood—than there are of pure-blooded Spaniards and indios, so the indios get their backs racked the bloodiest because they bear the greatest burden of fulfilling the demands of our Spanish masters.

Wars and rebellions by the indios have broken out periodically since the conquest by Cortés and collapse of the Aztec empire, mainly in protest of the Spanish taking the food from indios' mouths and the women from their arms in a gluttony of greed and lust for power and fortune.

Ayyo! Great wealth has come to the conquistadors, their heirs, their king, and their church. Only the millions of indios they have enslaved and the offspring from the rapes of indio women by Spaniards walk with dirt between their toes. Léperos like me—the poorest and reviled street trash—are at the bottom of the social cauldron.

Although there are people who have said they can see Spanish features in my face, I am not Spanish in heart or soul. I have always been a mestizo, a half blood, and have had to be careful not to show my lowly pedigree when I carried off the pretense of being a wealthy caballero.

But like the Spanish who lord over indios and mestizos, I am a lover of horses, almost as much as I am of women.

I admit that I have occasionally taken a horse that didn't belong to me, but only to protect the noble beast from its cruel owner. More or less. I also admit that I have made money from my charitable work with horses and that the owners of these horses considered me lower than a worm.

The group of Spaniards had grown quiet and the men were now coming toward me.

THREE

I HUMMED A little louder to calm the horse as it threatened to bolt while the men got closer with loud voices and their weapons rustling.

"You have anything to say to your god before you meet el diablo?" asked the man who defended my right to a priest.

Ayyo! Apparently his argument for divine intervention had failed.

"Yes!" I said. "I'm a Christian, and I'm entitled to a priest to give me the last rites."

What else could I to say? Hopefully, the closest priest was a great distance away.

"You do not deserve a priest, you thieving dog!" spit the man who argued the loudest against me. "You were caught red-handed, and you can do your confessing to el diablo!"

I felt the pull on my ankles from the fallen angel in hell getting stronger. Ay, el diablo wanted me to know he will welcome me with open arms and a place at his hearth.

"I told you that the mare followed me because it was attracted to the stallion and the little tune I hum."

"That mare didn't jump the fence; you took down a rail," the loud-mouthed—hang him without a priest—hacendado said.

"No! I never touched the rail. It was already on the ground; I swear by the holy mother—"

"Speak the Madre Santa's name in vain and I'll cut off your tongue before we stretch your neck."

I got a grip on my panic. "Señor Caballero, like you, I am a lover of horses and would never—"

"Listen to this slick-tongued, lying dog of a mestizo. He thinks he can talk his way out of what our eyes saw. Time for a hanging!"

"A confession! I need time to confess to a priest!" I protested, as the loud man stepped up to the horse's flank with his whip. "I'm a good Christian, a benefactor of the church!"

The lie flew from my mouth along with a spray of spittle. I pressed my legs against my horse's flanks. "Steady, amigo, don't move," I said under my breath. That was useless, of course; my mount would bolt the moment it got a good whack from the braided whip.

Perhaps I did need time in the confessional box more than most men, eh? Truth be told, I had many things to confess—sins besides the stealing of horses, even matters of the flesh that would shock—and titillate—a priest.

Ayyo! If I were a king, I would give my kingdom for just a few more gasps of life before I burned in the fires of hell.

PART 2

OAXACA, NEW SPAIN

A.D. 1556

LÉPEROS

These street people, who huddled, starved, and begged on every corner of the towns of New Spain, were known as *léperos*. Social lepers, they begged, did odd jobs, and robbed . . . They were the first Mexican bandits . . . The *Lépero* lived as he could . . . ready to cut either a throat or a purse, begging for food or work, screaming under the whips of the town authorities who frequently ordered them chastised . . .

Ironically, the *Léperos* were to survive, grow, and finally, inherit modern Mexico. They proved, not the degeneracy of man, but mankind's tenacity in the face of hideous adversity.

—T. R. Fehrenback, *Fire and Blood*

FOUR

"*BASTARDO! HIJO DE una puta!*"

It wasn't the first time I'd been called the bastard son of a whore, and the accusation didn't bother me. Not only was it true, but the speaker had the same birthright as I did, as did most of the other léperos on the street.

We léperos were not made on the streets, but we were born into a state of infamy.

The insult flew at me as I'd given the other bastardo an elbow in the face as the pack of us beggars charged into the street to plead for alms from people in a passing carriage.

There were ten of us, and I was in the lead on the wet, muddy street because I had spotted the coach before the others. It was an open carriage with a single coachman and carrying a man and woman who, from their dress, appeared to be on their way to a society ball.

It had been a miserable day, which is to say a lot when almost every day of my young life would have been called miserable by most people.

Sitting on the stone wall to the well in the town square, watching the movement of animals and people, I had been waiting for a passerby who would throw me something to eat or a copper coin.

Like all léperos who survived for any length of time on the streets, I had a finely honed sense of who was more likely to throw a bone to you or give you a bone-crunching kick with a boot.

Women had soft hearts but were quicker than men to slap a begging hand when they had little to give. Men were most likely to toss a copper when they were alone than in a group, and more likely to deliver a kick from a pointed-toe boot or a blow from a braided leather riding crop when other men were watching. Perhaps they didn't want to expose a side to themselves that might make them appear weak.

People on their way to enjoy a ball were often in a good mood and more charitable than they might ordinarily be, so I put in some extra effort to get to them first.

"For the sake of all that is holy, show God your charity!" I screeched as I neared the carriage, running as fast as I could.

Running alongside the carriage, I whined, "For the love of the Son and his Virgin Ma—"

Someone slammed into me, maybe the whole pack, and I skidded, my feet slipping out from under me as I slid toward the carriage and my legs went under, missing being run over by the front wheels.

I tried to pull back as I saw the big rear wheel coming and screamed as it rolled over my leg.

The carriage kept going down the street, the pack of léperos running alongside, loudly pleading for food or a coin as I lay in the mud too shocked and in pain to move.

I twisted onto my stomach, screaming as the movement sent a shock of pain through me from my leg. I started crawling back for the wooden sidewalk as another carriage came down the street. The pack of beggars abandoned the carriage that had rolled over me and raced back to get to the oncoming one without even glancing at me as I crawled in the mud, with tears from pain, not sorrow, wetting my eyes.

I would not have given a helping hand to any of the other léperos if I had been in their place. The first commandment of living and dying on the streets is that whether you were man, woman, or child, you killed your own snakes.

I crawled, dragging my bad leg behind me, until I reached the sidewalk and then pulled myself on it, crying out as my damaged leg hit the corner.

My breath coming in gasps from the pain and effort, I scooted on my rump until I got to the wall of the grain store. Leaning back, I whimpered because my leg screamed with pain—and it was a way to get a handout.

Passersby ignored me even though I whimpered loudly and held out my hand for a coin. Finally, a wrinkled old indio woman knelt beside me and tore her head scarf into two pieces, using the material to wrap the bleeding wounds on my legs.

The grain-store owner came out with a stick and whacked me with it.

"Get away from my store!"

Screaming from the pain and indignation, I refused to move until he threw me the core of the apple he had been eating.

FIVE

*H*UNGRY. AN EMPTY feeling that has been with me every day of my twelve years of life. Even the times I felt full were not satisfying because to get that way I had eaten too much of something not very appetizing. Sometimes what I ate would not have been appetizing to the wild dogs that roamed the streets and competed with us beggars for scraps in the gutters.

I live in Oaxaca, a town with an indio name that the Spanish find hard to pronounce. "Wa-ha-kạ," is the correct pronunciation, though to hear the word spoken by a Spaniard sounds much different than when a Zapotec indio speaks it.

Oaxaca is not a big city, not as large as Puebla, Guadalajara, or Guanajuato, and only a tiny fraction the size of Mexico City, the grand capital that lies three hundred miles to the north—about a week's journey from the capital during the dry season—but it is the extent of the world that I know. I have never been beyond its streets, not even to the fields and farms beyond the town.

Other than the whorehouse where I was born and the stable I sometimes sneaked into, I have lived my entire life on the streets of Oaxaca—streets where only the lucky and cunning have survived. And right now I was a wounded animal being watched by a pack of hungry beasts.

The mud had been deep and the load small, or my

leg would have been snapped in two. With broken bones and no one to care for me because I was an orphan, I would have been dragged to the churchyard and left there to die a slow, agonizing death as the demons that invade wounds attacked me.

Had I been Spanish or even indio I would have been taken by the nuns to the hut where they cared for the homeless sick. But as a casta, a half blood, and street trash, there was no sanctuary for me because I was damned by God.

I hobbled a few feet into the alley next to the store and crawled to a spot where I lay and slept until night fell.

When I awoke later I still kept up the pretense of being asleep because I knew the pack was watching me. The "pack" were léperos who shared the streets with me. I called them a pack, but, unlike wolves who cooperate and kill as amigos, léperos would run after the same morsel and fight each other over it even if it was enough to share.

I clutched a rock as I pretended sleep to let them know that I was capable of fighting if any of them came at me. The rock was only for appearances—tucked inside my shirt was a flint arrowhead attached to a hand's length of wood shaft. I had found the broken arrow on the outskirts of town after a group of Zapotecs had ambushed travelers.

For what purpose did I have the arrowhead?

If I was attacked, I would fake holding the rock with one hand while I shoved the piece of arrow into the gut of my attacker with the other.

As long as no Spaniard saw me, I would not even be hassled by the town constable—léperos who died on the street were dragged off to a pauper's grave. Like swatted flies, no one cared much about who killed them. It was assumed léperos were killed for offending a Spaniard or they had died fighting over a scrap of food.

I knew why the pack was watching me—they were looking for a sign that I was too helpless from my injuries to stop them from taking the rags from my body or finding a tortilla hidden under my filthy shirt.

That was how we lived and survived. If one of them had been injured, I would have showed the same lack of mercy. And avariciousness.

If I didn't steal well and fight every attack desperately, as if I was backed against a wall and facing the hounds of hell, I would not be alive to experience my twelfth birthday—though in truth I really didn't know when my birthday was, nor had it ever been celebrated.

One of the pack, called Juan the Mongrel because his twisted, ugly face had a big, flat nose like a dog, stayed to watch me even after the others left to hunt for a handout. With few having given names, most of us were called Juan, the most common name in the colony.

Like all the others, Juan the Mongrel was an old man even though he was only in his late teens. Few women lasted long as beggars because they were not as strong as the males—and few boys survived into anything more than a young manhood in which they looked old and battered.

The Mongrel didn't know what I was up to, but his instincts told him that I had found a source of food. I knew he caught on yesterday morning when I had not run for a bit of meat left on a chicken leg thrown by a passerby on the street.

He was right. I had found a source of food and didn't dare let anyone know it.

After a while he left to join other léperos outside a pulqueria where sour indio beer was sold. The hope was that a drunk might throw them a copper or be so intoxicated that they could follow him down a dark street and rob him.

As soon as the Mongrel disappeared around the corner, I forced myself up and crept down the dark alley. It was hard going—my stomach empty, my legs weak, and my head full of angry pain.

Using the walls of buildings for support, I limped along, glancing back frequently to see if I was being followed.

Night had fallen, but that only gave predators on the streets more places to hide.

That I was up and on my feet, able to hobble along stiffly, was a result of hunger that I could satisfy only by one means—stealing.

SIX

THIEVERY WAS MY birthright. I possessed nothing except the rags on my back and the dirt between my toes.

I had no family or even a memory of being loved except a vague feeling sometimes as I lay on the cold ground at night—a feeling of being held at a time when I had a mother. I saw other women carrying babies and was sure that what I felt was having been held in my mother's arms, pressed against her tender breasts as she hummed a tune.

The tune had stayed with me, helping me stay unafraid in the darkness, with a warm feeling that I had once belonged to someone.

I had no recollection of the features of the woman who had held me, although sometimes on the street I would see a woman who, for reasons I couldn't define, stirred in me a feeling of familiarity and created a longing to be held tightly. But I had no mother I could put a true face on even in my imagination.

The feeling of being held and loved and protected lasted only for a moment before I would roll over on the hard ground and go back to sleep, often dreaming of gorging myself with so much food that the hollow pit in my stomach no longer ached.

One might think that we street people would huddle together for companionship as I said wolves did, but the truth was that street dogs got along better than we two-legged animals. Since there was not enough food to feed all the beggars, one killed under a horse's hooves or wagon's wheels or by a foul disease that left him screaming with his brain on fire and boils on his skin until el diablo yanked his soul only meant there was one less scavenger to fight for garbage.

It bears explanation that this caste of people who begged on the streets for scraps and were barely recognized as human by the government, church, and other people came not from divine intervention by God but the bawdy urges in the loins of Spaniards.

From the first time the Spanish landed on the shores of what was then called the One-World by the indios, the invaders came without women but not without their lust for female flesh.

Even after the conquest and total destruction of the indio nations and the creation of a slave state the king in Spain called a colony, Spanish men came to the land they named New Spain in far greater numbers than the women of their country.

Not only did that encourage the men to bed down with the conquered indio women, but the fact that the women were helpless against rape made it easy and convenient for Spaniards to relieve their urges by spreading the legs of indio women.

Not all the women were taken by rape, of course. Some were attracted to the male conquerors, perhaps out of the hope that they would make them legitimate wives. But marriage in the eyes of God, which the Spanish priests tell us can only be sanctified in God's house, happened rarely for the indio women.

The product of those rapes and other unions created people like me, a person of mixed blood that the Spanish called mestizos.

Ayyo! It would have been better for me to have dog's blood in my veins than the blood of two races.

The pure bloodline of a murderer is more respected by the Spanish than that of a saint who possesses the blood of two different ethnicities.

The Spanish hatred of mixed blood runs deep in their history and emotions, while the sight of the offspring of Spanish men and indio women is an insult to the indio. The result is that few with mixed blood are fortunate enough to be accepted as respectable members of the colony by either the Spanish or indios.

That left mestizos in a state of utter poverty, disgrace, and infamy. Looked down upon as inferior and even cursed by God, unable to find respectable employment, we end up on the streets as beggars—a notorious breed shunned as lepers and contemptuously called léperos.

The umbrage toward street people was even reflected in the names we were known by. I was called Juan the Lépero. The Spanish could have added the more respectable appendage of Bastardo instead of Lépero because I was conceived in sin rather than holy matrimony, but a lépero bore much more disrespect than a mere bastard.

As I said, the reason léperos were shunned like lepers and those people called Untouchables in the land on the other side of the world called India was because of their mixed blood and because a loathing of what the Spanish called impure blood ran deep in a Spaniard's character.

I have been told that this aversion of the Spanish for mixing blood arose because Spain—which many Spaniards refer to as the peninsula and those born there as peninsulares to distinguish them from those of Spanish blood born in the New World—had a mixture of different peoples.

For the past thousand years the peninsula had been occupied with people of conflicting race, religion, and culture. Three different religions thrived in the region—Islam, Christianity, and Judaism. And a wide range of skin color was present—the darker complexion of the Muslim Arabs called Moors from North Africa dominated the southern part of the country, the lighter-complexioned Christians of European stock held sway over the northern regions, and those of the Jewish faith were spread throughout the region.

After long and bloody wars, the Christians won the entire peninsula and drove out the Moors and Jews who refused to convert to Christianity.

The end result was a country that was a part of Europe and had been made Christian by sword point, but whose people had a wide assortment of skin color, ranging from lighter skin in the north to the olive and darker complexions of many of the peoples of the southern Mediterranean regions.

To impose social order on a nation with such diversity, the Spanish monarchs classified people by racial blood lines rather than skin color. From a social and legal perspective, what made one inferior was having a mixture of blood. *Pureza de sangre*—purity of blood—was more important than the color of skin.

The clever Spanish carried this concept of the "color" of blood deep, not just in their social attitudes, but in implementing laws that defined a person's status by the purity of blood, with those of mixed blood at the bottom of the ladder.

In Spain or in the colony, to be considered for high office or marriage to a full-blooded Spaniard of European ancestry, one was subjected to the *limpieza de sangre*. If your blood was mixed—and by that the Spanish meant "tainted" by the blood of Moors or Jews—you were considered socially inferior and lacked the same legal rights as those with pure blood.

However, it was only the mixing of blood that was prohibited, not the ethnicity of it. Thus those of "pure blood" were not ostracized regardless of whether their bloodline was Moorish or European, as long as it was *pureza de sangre*—pure blood.

Not even riches or great abilities in the arts made a person of mixed blood an equal to the lowest pure-blooded Spanish street sweeper. To the Spaniard, pure blood gave people moral strength in life; it even gave men courage in battle and domination over weaker people.

The Spanish brought their concept of purity of blood to New Spain, with pure-blooded Spaniards at the top of the social heap.

That left half-caste léperos at the bottom of the social heap, damned by the fact we carry what the Spanish called a blood taint.

Ayyo! Accepted by neither the masters nor their peons, not educated or trained in a trade, we with the blood taint became street people, beggars and thieves, jail bait, and born to be hanged. Life on the streets among my lépero "brothers" was not comforted by brotherly love—all léperos were thieving bastardos who would cut my throat for a tortilla.

I had no knowledge of the man who fathered me. A whore who knew my mother told me that my mother had not been a whore but a girl driven out from her family and village when they found out she carried a child out of wedlock, but the whore did not know who my father was.

Not that it mattered—bastardos had no rights in

the colony even if their father was known, unless the father legally recognized the child as his.

Ayyo! If Spaniards had to be responsible for all the children they sired with indio girls through rape and coercion, they would leave the colony and return with their booty to their homeland.

After my mother died when I was an infant, I was raised with the pack of other children born in the whorehouse; most of us doubly orphaned because our fathers were unknown and many others because their mothers were wiped away in childbirth or by the periodic maladies that struck down many.

I was on the street by the age of eight, forced out of the whorehouse, though the prostitutes sometimes took pity on me and gave me food, but this was one of the many nights when even they went hungry because of fighting in the area.

An indio rebellion in the region resulted in the town being taking over by Spanish soldiers, who confiscated all the available food.

Which left me with nothing but dirt to eat.

Dirt was also part of my life. I slept on the ground covered by a dirty blanket and wore clothes swaddled in dirt. My clothes were rags that only got washed when it rained on them.

My body was as dark and grimy as my clothing, and if the people of quality that I ranted at for coins were being truthful, I smelled worse than a pile of manure.

The fact that I had even survived this long was itself truly a miracle. Only the biggest, the cleverest, and for sure the luckiest lépero survived for long on the streets.

Today I was doubly lucky because the carriage ran over my leg instead of my head.

Doubly lucky today, but tomorrow I might get my head bashed in by a rock wielded by another lépero as we wrestle in the dirt for a small coin thrown like a bare bone to a pack of hungry dogs.

Eh, that is the life of one with the blood curse. We are the "leftover" people, the ones who have no place in society because all the other positions are filled by Spaniards who believe the purity of their blood makes them superior and by indios who sulk and wait for the day when they can spill some of that "pure blood."

Unwelcome, uninvited, spit upon—that left us léperos not in purgatory but in the hell of the streets.

One would think that because of the way the Spanish treated them, the indios would have more sympathy, more empathy for outcasts, but they resented the half-castes even more than they did the Spanish.

I don't know why I empathized with the indios rather than my Spanish side. The indios treated léperos with the same contempt that Spaniards did even though in many ways they were themselves mistreated. But at least they did not kick us.

There was a pecking order, and although the indio appeared near the bottom, there was always the mixed bloods one step down from them.

Ayyo! It was painful being the smallest bug.

SONG OF THE LÉPERO

Whilst I am writing, a horrible *lépero*, with great leering eyes, is looking at me through the windows, and performing the most extraordinary series of groans, displaying at the same time a hand with two long fingers, probably the other three tied behind.

"Señorita! Señorita! For the love of the most Holy Virgin! For the sake of the most pure blood of Christ! By the miraculous Conception!—"

The wretch. I dare not look up, but I feel that his eyes are fixed upon a gold watch and seals lying on the table . . .

There come more of them! A paralytic woman mounted on the back of a man with a long beard. A sturdy-looking individual . . . holding up a *deformed foot* which I verily believe is merely fastened back in some extraordinary way!

What groans! What rags! What a chorus of whining!

—Fanny Calderón de la Barca, *Life in Mexico*

SEVEN

AT THE FAR end of the alley I stopped to rest my painful legs behind the town stable.

The stable was where visitors and the postal stage quartered their horses in Oaxaca. It also had become my source of food.

All of the windows of the stable were glassless and at night were shuttered to keep out intruders, but the center of the building was an open-air courtyard surrounded by horse stalls. Reaching the roof with the help of the grapevines permitted me to drop down into the courtyard.

I grabbed a handful of the vines, then lifted my legs, gasping from pain as I bent my knees to get footing.

I was only a few feet off the ground when I heard the crunch of feet behind me. A pair of hands grabbed me and pulled me off the vines.

I fell backward, hitting the hard ground, crying out as pain exploded in my injured leg.

"I know your secret now, bastardo!"

Mongrel.

He swung at my face with a rock.

I brought up my shoulder and the rock hit bone, sending another shot of pain through me as the rock made contact and flew out of his hand.

He was the biggest lépero in town and the meanest.

I knew I could not beat him in a test of strength. He stamped on my leg and I cried out again.

He began kicking me and I rolled, but he kicked me in the back.

"I have a copper," I said. "Take it! Take it!" I pleaded.

I patted my left pocket to draw him to it as I stuck my right hand under my shirt and got hold of the piece of arrow.

"Give it to me," Mongrel said. He knelt down, setting his knee into my stomach.

The wind exploded out of me when his knee sank in, and the arrow slipped out of my feeble hand.

He reached down, tearing at the ragged pocket to get it open.

I knew he would not be satisfied with the coin even if I really had had one. He was going to kill me. That was the way of the street. You didn't hurt someone and leave them alive to stab you in the back later, because it was inevitable that the enemy would be at your back again one day—and no one on the street watched your back except your enemies.

I put out my hand to try and force myself up. My right hand hit the rock. I got a grip on it and swung up.

He turned to face my upcoming hand as he saw the movement, and the rock impacted, catching him on the nose.

He went back with a spray of blood, falling on his rump.

As he started to get up, I reached over, stretching as far as I could, and hit him over the forehead with the rock.

I saw more léperos coming, and I hobbled away and hid.

They saw Mongrel sitting up, holding his bleeding head.

I turned away, shutting my eyes as they fell upon him.

It was his turn to be the wounded prey.

EIGHT

I WAITED, MY eyes turned away, my heart empty, as the pack beat Mongrel to death.

While his body was still twitching and his lips foaming with blood, they stripped off his clothes and kicked him until his spirit had left for hell.

They found his clothes too foul and ragged even for léperos and threw them on the ground as they walked away, squabbling over a tortilla found in his pocket.

I knew they would return to the main square and hang around the inn and the pulquerias in the hopes of picking a copper or getting a bone thrown to them, leaving behind without thought someone who for years had begged, stolen, squabbled, and whined with them.

When it was safe, I approached the naked body slowly, worried that el diablo was still taking his soul and might reach out and grab me if I got too close.

I gathered up what I could of his torn shirt and pants and laid them on Mongrel's body, giving him more dignity than he would have given me if he had managed to kick me to death.

I don't know why I bothered. I felt nothing for the vicious animal. He was ugly-mean and had often hurt others because he took pleasure from their pain. Being cold and hungry and abandoned had not made any of us street people saints, but few struck out at anyone smaller or weaker, as Mongrel did for no other reason than he was bigger and stronger.

He would be forgotten quickly even by those he had stolen from and abused. Though I and the rest of Oaxaca's street trash had been aware of Mongrel's presence on the earth, and not a few of us had been kicked and punched as he stole a juicy morsel, none of us cared that he had come and gone, not even God, who had long ago abandoned him to el diablo.

I heard growling and saw shining eyes and dark forms coming at me from both directions in the alley.

They came out of the darkness—a pack of hungry dogs. They had smelled the blood and there was nothing I could do. I had blood on me, too, on my legs and my pants.

Like me they were gaunt and hungry, but their teeth were sharper. I stood no chance against the pack.

I turned away to climb back up the wall, shutting my mind from the snarling, snapping, and ripping I heard as the dogs pulled flesh off the body and fought over the pieces.

My foot kicked a rock and I got a grip on it as one of the dogs that got shoved out of the feast turned and came at me.

I swung around, bringing the rock with me, hitting the animal across the side of the head as he flew at me with jagged jaws. I connected good and the blow sent him stumbling sideways and down to his knees, a bloody gash open between his eye and ear.

I backed away as other dogs coming down the alley went for the dog with the open wound.

NINE

GRABBING A HANDFUL of vines, then another, I pulled myself up slowly, getting a handhold, then a foothold, stretching to reach upward, my arms doing most of the work of bringing up my wounded leg, which trailed almost useless behind me.

Vines ripped, and I slipped and started to fall as more vines broke loose. I clawed at the vines, breaking my fall, hanging frozen on the wall as I tried to get my breath and slow my pounding heart.

The sounds of the dogs growling and snarling as they ripped off pieces of flesh gave me the desperation I needed to move again, testing the strength of the vines before I put more weight on them.

I had lived like a wild animal for so long, rarely treated better than one because domestic animals gave value while léperos were thought of as festering maggots who spoiled the soup for all, that I understood why God gave the dogs sharp teeth and a hunger for red meat, regardless of where they found it.

I had an urge to slip back down to the ground and rip pieces off the bloody stump to satisfy my hunger.

Ayyo! Did my sudden lust for human flesh come from being so weak and hungry that I was mindless . . . or some primeval instinct for the taste of human flesh I had inherited from my indio ancestors?

The barbaric hunger of my indio ancestors was rarely far from the thoughts of people because it was a favorite subject for Spanish priests to harp upon as they reminded us at church services that indios were little more than half-naked savages with strange appetites before the conquistadors arrived to "civilize" them.

The priests always neglected to add that the Spanish system of "civilizing" the indio was similar to the way they broke farm animals to the harness and plow.

Weak and dizzy and only halfway up the wall, I stopped, forcing my knees to lock to keep from sliding back down as I hung on, my arms feeling as if they were being pulled from my shoulder sockets.

Rubbing against the thick, rough vines had spread open my wounds, and I left a trail of blood as I fought my way up.

I began to feel light-headed, almost dreamy—

"*Stop it!*" I gasped aloud.

The pain was almost insurmountable, but I knew there was food if I made it up the wall, and pain is suffered easier without the added ache and weakness caused by hunger.

A man who once watched me climb a tree to fetch a toy his son had tossed into the branches had called me a squirrel, but tonight I was a wounded one and the hardest part was yet to come.

When I reached the top, I would have to drag myself over the edge to lay on the roof, with my breath coming fast and my legs screaming from pain.

Why would I suffer the pain and nearly kill myself to climb up a stable wall at night?

What was the gourmet meal that I would sup on once I had conquered the "mountain" and reaped my reward?

Horse feed, of course.

Horses are the pride and joy of caballeros. More

than that, horses are their treasures. A man's horse often costs more than his house. Spanish gentlemen boast more about the accomplishments of their horses than those of their children.

Men call themselves caballeros, and the title is proudly used by even the plumpest merchant who would have to be lifted onto the back of a very big horse in order to justify the title.

Any horse in the colony ate better and slept warmer than a lépero.

Ayyo! Even a mule was treated better than a lépero.

Mules and carriage horses were fed hay, but the fine riding horses of the rich caballeros also got oats and corn—even apples!

The only apples I had ever bitten into were over-ripe ones with large brown spots tossed from a farm wagon that I ran after while loudly begging.

I understood the Spaniard's love of horses, though I had never ridden one. The great beasts created a sense of awe and wonderment in me as I watched them carry a grown man or pull a full wagon, their beautiful coats shiny, powerful muscles rippling, hooves pounding.

Watching the caballeros on their horses, I had many times tried to imagine what it would be like to ride on one. I would be high above people who were walking, the power of the great beast warm between my legs, the wind in my face pushing harder and harder against me as the horse galloped under me, carrying me with no more effort than I could carry a puppy.

The indio has been in awe of and even in fear of horses since these animals first arrived in what Europeans mistakenly call the New World. Those mounts left the first horseshoe prints on the mainland on the beaches near what is now Vera Cruz when they were unloaded from the ships that carried Hernán Cortés and the other conquistadors to this land.

Although many thousands of horses have since arrived from the mother country and even more of them have been bred in the colony, the most prized and expensive mounts in New Spain were in the bloodline of those fourteen original warhorses that Cortés brought with him.

Ayyo! Any horse was valuable, and the ones whose bloodlines could be traced to a champion because of its appearance, speed, or stamina went for more gold than ordinary horses.

However, a mount whose bloodline could be traced back to the fourteen warhorses that carried Cortés and his highest-ranking officers to victory was prized among none other, perhaps even more than any other class of horses in the entire world. The king in Spain, who sits at the right hand of God and is the mightiest monarch on earth, with an empire so vast and far-flung that the sun never set upon all of it at once, had horses of the conquest bloodline in his stable.

Sí, I was nothing but a thieving, begging, lying lépero, but like the Spanish, I loved horses. And my indio blood also sensed a spirituality with the animals, just as it did with jaguars, the mighty beasts of the jungle who could kill a man with a single blow.

In truth, I have an affinity with horses, a special connection that I never understood and only discovered accidentally when I approached horses that their masters had left with their reins secured in the iron rings in front of the inn.

When I petted the smooth, shiny coats, I hummed a tune that slipped out through my teeth. A prostitute who helped raise me said it was a melody that my mother always used to sing to calm me when she held me in her arms.

Like my mother, the prostitute was long dead, swept away by one of the deadly maladies that occasionally seemed to blow across the land like a storm wind, carrying lives away with it.

One time when I was begging at the house of prostitution I had asked other girls about the song, but none of them had known my mother nor had they ever heard it sung.

I don't know why the tune calmed horses. It was as if I spoke a language that they understood.

I knew of no one else who hummed the same sound, and the léperos who saw me do it simply laughed and said I was dumber than the horses to which I sang.

Ayyo! If just one of them were as smart as a horse.

With my last bit of strength, I dragged myself onto the roof of the stable.

TEN

MY BODY WAS shaking from pain and exhaustion as I sprawled out on the flat roof and gasped for a breath, empty of strength and will, faint and dizzy. I needed food and rest.

The cursing shouts of a man bellowed from the street below, followed by the painful yelp of a dog—the town's night watchman had discovered Mongrel's body and was driving off the dogs.

Once the watchman found out it was a lépero, he'd load up the body onto his horse cart and take it to where paupers were buried. He'd have little curiosity or concern about how Mongrel met his maker. That the deceased person was a lépero was reason enough for him to be dead.

I lay quiet, trying to silence my breathing, because if the watchman spotted me I'd get a severe beating from the club he carried.

As I rested, the horse smells of straw and manure rose to my nostrils from the stalls below. Odious to others, to me it was a friendly scent because my love of horses was the only comforting feeling I had about life.

The sole public stable in town, the inn for horses was a long narrow building with a front entrance facing the street. The owner's house was attached to the right side of the building.

The stable entrance had a set of double barn doors

that opened into the receiving and working area. A space on one side was used for carriages brought in for repairs, with the other side of the room utilized for an anvil, furnace, and other blacksmith equipment along with saddles, bridles, harnesses, and other tack for sale or brought in for repair.

Beyond the front entrance were two parallel rows of stalls facing each other across a space open to the air. Each stall had its own door split so the upper half could be left open. The horse owner's tack hung on the wall next to the door. Saddles and harnesses studded with silver and turquoise were usually taken to the inn or wherever the horse owner was staying.

For me, the stalls were a virtual palace! I had never enjoyed the luxury of sleeping in an enclosed area with a roof, walls, and a door like these kingly animals had. There was even hay to lie on.

Most of my nights were spent under the roof of an open-air alcove behind the inn. The innkeeper had a pig tied there to receive the slop from the kitchen each day.

The pig permitted me to snuggle up next to him for warmth at night, but nearly took off my fingers when I tried to reach for a bit of meat on a bone in the slop. Had he known that he was simply being fattened up to be served to the inn guests he might have been more generous.

When I made my late-night visits to the stable, I normally jumped from the flat roof down to a stack of hay, but tonight my legs would not take the impact. Instead, I crawled to the rain gutter and shimmed down a drain pipe, whimpering with pain as the rough-surfaced clay pipe rubbed against my leg wounds.

Hobbling on my feet in the courtyard, I half-filled

a copper ladle with water from a trough and added maize from a horse's feed bin, then placed the ladle on the dying coals in a blazer in the horseshoeing area.

Blowing air at the coals with a handheld bellows as I'd seen the stable owner do, who was also the blacksmith, I heated the concoction until it softened into a corn mush.

I greedily gobbled up the cornmeal and whatever bugs infested it as I sat on a bench with my back to the stall wall. Another ladle and my stomach felt warm and full.

I topped off my dinner with a sour apple taken off the ground.

Ayyo! Maize was the food of the gods! And a privileged horse got more of it every day than what I begged and stole in a month.

"Gracias," I whispered to the horses, thanking them for their contribution to a fine meal. No king had enjoyed a banquet more than I did on the food I stole from the horses that night.

Despite my body telling me that it was broken, I felt myself relaxing because I loved the stable, with its smell of horses, their snorts and neighs as they spoke to each other, the sound of their hooves as they shifted their weight in their stalls.

Humans were unpredictable and not infrequently brutal and dishonest, but horses lacked vices.

Since I left the house of ill repute when I was eight years old and had to fight for survival on the streets, I had never felt safe and comfortable until a month ago, when I sneaked into the stable, cooked my corn mush dinner, and slept peacefully.

I was careful to awaken before the crack of dawn

to get out before the stable owner arrived to open for business and feed the horses.

I yawned, ready to curl up, my eyes heavy when I heard the snort and whinny of a stallion—a sound full of power and arrogance.

I knew immediately that this was no ordinary horse.

ELEVEN

HOBBLING OVER TO the stall where the stallion was being boarded, I stopped and stared at the tack hanging on the wall.

Mi Dios! Never had I seen such a saddle and bridle.

I ran my hand over the smooth and velvety leather, the finest I had ever seen hanging in the stable or on horses in the streets. And while caballeros were generous about enriching their horse tack with silver and semiprecious stones like turquoise and jade, the pieces on this one also had diamonds and pearls.

Even I knew that this was not the horse equipment of a caballero, but that of a king.

Still more mysterious, besides who owned the tack, was why he would leave it hanging in the stable. Stealing a fine saddle would get a rope as tightly wound around one's neck as stealing a horse, but men still did such things.

To leave such richness casually hanging outside a rented stall was so incredible that I could only imagine that no amount of riches would impress the wealthy owner—or the owner was so greatly feared no one would dare steal from him.

The stall itself was the only double one in the stable and was reserved for mares about to give birth.

I heard the snorting and stomping of great hooves as I drew closer. Peeking over the open upper half of the stall door, I could see that it was no mare, but a king of horses.

The stallion's coat was the reddish-brown called chestnut, and it was the biggest horse I had ever seen—at the withers, the point where the neck meets the shoulders, it was taller than me. And the beast was broad, what I imagined Cortés's own warhorse to have been like from the stories that were told.

More than just size, the big stallion possessed a powerful spirit and energy, with rippling muscles. It stared at me and stomped its big hooves, trembling the ground beneath my feet. Snorting, it gave me a contemptuous glare, as if it dared me to invade its territory.

Something else struck me.

"You have a bad temper," I told the stallion.

The horse snorted.

I knew a lot about horses just from hanging around the card tables on the sidewalk in front of the inn. Horses, women, and luck at cards dominated the table conversations.

A horse was called a colt or a filly up to four years old, and after that it was called a stallion or a mare. Stallions developed into more powerful horses than either mares or geldings, which were castrated males. And stallions were inherently more aggressive than other horses.

It was easy to tell from the way the horse was staring at me and impatiently stamping his hooves that this one was obviously more territorial than most, even in a stable stall.

While stallions were the largest and most aggressive horses in a herd, the leader of a herd was a mare called the boss mare. A stallion protected the herd from predators and the attempt by other stallions to take over, but it was the boss mare that led the herd to food and water and decided the direction to take from danger.

The stallion looked at me like I was a coyote ready to be stomped.

"I am your amigo," I told him.

I undid the lower door bolt and slowly opened the door just enough for me to slip in and pull the door shut behind me.

The stallion stamped its hooves impatiently, volatilely, as if it was ready to break into violence and stomp me into tortillas. I felt as if I was facing a keg of black powder on a short fuse.

Horses are big—the bigger ones ten times the weight of a grown man—and this was a big stud whose size alone would make it desirable for breeding.

The stallion took a step forward, and I went back against the door I had latched behind me, my painful knees trembling.

I began to hum the tune I had learned from my Aztec-Zapotec mother. Still the stallion snorted and pounded its hooves. I felt like a bug about to be squashed.

Barely able to keep my knees from giving way, I continued humming and stepped forward, not aggressively but slowly, reaching out with a shaking hand to touch the horse's broad chest.

The image of a hummingbird suddenly came to me. I don't know how or why or where the image came from—I had never gotten it before—but as the tune came out of my mouth, the sound became louder, piercing, and I got a vision of Huitzilopochtli, the Aztec war god, who appeared as a hummingbird.

I had seen drawings of Huitzilopochtli on indio

pottery, but I had never thought of the ancient god before.

I heard a voice in my head, a soft, warm female voice, telling me that Aztec mystics had used the hummingbird war-god tune to quell the rage of jaguars.

I knew then for certain that it was my mother who had whispered the sound into my ears and that, for reasons I could not decipher, she had had the knowledge of ancient kings.

HUMAN TREASURE

[The Conquistadors] carried with them a detailed account of their hungry periods, their wounds, even their scratches; they talked incessantly about their perils and their incredible exploits; they composed moving stories of their immense efforts and sent them to the king. In exchange for their suffering, they solicited him for a small piece of land and a handful of Indians out of the millions they had won for him and for Christianity by the might of their swords.

—Fernando Benítez, *The Century After Cortés*

TWELVE

SANCHO, A MULETEER coming up the street toward the inn, had just left the town whorehouse. It was already daylight, and he had to pick up his bedroll at the inn and get back to his animals.

He had treated himself to a night at the inn after a hard two-week journey leading a pack train of cantankerous mules—the only kind God made—from Mexico City to Oaxaca. However, human nature had taken its course, and instead of spending the night in a comfortable bed at the inn he had chosen a softer bed in the arms of a prostitute, or two or three—he couldn't remember how many.

Men of his ilk were the lifeline that kept the commerce of the colony flowing. Starting at Vera Cruz for the vast shipments that arrived from mother Spain, or at Acapulco for the periodic Manila galleon that brought the riches of the Far East, goods were unloaded from mules to be put aboard the ships, and the mules were then reloaded to haul the products from ships through the thousands of miles of dirt roads in the colony, many of them little more than goat paths.

Head muleteers like Sancho who came over from Spain to earn more money in the New World were invariably Spanish and assisted by indios.

Sancho had working with mules in his blood. His family boasted that they had been running pack trains in the Granada region of the Sierra Nevada mountains of Spain since the time of the Romans. He had come to the New World with a brother to start the business here and had spent the last twenty years at the task that kept him on the road most of the time, with an occasional stop to spend time with his wife and children at their small rancho half a day from Mexico City. His two boys were old enough to help his wife tend the herd of mules being raised at the rancho.

He was nearing the inn when he saw a man come out of the building and turn in his direction.

Sancho almost stumbled. He had seen the man in Mexico City months before, pointed out to him as the man rode a horse in the capital's main square. The man was of such great distinction that Sancho had made a special trip home to tell his wife and children whom he had seen. Encountering him here on the street created an instant social dilemma for Sancho.

Among the Spanish community, a muleteer—even with his own animals—ranked low on the social scale, below a small merchant, above a common laborer, but, for sure, not a person of importance.

The man coming down the street was the second most famous man in the colony. And a possessor of vast wealth.

More than name recognition and riches, the man carried the blood of Hernán Cortés, the immortal conqueror himself, a legendary hero whose name was spoken in a reverence used for God and with more awe than mention of the king.

Sancho was about to pass Martín Cortés the Elder—son of the conqueror.

There were two sons of the conqueror . . . both named Martín.

The man Sancho was about to pass was the *first* son born.

Had the man been the *second* son, Martín the Younger, Sancho would not have had any question or hesitation about how to greet the man: he would have stepped off the wood sidewalk to give the son of Cortés the full width, even though the walkway was wide enough for two men to easily pass, then removed his hat and dropped to one knee as if the man were an archbishop or prince of royal blood.

Sancho would have been correct in his show of respect because Martín the Younger carried the noble title of Marquis del Valle de Oaxaca.

As the marquis passed by, Sancho would have lowered his head and said, "God bless you, Great Sir."

But being the firstborn son of Cortés raised an issue of *blood*—his mother had been an india girl; thus the elder Martín carried the taint of mixed blood.

Sancho, a lowly muleteer, was a full-blooded Spaniard.

A Spaniard of pure blood, whether a nobleman, merchant, or a stable hand who shoveled manure, had higher social rank than a person of wealth and power who carried the blood taint.

That the "indias girl" was Doña Marina, an india princess who was a heroine of the conquest and whose help in translating and advising Cortés about the plots and conspiracies of the Aztecs helped bring victory, did nothing to raise the elder Martín's social status.

The muleteer would have considered the Holy Mother herself beneath him had she been of mixed blood.

THIRTEEN

MARTÍN CORTÉS THE Elder recognized the muleteer's dilemma as he approached the man on the sidewalk. He had experienced it since childhood, when his younger brother, son of Cortés's Spanish wife, was treated as royalty while he was treated as a curiosity—one that commanded respect and even a degree of awe, though not the reverence given the Spanish son.

Although he bore the same name as his younger brother, his status was perfectly described by the name by which he was universally known:

El Mestizo.

The name implied both a description of his bloodline and a historical point of interest: the mating of Cortés, the Spanish conqueror, and Doña Marina, the indias princess, had created the first person to carry a mixture of Spanish-indio blood.

More mating would follow as the conquistadors lay with indias and more sons of Spain came to the colony, until now there were many thousands of mestizos in the colony, though the number of them was small compared to the huge indio population.

As the muleteer approached El Mestizo, the Spaniard touched his hat, lowered his eyes, and muttered, "Buenos días, Señor."

"Buenos días," El Mestizo said.

The responses between the two men were about par for the way El Mestizo was acknowledged by even higher-ranking Spaniards. While he carried the blood taint that made all mestizos less than respectable and léperos outcasts, he still had the blood of Cortés in him. Cortés the conqueror had been dead for nearly ten years, and his Spanish son had assumed the title. That made El Mestizo the brother of the most respected living personage in all of New Spain—and anyone who showed disrespect to him would be treated as if they had shown it to the marquis.

El Mestizo was well aware not only of how the Spanish thought of him but also that indios had even less respect for him because they considered his indias princess mother to be a traitor.

Thirty-five years had passed since the 1521 defeat of the Aztecs by his father, Hernán Cortés, and his father's conquistadors, but the tale of how the brave and cunning Cortés conquered twenty-five million indios with fewer than six hundred Spanish soldiers, fourteen horses, and fourteen cannons was still being told and retold, with no Spaniard tiring of the most trivial detail.

El Mestizo was always secretly amused whenever he heard a Spaniard tell the story, leaving out the fact that the Aztecs were defeated not just by Cortés's small force, but by the thousands of indio warriors who fought beside the Spanish because they hated the much-feared Aztecs. The Spanish versions also left out how much of the victory was accredited by Cortés himself to the incredible ability of the indias girl Doña Marina to correctly interpret the actions of the Aztecs.

But he also knew that the assistance Cortés got from the indios took nothing away from the courage and strength of the conquistadors or of their daring leader. In one of those moments in history in which a leader showed more intrepidness than Julius Caesar crossing the Rubicon or Hannibal climbing the Alps with elephants, Cortés had his own ships burned to keep his men from fleeing when it appeared they were hopelessly outnumbered.

Ayyo! His father was quite an hombre! The man had cojones bigger than cannon balls. He was lucky that his men didn't cut off his cojones and shove them down his throat after they found out he deliberately burned their ships, stranding them with their backs to the sea to face a hundred thousand Aztecs.

Unlike his father, who was a leader of men, or his brother, who was a leader of society, El Mestizo was rather quiet, dignified, conveying a soft-spoken strength that commanded respect.

His first love was horses, and the bloodline of his horses was recognized as among the finest in the land.

It wasn't the power of the horse that attracted El Mestizo, though horses could make a man—or a race of mankind—dominate others. More than anything else, the horse represented superiority of the Spanish over the indios and mestizos. On a horse the ordinary Spaniard was almost twice as tall as most indios. And the Spanish instinctively guarded their predominance over the indios whom they stole the land from and over the mestizos whom they stole dignity from.

For El Mestizo, it wasn't the horse rider's dominance over others, but the beauty of the great beast, its power and rhythm as it galloped, flowing almost as if it were a piece of storm, a tornado, knocking down any man or animal that stood in its way.

El Mestizo was rarely in Oaxaca despite the fact that his brother, the marquis, had inherited a vast estate from their father and El Mestizo managed much of the marquis's property. Like his brother, he had a palatial home in the capital and a horse ranch an hour's ride from there.

Most of the family wealth didn't come from the ownership of land, though El Mestizo and all the Cortés family had large haciendas, but from the encomienda originally given to his father following the conquest.

The encomienda system enslaved indios to the owner, an encomendero, by requiring the indios to pay the encomendero a percentage of their productivity as a tax. Since the indio was mostly tied to the land and worked long hours to produce little more than necessary to feed his family, the system literally took the food from the mouths of the poor and gave it mostly to the heirs of now dead conquistadors.

As a man of compassion for all people, despite the lack of complete respect he was denied by others, El Mestizo disliked the encomienda system and had frequently suggested to his brother that the family had more than enough wealth and that the system should be eliminated.

The suggestion was never well received by his brother, who at twenty-one had inherited his father's noble title and control when his father passed away. For some people "more than enough" was never enough, and perhaps because the younger Cortés had never accomplished anything, he wanted even more.

El Mestizo suspected that rather than the wealth the system brought them, the fact that an encomienda was akin to a feudal domain fed his brother's grandiose visions.

The system got its start as Spaniards set out from the mother country to find riches, either in treasure, land, or human "livestock." Cortés was one of the early adventurers, a conquistador who was to conquer an empire and hand it over to the king of Spain.

However, the king of Spain did not finance Cortés or the leaders who followed in his footsteps. Instead, men like Cortés were adventurers who raised money for ships and supplies and recruited soldiers and other adventurers with promises of treasure.

While treasure got passed around generously following the collapse and pillaging of the Aztec and other indio empires, the king also rewarded the conquistadors with the encomienda grants, which were later extended to the Spaniards who came along after the conquest to tame the land and extend Spanish rule over it.

The encomienda plan was inspired by the feudal system long in use in Spain, whereby individuals were given control and the right to collect certain revenues from towns and villages in return for their services to the Crown.

That feudal system wasn't a far cry from the way the indios had been living under their own empires, in which ascending orders of nobles ruled over regions.

When it came to parceling out the right to tax indios as a reward to the conquistadors, the number of indios awarded was based upon the individual's rank and contribution to the conquest.

Being granted the right to collect from several thousand indios was common. Naturally, Hernán Cortés got the biggest piece. Besides his share of the booty and rights and privileges that came with being made the Marquis del Valle de Oaxaca, his encomienda included over a hundred thousand indios.

Even with the death of indios from plagues and

other maladies, Cortés's younger son, the marquis, still collected encomienda rights from over fifty thousand indios.

El Mestizo knew that the sheer size of the marquis's holdings was a dangerous blessing because it caused envy and jealousy not just in the colony but at the royal palace in Madrid. The income generated by the encomienda was substantial enough for the king to view it as a nice prize if he could grab it.

That also went for the rest of the encomiendas in the colony. And countering the royal desire to be rid of the system was a desire by the aging conquistadors and the heirs of those who had passed to have their encomienda rights converted into a permanent lord-vassal system like baronages that passed on to their heirs in perpetuity.

The encomenderos pointed out that, like knights and nobles, they had the duty when called to arms to support the king with horse, lance, sword, and other arms.

The king had extended the system to the heirs of the current encomenderos, but the fact that he had not extended the rights in perpetuity was a sign that the privilege may end someday—a situation feared by those who had grown rich and fat from the sweat of indios.

Perhaps it was his indio blood, but El Mestizo passionately hated only one thing, and that was the encomienda system. It was a form of brutal slavery in which the indios subjected to it had the deepest cuts from the "wearers of spurs"—the gachupins.

The notion put forth by encomenderos that the levies upon the indios were not harmful was nonsense. Most indios were poor farmers and the burden of paying a percentage of their crops to Spaniards who most often lived hundreds of miles away in the capital was a terrible injustice.

Worse, to increase their income, encomenderos frequently kept indios tied to the land—some even branded them like cattle to make sure that they didn't leave the area.

"It's medieval," El Mestizo had told his brother during a heated argument, "even worse the way some owners treat the indios, as if it were the Dark Ages."

El Mestizo was also critical of the way the entire colonial governmental system was fastened. It began with wealthy Spaniards "buying" the license to perform a government service, such as being a judge, an administrator, tax collector, or almost any other governmental function.

In return, the king granted the license holder the right to collect and keep part of the revenues generated by his office. Thus a licensee would buy the right to be a judge and share with the Crown what he collected from fines, or buy a license to collect taxes for a region and again keep a share and give the rest to the Crown.

The system created an inherently corrupt and ineffective system of administration in which avaricious license holders collected as much and as fast as they could before the term of their license ran out. They then returned to Spain much richer than when they had arrived. Some *very much* richer.

The result was a gutting of the colony, in which the cream of New Spain was siphoned off and shipped to Spain, leaving behind a heritage of public corruption and ineffectiveness.

The entire system by which Spain controlled the colony rankled colonists and caused secret whispering of sedition. Madrid created the system because, with the discovery of vast quantities of silver, New Spain became a treasure house that not only was the jewel of the Spanish colonial world but also financed the rest of the nation's vast colonial empire.

The king was determined to retain tight control on New Spain to keep it within its fold. The Crown accomplished this by ensuring that all important public offices, from the viceroy to the military commanders, were held exclusively by Spaniards who were born and raised in Spain and loyal to the Crown and, most important, to the king. Another requirement was that they planned to return to Spain after their time in the colony, thus were called peninsulares by the criollos.

The word made reference to the fact that Spain occupied most of the large Iberian Peninsula.

This created a structure in which the main governing officials came over from Spain not to live and raise families but, like military officers serving "overseas," to serve a period of duty, during which they would enrich themselves, and then return home.

With no loyalty to the colony itself, there was little motive to ensure that long-term policies had to be best for the colony rather than the mother country.

El Mestizo found it ironic that these European-born Spaniards considered themselves superior in all ways to the full-blooded Spaniards called criollos who were born in New Spain.

The peninsulares claimed it was the warmer climate that caused a more relaxed lifestyle among the criollos, making peninsulares superior to govern.

But El Mestizo and the criollos knew that was a lie.

The peninsulares kept control of the government because the criollos were a step removed from control of Madrid, thus a step removed from the king's trust, while the peninsulares were only temporarily in the colony and would have to someday come face-to-face again with the authorities in the "old country."

The criollos resented the fact that they made up the largest number of the wealthy aristocracy that ruled New Spain, owning most of the mines, haciendas, and commerce, but had to bow to the peninsulares, who maintained a tight grip on political control and funneled much of the wealth of the colony back to Spain.

The criollos, in turn, treated the indios as little better than slaves. The indios were possessions of the hacienda and were hunted down if they strayed or tried to return to the jungle.

When silver was discovered, becoming the "money crop" of New Spain, unscrupulous mine owners enslaved indios and half-castes as work animals in the mines, often forcing them to work in chains so they couldn't escape. Some mine owners, like some encomienda owners, branded the faces of indio workers with the mark of ownership.

To the indios, mestizos, and léperos, it didn't matter what Spaniards called each other; to them, Spaniards were gachupins with their sharp spurs.

Spurs that roweled the lower classes at every turn—bloodying their backs whenever the gachupins wanted their money, women, or lives.

BRANDING INDIOS LIKE ANIMALS

The encomendero treated the indio not just as slaves, but as work animals, even branding them with their initials.

Somewhere along the twisted road in which the entire structure of their society was destroyed, the indios lost their image of themselves as a great and mighty people.

They lost their faith in their gods and in themselves. People who once built dazzling cities and perfected science and medicine now sat with dull eyes in front of thatched huts and poked sticks in the dirt.

—Gary Jennings, *Aztec Blood*

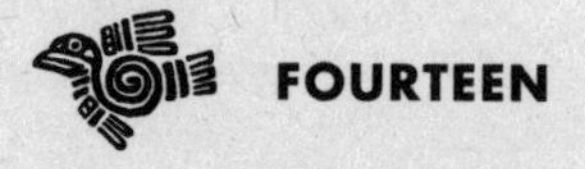

FOURTEEN

GOMEZ, THE STABLE owner, had just swung open one of the big doors to the stable entrance, signaling that he was open for business, when El Mestizo approached.

"Buenos días, señor," Gomez said. "Come to take that bad-tempered stallion off my hands?"

"He's not bad-tempered, just temperamental. But I hope the scent of the mares you're boarding wasn't enough to make him kick down the walls to get to them."

"If he did, I hope it was my own mare he got to."

Wishful thinking, El Mestizo thought. The offspring would be worth more than the stable itself. The stallion was in the bloodline of the warhorses ridden by Cortés during the conquest, though not the warhorse he rode for the final victory against the Aztecs at the critical battle of Otumba. That prized stallion was owned by a sister of El Mestizo and considered perhaps the most valuable stallion in the world.

Leading the son of the conqueror down the open-air center of the facility, Gomez spotted a copper ladle that still had the residue of cooked corn on it.

"Look at that. I've been wondering if someone wasn't coming over the walls at night. Some lépero has found a way in."

His eyes quickly shot to the stallion owner's tack and then relaxed—it was still there.

"Your stallion is sleeping," Gomez said as they approached the silent stall. "Way he stomped around when you brought him in, thought he'd be up all night kicking out my walls and doors."

"He never sleeps soundly until he's had a few mares."

Gomez looked over the half-open stall door and gaped. "*Madre santa de Dios!* The stallion has killed a boy!"

Juan stirred from sleep on the hay beside the horse and sat up, staring at the two surprised men.

The stallion neighed and leaned down with its head, gently brushing the boy's head.

"You dirty little lépero! I'll teach you!" Gomez shouted. He pushed open the stable door, slamming it against the wall.

The stallion got excited at the shouting, stamping its feet. El Mestizo was sure it was ready to bolt—right over them.

Juan stood up and hummed as he petted the horse's muzzle.

Neighing, the stallion calmed down as the two men watched in amazement.

FIFTEEN

WHERE DID YOU learn that sound?" El Mestizo asked me.

"From my mother."

We were seated in the shade at the far end of the stable, where there was more privacy.

El Mestizo had had Gomez bring me a tortilla filled with juicy pork, tomatoes, and onions. I chewed on it as I answered the man's questions.

"What was your mother's name?"

"Maria."

"And your father's?"

I shrugged. "Only God knows his name. I am a bastardo."

"What do you know about your mother?"

"Very little, señor. She came to the house of the prostitutes alone and with a swollen belly. I was born there and stayed until I was old enough to go out onto the streets."

Despite his grand clothes, the prize stallion, and expensive tack he owned, I recognized the man as a mestizo like myself. It wasn't his skin color, which was about the same as mine; Spaniards came in many different shades, from pale white to olive. But I could see from his features and the thickness of his coal black hair that, like me, he also carried indio blood.

A few mestizos owned small ranchos, most were laborers or léperos, though I had heard that there were also mestizos who were like grandees, but I had never seen one.

"Did your mother tell you anything about herself?"

"No, señor, my mother left the world when I was very small, before I was two years old, I think."

"So you know nothing about your mother or her family, and nothing about your father or his family."

"True, señor, I am a miserable bastardo," I whined, "and God will reward you if you—"

"Stop!"

I clamped my mouth shut.

He leaned toward me, his eyes blazing.

"You are never again going to beg. You understand that?"

I stared at him, confused. "Then how will I eat, señor?"

"How will you eat?"

The question was asked of himself, and he appeared to muse over it, rubbing his jaw.

He suddenly stared at me so intently I drew back, frightened.

Reaching out, he gave me a gentle touch on the shoulder. "Don't be afraid, chico. I'm just puzzled because you remind me of someone."

"Who do I remind you of, señor?"

He hesitated and his features darkened.

"No one. I was mistaken . . . you remind me of no one."

The grandee mestizo confused and scared me. I wanted to bolt, but my sore legs would have been unable to outrun him.

He stood up.

"Come, I must talk to the stable owner."

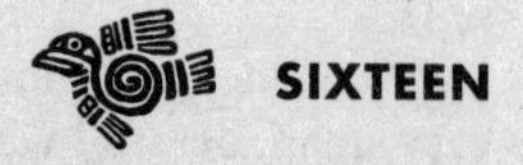

SIXTEEN

"DID YOU HEAR what that boy hummed?" Gomez asked El Mestizo. "There's a legend about a Zapote tune taught to princesses that could tame a jaguar. I heard the princesses would use it to calm their crying babies."

"It wasn't the noise the boy made that calmed the horse. The stallion doesn't mind small boys."

El Mestizo's rebuttal was a lie. He, too, knew of the story about a tune hummed by Zapote princesses, but he didn't want the tale identified with the boy.

Gomez started to say that he didn't think the stallion would tolerate the stinking little street boy short of an act of God, but shut his mouth. He was in awe of El Mestizo even though he himself was a pure-blooded Spaniard. What the Cortés family didn't own in the Oaxaca region, it controlled, and even a half-blood Cortés was considered Oaxaca royalty.

El Mestizo asked enough questions of the stable owner to determine that the only thing Gomez knew about the boy was that he was part of the pack of thieving léperos that polluted the streets with their cries and crimes.

When Gomez showed some curiosity about why a Cortés would be interested in a street boy, El Mestizo said, "My priest says I must do penance for a sin." He gave the stable owner a wink that told the man the sin was of a sexual nature, something the other man would quickly relate to.

"I have decided to do penance by helping out the boy, making sure he has an opportunity to rid himself of not just the lice he carries on his filthy body, but the disgusting habits he has picked up on the streets."

El Mestizo courteously asked Gomez if he would assist him with his penance, offering to pay for the boy's keep if Gomez would clean up the boy and train him to work in the stable.

"Sí, señor, but would the boy also not get training on your hacienda?"

"True, but I will be leaving with my brother for Madrid shortly," El Mestizo said. "I'm not certain how long we will be gone. We do the king's work and will stay as long as he commands it."

"Of course," Gomez said, nodding, "of course, at his command."

"It would be better for the boy to adjust to life here, in town, where he is used to living." El Mestizo gave Gomez a look. "Your assistance to my brother, the marquis, and myself would be greatly appreciated, but if it's not something you feel you can do . . ."

The mention of the marquis had an electrifying effect on the stable owner.

Gomez got down on his knees and begged for the opportunity to take the street boy in.

El Mestizo was careful to name a sum to pay for the boy's upkeep that wouldn't cause suspicion, but he also slipped the man a gold coin to prime the pump.

Leaving the stable, El Mestizo's knees were shaking. He prayed he had pulled off the pretense about penance with the stable owner.

He knew exactly who the boy was—and the child would not live long if others learned his heritage.

"Penance for sins against the boy," he mumbled to himself.

He had not lied about that.

SEVENTEEN

AS SOON AS the stallion owner had left, Gomez cuffed me on the side of the head.

"You stinking bastardo! You've been sneaking in, stealing my corn."

"Just a handful, señor."

"Well, you're the luckiest dirty little lépero in the colony. El Mestizo has arranged for you to work in the stable."

I was stunned and puzzled. "What does that mean?"

"It means you get to sleep in one of the stalls and eat what the horses eat as long as you work hard, don't steal, and don't talk back." He waved his hand in front of his nose. "Phew. And take a bath once a year. Understand?"

"Sí, señor."

But I understood nothing, though thoughts were buzzing in my head like an angry hornet's nest. It sounded like the stable owner was saying that I could live and work in the stable, that I would actually have a home among the horses, but the idea was too incredible, too incomprehensible to be true.

"You're lucky the stallion didn't stomp you into the ground," Gomez growled at me.

"Sí, God was watching over me."

"God doesn't watch over lépero trash. Phew!" Gomez again waved away the stink flowing from me.

"You smell worse than the manure. Go wash yourself down at the river."

"I can use the horse—"

"You'd poison the horses if you used their troughs."

I stopped him with a question as he started to walk away.

"This man, my benefactor, who is he?"

"He's the son of the conqueror, birthed by Marina, the india interpreter that helped our heroes fight the Aztecs."

A son of the conqueror! Even an ignorant lépero like me knew about Hernán Cortés.

"The Marquis del Valle de Oaxaca?" I asked.

"Of course not. That is his brother, a pureblood and conceived in a marriage bed sanctioned by God. El Mestizo is a bastardo who carries the blood taint." The stableman spit. "A mestizo bastardo has less rights and fewer brains than a jackass."

Gomez quickly looked behind him to see if El Mestizo could have returned and heard the insult.

"Get out of here," he told me. "Leave that stench at the river or don't come back."

The hornets in the nest in my head swirled as I hobbled to the river. I no longer actually felt any pain. I was too numb from what had just happened to feel any pain.

A mestizo bastardo who wears fancy clothes, owns a valuable horse, and is the son of the conqueror.

And he had arranged for me to work in the stable.

I had never realized that a mestizo could be more valuable than a toad, much less own a champion stallion.

Was it possible that even I had as much worth as the horses I stole grain from?

PART 3

OAXACA

A.D. 1565

OAXACA

We came to the city of Oaxaca . . . and though not very big, yet a fair and beautiful city to behold. It standeth fourscore leagues from Mexico in a pleasant valley from whence Cortés was named Marqués del Valle . . .

The valley of Oaxaca is of at least fifteen miles in length and ten in breadth, which runneth in the midst a goodly river yielding great store of fish. The valley is full of sheep and other cattle . . . but what doth make the valley of Oaxaca to be mentioned far and near are the good horses which are bred in it, and esteemed to be the best in all the country.

—*Travels of Thomas Gage*

EIGHTEEN

PUSHING THROUGH THE crowd of jubilant people in the town square, I made my way past the card tables set up under torchlight in front of the inn. I pretended to show little interest in the game that had just started, but it was the reason I had come to the square.

I was up to my first larceny since I had found a home in the stable nine years before and left my life as a lépero.

Well . . . perhaps not really my first—old habits are hard to break—but it had been a very long time since I had stolen anything. Even though life had some bumps and rocky places, since the day I was taken in at the bequest of the eldest son of Cortés, I had had food and shelter and worked with horses—what more could a young man ask for? Perhaps a good woman to share his bed? That would come when I could afford to have a wife.

Yes, there was that one more burning necessity, but since I was not ready for marriage, I satisfied my lust on Saturday night at the whorehouse and obtained absolution Sunday morning at confession.

My Saturday-night enjoyment kept me broke for the rest of the week, but it took the edge off of my urges, too.

Sí, I am no longer a stinking, dirty, hungry, thieving lépero, though as a half-caste, I still sleep in the stable and I am only one rung up the social ladder from the léperos on the street.

Even though I am granted a tiny bit of respectability from gachupins because I care for their horses, I have a place to sleep and plenty of tortillas, frijoles, peppers, and even carne . . . but in truth I still thought like a lépero. That cunning and alertness to watch my back was still part of me, hidden inside my soul.

When the time came that it was needed, my lépero sense of survival and larceny would come to the surface. That included the ability to climb walls, a feat I planned to perform tonight, though not in view of the hoards of people who have come to the festival.

People around me were happy and drunk; there was food, drink, gambling, dancing, and music. I was eager to join them as soon as I accomplished the task I had agreed to perform.

The laughter and dancing seemed to have broken the tension that had gripped the town for days after another indio incident in which a Spaniard was killed. Many indios, almost all of them only guilty of being nearby when the drunken gachupin was killed in a struggle with a man whose daughter he was raping, were murdered by a posse of Spaniards in retaliation.

The dead Spaniard had an evil reputation for cheating indios and raping their women, but because he was a wealthy landowner and the victims were indios, Spanish legal administrators looked the other way as a group of Spaniards took action against indios to ensure that they would not get up the courage to kill another gachupin.

It wasn't that the Spaniards were totally insensitive to the evil that their deceased amigo had done—more important to them was to keep the indio population, which vastly outnumbered them, frightened and submissive.

Night had fallen and Oaxaca's main square was lit up with torches as more and more people crowded in for the festivities. Most of the people were indios, with a small number of Spaniards, a few mestizos, and too many whining, drunken, begging léperos. Even I found the stinking, whining street trash insufferable.

I was no longer Juan the Lépero—now I was Juan the Mestizo—but the size of my physical world had not grown much. I had still never been farther than the river at the edge of town and the pasture along the river where horses were traded and trained. But I had learned many things about the colony and what had happened outside of Oaxaca since I had become respectable—at least as respectable as one who bore the blood taint could be.

On the surface it appeared that I had gained little of consequence. For sure, I had a warm place to sleep and a bellyful of tortillas, but I was still just a stable boy. But the effect on me wasn't just that I didn't smell worse than manure anymore—once I realized that a mestizo was at least as valuable as a horse, I gathered knowledge, though I had avoided learning how to read and write, turning down the help of a young priest who thought he could save my soul if I could read stories about the prophets in the Bible.

Learning about horses, how to stable them, shoe them, and treat their illnesses and injuries, had more meaning to me than lifeless words on a piece of paper.

I learned that Oaxaca was not the center of the world, was not even one of the grandest towns of New Spain; that Mexico City, Puebla, Vera Cruz, Guadalajara, and the northern silver mining towns were all larger; and that many of the larger cities had cobblestoned their main square and even many of the main streets, while Oaxaca's were packed dirt that turned to mud during the rainy season.

Rather than being a crossroad of trade or sitting atop mountains of silver, Oaxaca was a quiet farming community; only instead of just the beans, maize, and peppers that had been grown here since indios first scratched the land, the Spanish brought with them horses, mules, cows, goats, sheep, chickens, and oxen, all of which thrived in the green river valley.

But the Spanish also brought with them things that were not as beneficial as farm animals—disease.

The priest told me that in the days before the 1521 conquest, the valley supported around a million and a half indios, but ninety percent of the population had been wiped out by the diseases that the invaders carried with them from Europe. The population number increased little over the years because so much of the food and other products indios created ended up being taken from them without compensation.

Ayyo! Tonight, with my help, a little of what was stolen from the indios and mestizos was about to be returned.

The noisy festival in the town square was the Guelaguetza celebration, which, like many traditions in New Spain, was held to attract the indios with what they were already familiar with; the church had converted a traditional indio fete to one with Christian religious principles—leaving out the bloody indio rituals, of course.

Before the conquest, the celebration honored Centeotl, the Zapotec and Mixtec goddess of corn, and a virgin slave girl had been sacrificed in the name of the goddess.

What a waste of womanhood!

As soon as the indio empires collapsed, Spanish priests set out to completely destroy the religion of the indios, burning their books and using the stones of their temples to build churches. That left a religious void for the indios because they were not able to instantly convert to the religion the invaders brought with them.

The clever priests realized that it would be easier to get indios to participate in a festival that was familiar to them than trying to teach them a Christian one from scratch. So they eliminated the indio sacrifice of a virgin girl and instead made Guelaguetza a celebration in honor of the Virgin del Carmen, with music, dancing, gambling, and games of skill.

While the celebration was going on in the main square, the governor had posted constables armed with muskets at strategic points to ensure that the fete stayed peaceful.

The precaution was a reminder that, despite the destruction of the indio culture and the substitution of a Spanish one, the conquerors did not have a firm grasp on all of the colony they called New Spain.

Nor was the colony completely "civilized" by Spanish standards. Only the heart of the territory—Mexico City, Guadalajara, Guanajuato, Vera Cruz, Acapulco, and their environs—were firmly dominated by the conquerors.

The Oaxaca region was on the fringes of being completely under the control of the Spanish, but Zapotec and Mixtec uprisings still spontaneously ignited, only to be put down harshly.

Beyond the silver mining regions in Guanajuato and Zacatecas to the north of Mexico City and Oaxaca to the south, much of the colony was still dominated by indios, many of whom carried on continuous resistance as the Spanish pushed farther and farther north in the search of more silver, gold, or valuable farmlands, destroying what little the indios had, impoverishing them, and forcing them to work for Spanish masters in order to survive.

The Maya region to the far south was not completely under the control of the Spanish. The jungle terrain was difficult, the people stubborn, and the lack of land that could be farmed all worked against total subjugation.

Even where the Spanish did not completely dominate, they had scattered settlements and mining towns that were armed camps and missions that were little more than church-fortresses.

These entities outside the direct control of the colonial administration existed in an uneasy peace with the surrounding indios that sometimes turned violent.

Tonight I would strike a small blow against the Spanish, at least against one particularly cruel Spaniard.

NINETEEN

PASSING BY THE card tables set on the sidewalk in front of the inn, I gave one table a quick glance as two players were getting prepared to engage in a play-off.

One of the players was a mestizo, a small ranchero I had become friendly with because he owned two horses, a mare and a stallion, and I had treated the stallion for a hoof that had become infected after suffering a cut.

A Spanish hacienda owner would have considered the horses that the mestizo owned only good enough to pull a work wagon, but to the mestizo they were a treasure trove that would become the beginning of a herd when the mare became pregnant.

The owner of the hacienda bordering the mestizo's small property resented the fact that a mestizo had two horses, much less that he had what could be the start of an actual horse ranch.

Getting the mestizo drunk in town one night by pretending to be friendly to him and supplying strong brandy, the hacienda owner cheated him in a game of cards and took the horses as payment.

Tonight the mestizo was playing against the Spaniard again, but this time he was putting his rancho into the pot while the hacienda owner's ante were the horses he had cheated to get.

If the ranchero won, he would only get back what

he had lost, but when a mestizo is pitted against a Spaniard, that would be a miraculous victory.

If he lost . . . he would have to build a shack for his family to live in and hope to raise a crop of corn before they starved to death.

The hacienda owner had a reputation as being both arrogant and vicious, a man who enjoyed hurting people and animals when he had a bellyful of booze. I witnessed him hit his horse across the head, blinding it in one eye, after he fell off trying to mount the horse when he was drunk. Onlookers had laughed when he fell, but that was enough to put the man into a rage against the helpless animal.

I had gone to the aid of the horse, and the drunken lout had struck me with his quirt.

I took the blow because to have hit back would have put me in the constable's jail if I wasn't killed on the spot by the hacienda owner's Spanish friends.

The hacienda owner thought of himself as particularly good at cards and had invited his friends to watch him humiliate and destroy the mestizo he had once cheated.

Of course, the Spaniard had not counted on the ranchero having a friend who had once been a thieving lépero—and loved horses.

The horse he blinded in one eye was in my thoughts as I made my way past the table.

Leaving the packed square, I went down a deserted alley at the back of the inn. It was familiar ground to me because I had once shared a space under the eave with a pig—that was before I got a roof over my head at the stable.

Years later, another of the swine's fellows was tied up there, waiting for slop to fatten up on until the day he is invited to be the guest of honor at the dinner table.

Looking around to make sure I was not watched, I started up the grapevines attached to the back wall, going quickly all the way up to the open window of the room at the top. The windows were glassless and the shutters were closed only for rain.

I was heavier now than in those days when I could climb like a squirrel, but the vines were thick and would hold my weight—I hoped.

An indio servant told me that the room was rented by an important Spaniard visiting from Mexico City and that the man was a guest of the bishop and would be watching the festivities from a raised pavilion in front of the church.

No one was in the room as I entered.

I looked around, curious as to how the wealthy gachupins lived. The only room in a house I had been in was the front room of the stable owner's quarters next to the stable. This one here was much fancier, with a big bed that had a canopy over it.

The door to the dressing room was open and I took a peek in. The man's carriage trunks were inside and his clothes neatly laid out. The silk material and other fine cloths belonged to a personage of importance.

A jewelry case was open on the dresser and I paused to look at the pearls and other gems just long enough to remind myself that this was forbidden fruit. I might get away with taking a fancy handkerchief, claiming I found it on the street, but it would be impossible for me to wear or sell jewelry in Oaxaca without finding myself with a date for the hangman.

Besides, I was on a mission that even the good

Lord would approve of even though cheating at cards was needed to bring about a just ending to an injustice.

Then I spotted something I could steal without risking arrest: his perfume bottle on the dresser. I shook a generous amount of the lilac-smelling liquid into my palm and stuck my hand inside my shirt to rub it under one underarm and then the other.

Ayyo! I smelled like a gachupin!

But it was time to go to work.

I got down on my hands and knees and crawled out onto the balcony, staying low enough to avoid being spotted. The inn was the tallest building in town, outside of the church, and I would not be seen even if someone was in the church bell tower because the railing was covered with flower vines.

I slipped a short spyglass I had "borrowed" from the stable out from under my shirt.

The vertical supports of the railing were spaced far enough apart to permit me to push aside the vines and stick my head through to look down at the card game with my spyglass.

The two players had their sides to the inn. The fancy playing cards, being dealt by another gachupin, were about the size of a man's hand, and I could easily make out the details.

The cards were not the typical ones based upon the French design with kings and queens and jacks but had swords and wands, goblets and coins for symbols. The game to be played was a simplified version of Cacho, in which the winner has the highest three-card combination.

If the mestizo had a winning hand, I would nod the spyglass up and down; if a loser, side to side. The mestizo's wife was across the way, watching for my signal. She in turn would pass the signal to her husband.

Easy, no?

TWENTY

NINA ALVAREZ OPENED her room door on the top floor of the Oaxaca inn and peeked out. Two women guests were in the hallway chatting, and Nina quickly closed the door.

She would check again in a couple of minutes to see if the coast was clear. If it was, she would scurry down the hallway and use the key her lover gave her to enter his room and wait for him.

Carlos de Rueda, her lover, was married to a sister of the marquis. Carlos had come to Oaxaca for a Cortés family gathering to celebrate the return of the marquis from Spain. His wife remained in Mexico City because she was ill.

Carlos had come in his own carriage, and Nina had followed in the public stage that made the trip from the capital to Oaxaca in considerably less comfort, but she had made the journey for love.

His wife's serious illness had made it even more difficult for them to meet in the city. Under ordinary circumstances, little comment would be made when a man takes a mistress, but Carlos feared that the marquis would be offended because of his sister's serious condition.

Nina wondered if Carlos would marry her if his wife passed away. She had hinted about it, but had not gotten a response. Despite her yearning, it was doubtful that such a match would be made because of her lower social position. She was of the merchant class, while Carlos was a wealthy caballero and related by marriage to the most noble family in the colony.

Nina was a rarity among even the merchant class because she was a woman who made a living on her own. Few jobs were open to women other than as servants or laborers washing clothes in laundries, sewing, or weaving.

Known as the best seamstress in Mexico City, she designed gowns for the wealthiest women in the colony. It provided her a good living, though she eyed many of the women with resentment, especially the wives and daughters of the merchant class to which she herself had once belonged.

Her father had lost his wealth and took his own life after speculation on a silver mine made his family homeless and put him in debtors' prison. Silver—which made the colony the richest in the empire and created many a great fortune—had cost more men their lives and fortunes than card games.

Nina was famous for her fine, fancy weaving, creating intricate patterns with her small fingers. She knew that Carlos also delighted in her tiny fingers and quick tongue when it came to their lovemaking.

Impatient now, she went to check the hallway again to see if her lover had managed to slip away from the bishop's company.

TWENTY-ONE

AS THE GAME below progressed and the stack of pieces of eight coins on the hacienda's owner's side of the table shrunk while the stacks increased on the ranchero's side, I could see that the hacienda owner's temperament grew meaner at about the same rate as his losses.

The match wasn't about the number of silver coins. Rather, the coins were used as chips, and when the hacienda owner lost his last chip, he had to turn over a paper giving ownership of the two horses back to the ranchero.

I was surprised when the hacienda owner calmly handed over the paper when his last silver piece was lost.

The elated ranchero, bubbling with joy, bowed and profusely thanked the man. In response, the hacienda owner slipped his quirt off the hook on his belt and hit the ranchero in the face with it, slicing open the side of his face from hairline to jaw.

Ayyo! I had run on the streets with léperos who were finer human beings than that bastardo.

I left my position at the railing, resisting the temptation to drop a heavy clay flowerpot down on the hacienda owner because it would have also brought hell into the ranchero's life. At least he had his horses back and knew never to trust gachupins.

As I entered the room, the door to the hallway

began swinging open and I dived to the floor next to the bed. I froze for a second in pure terror that I was about to be discovered and about to have my gut sliced open with a gachupin's blade, then scooted under the bed.

I heard footsteps walking across the room, but not the sounds of a man's heavy foot.

In the dim light I could see the bottom part of a woman's dress and shoes as she moved across the room, turning off the lamps and then pulling the curtains, until the darkness in the room was relieved only by a single candle next to the bed and a little lamplight coming through the open door of the dressing room.

She was either very romantic or a damn bat, and I didn't care which as I lay motionless with my heart pounding, expecting to be discovered at any moment, her screams sounding an alarm that an intruder had invaded the room.

If I got out of this without my neck stretching on the gallows, I would be paying the india servant a visit and taking back the coin I gave her for information about the room's occupant—she hadn't told me that the man's wife had accompanied him.

The woman stopped moving. I saw her feet turn halfway around—in my direction. Had she spotted me under the bed?

I looked down at my own feet in sudden fear that they were exposed. Relieved that they weren't, I lay as still as possible, and waited, hoping I wouldn't have to sneeze or cough—dust under the bed from the coal bed warmer was tickling my dry throat.

What was she doing? I felt the beads of sweat forming on my forehead and under my arms. Being caught in a room with a Spanish woman would mean the end of me—quickly. The chief constable would simply turn me over to the mob of gachupins who came to the jail with a rope.

I could see that her feet still stood planted on the floor, but now I heard the swishing movement of a dress.

Impatient, I slowly inched my head farther out to see why she halted in the middle of the room.

Ayyo! The woman had stopped in front of a full-length oval mirror on a stand. Swaying seductively back and forth, she hummed a little song as she examined her figure in the mirror.

She glided her hands along the tight-fitting bodice that accentuated her ample breasts and round figure, admiring herself in the full-length mirror, before she finally began to undo her layers of clothing, removing first her silk dress and then the mountains of petticoats underneath. Her shoes were the last to come off.

Madre de Dios! She stood totally naked now, except for a strand of pearls around her neck, and a distinguishing mark on one of her breasts that I couldn't quite make out.

Watching her voluptuous body moving in the faint light had awakened the private part between my legs. I wanted to spring out from my hiding place underneath the bed and have this sultry woman.

She had a presence of self-assurance and assertiveness about her, unlike the young señoritas that I had seen in the city, all of whom appear too innocent and naive. I doubted if this woman had any trouble enticing men to give her what she wanted in exchange for giving them the pleasure they desired.

How long would I have to hide underneath the bed and have her torment me like this? I had no control in the growth of my manhood, and it was beginning to ache pressing against my pants because I couldn't make an adjustment that would have made it more comfortable.

There was nothing I could do but wait in agony, even though my body screamed for me to dive out and shove my pene into this woman so I could satisfy my lust.

The woman finally went into the dressing room.

I knew this was my chance to escape. I slipped out from under the bed but hesitated a moment. I had to get across the room and the door to the hallway without being seen or heard.

The problem was the candle next to the bed. It gave off just enough light to reveal that there was a stranger in the room if she stepped out of the dressing area.

I pinched out the candlelight, turning the room almost completely dark.

The path to the door was clear of furniture, and I moved soft-footed on the floor. Reaching the door, I quietly opened it, and shut it as I saw a man and woman topping the stairway across the hallway.

The latch scraped as it dropped into place—*it sounded as loud as a church bell.* I didn't breathe, didn't move.

"I'm coming, darling," came from the dressing area, and the bedroom was cloaked in darkness as she extinguished the lamp in the dressing room.

She *was* a damn bat!

I headed for the window I had climbed through from the vines earlier and hit a table, knocking something off and onto the floor.

And then she was on me. It was too dark to see her and I smelled her before I felt her grab my clothes. She put her arms around my neck and kissed me, hard, her mouth eagerly kissing my neck, my cheeks, my lips again, and I realized as she pressed against me why she had turned the room completely dark—she was still bare-ass naked, her body hot and moist from the bathtub.

"Oh, darling, I missed you . . . your arms around me—"

She guided my hands to her full breasts, and I squeezed them as she pulled my head down to her chest.

I had to pretend I was her man. What else could I do?

I kissed the big luscious mounds, first one, then the other, taking each nipple in my mouth and caressing it with my tongue.

She undid the front of my pants and her hands slipped down.

"I know how much you love my nimble fingers," she said.

Ayyo! I almost jumped out of my pants as she grabbed my swollen stalk with one hand while her other hand squeezed my cojones until I had to force back a gasp that wouldn't sound like her husband.

"My darling . . . you feel even bigger and harder than you ever have been before," she whispered seductively.

Suddenly my pants were half off and she was on her knees, taking my engorged stalk in her mouth, keeping a firm grip on it as she sucked, up and down, again and again . . . Ayyo! The pumping was making me dizzy and ready to explode in her mouth when—

The door unlatched!

I broke off the mouth pump immediately and ran for the window, pulling up my pants on the way as best I could.

I heard her scream behind me as I flew into the drapes and pulled up the window.

It was the wrong window—no vine and a sheer drop to the ground three stories below!

"Get out of here!" she shouted to the person who entered the room.

"Pardon, señora, coals for the bed!"

I was confused and crazed with panic.

Staying in the drapes, I moved toward the window where the vine came up, freezing in place when I heard her pulling aside the drapes.

I couldn't see her but I knew she was checking out the window, looking to see if her phantom lover was below, muttering to herself in sheer bewilderment.

The door being unlatched sounded again, and I heard her exclaim, "Carlos!" as her bare feet patted away from the window and drapes.

"That damn door latch was jammed," a man said. "What's the matter, Nina? You look like you saw a ghost."

"I—I—"

"What's happened? You're ready to faint."

"The—the coal man, he brought coals."

"Coals?"

"For the bed. He opened the door and I was waiting for you—as I am now."

Carlos chuckled. "Well, you made his day exciting, perhaps his whole life, since he will be talking about the naked woman he saw. I'm just happy you weren't seen by anyone of significance. If my wife's relatives found out—but enough, come to me, do those things with your fingers and tongue that I love so much."

Ayyo! I agonized as I heard his shouts of glee about how much joy those fingers and tongue brought him.

TWENTY-TWO

I STOOD PERFECTLY still, for an eternity it seemed, knees locked, my swollen stalk already deflated, as the man greedily spent his passions under the woman's erotic touch.

When it came for her turn to be satisfied, he apologized for not being able to perform his manly duty.

"It's been a trying day with my wife's relatives," he alibied.

"I think it's the sheepskin you cover your pene with to collect your manhood. I wish you didn't wear it."

"Darling, you know why. I have to make sure I don't impregnate you. It wouldn't matter if you were an india, but you are Spanish and a Spanish bastardo is much harder to deal with and keep quiet. I don't want a problem with the marquis. He already complained to me that I am not doing enough to make sure his sister is comfortable."

"It's her last illness, isn't it? Then we can be—"

"Don't start that again. You know that I will have to marry a woman whose dowry can maintain my lifestyle. You are a seamstress and have no dowry. What you do for my stallion has kept me in gold so far, but as the animal grows older, suspicions will arise."

I found the conversation strange and wondered what he meant by her keeping him in gold because of his stallion.

As their conversation droned on I found my head

nodding and nearly lost my balance as I started to fall asleep.

When I finally heard them both snoring, I gently raised the window behind me. Gently wasn't enough because it made a screech. I jerked it up quickly and prayed that I was going out the window that had the vines.

I went through almost headfirst, grabbing hold of a vine, swinging back against the wall, barely getting a grip to break what would have been a plunge to my death.

Cursing came from above as the man stuck his head out the window, but I didn't look up as I scrambled halfway down the wall before I let go and dropped to the ground.

I hit the dirt that the pig had softened with its hooves and droppings and rolled in pig shit, getting to my feet and running like hell away from whatever or whoever might be running after me.

TWENTY-THREE

THE NEXT MORNING as dawn broke I left the stable eating a tortilla filled with carne, eggs, and peppers and headed for the corral outside of town where horse traders gathered to make deals and buyers of unbroken mounts paid to have their new purchase carry a rider for the first time.

I led a horse beside me that had been stabled and that the owner wanted taken to a trader.

Since that time of being discovered under the hooves of a stallion and finding a home as a stable boy, I had learned much about horses and people. I had learned that there were good people and bad people, and more sinners than saints.

I had a natural affinity with horses right off, but had to learn how to recognize and treat their maladies and injuries, when to put them down to keep them from suffering if they were no longer able to function, and the craft of horseshoeing, an art that Atlas himself would have found more perplexing and demanding than holding up the sky.

Anything I earned, of course, went to the stable owner, so I had owned nothing but the clothes on my back and a few copper coins that jingled in my pocket. But I ate well, slept soundly with a roof over my head, and enjoyed living, working, and breathing with horses.

Things had changed during the past few months,

but I still hung on to my job and the stable stall where I slept.

Perhaps because he had no family of his own, Gomez had begun to treat me with some of the respect and endearment a father gives a son. He had told me that his only family was a sister whom he disliked intensely and that when he died, the stable would go to me.

"I went to the lawyer and signed a paper giving you the stable after I pass," he told me one night after he had returned from the inn with a bellyful of wine.

The lawyer had argued with him, he said, telling him that people would be angry if the stable came into the ownership of a lépero.

"But I don't give a damn what they say. I want you to have it," he said.

Gomez passed beyond sorrow six months ago after he got kicked in the head shoeing a mule. Within a day, his sister and her husband, Héctor, came and took over the stable as the new owners.

A Spanish friend had also been told of Gomez's wish in giving me the stable. The friend took me to the lawyer and had me sit outside when he went in to talk to the lawyer. A few minutes later the town mayor arrived and gave me a dark look as he went into the lawyer's office.

When Gomez's friend returned a short while later his attitude was gruff and even angry toward me.

"Go back to the stable and do your work. It will never be yours. A lépero can't own such a thing."

I am not completely stupid about the ways of the world, and I knew the man spoke the truth. The ownership of the stable had been decided based upon blood, not Gomez's wishes.

The notion that I could have owned the stable had

never been real to me, anyway. I had never possessed anything more than the clothes on my back and the dirt between my toes.

When Gomez told me that he would leave the stable to me, in my mind it only meant that I would continue to have a place to live and work after he was gone. But when the new owners arrived, I quickly learned the difference between owning a stable and working there.

Gomez knew every aspect of the business and worked hard alongside me, whether it was shoeing or shoveling, feeding horses or treating their problems—it didn't matter what the task was, he carried part of the load.

The sister and her husband were lazy and stupid. What she did best was eat, and her husband had mastered the art of drunkenness so well he got in that state even during the workday.

They knew nothing about horses and less about running the stable except to have their hands out to collect the money and keep their tongues wagging to give me orders and complain that I wasn't working fast enough.

I didn't mind the work, but hated working for people who were more greedy and stupid than the swine—two-footed and four-footed—I had once slept alongside on the streets.

Since the drunken husband took over, I was appalled over the way he treated the horses. Héctor had never owned a horse and knew nothing about how to handle a horse except with a whip.

When I tried to show him how to lead a horse correctly, he raised the whip to hit me.

I took it from him, jerking the whip out of his hand. He fired me, but his wife was a little smarter than he was—she told me I could still work at the stable, but must learn to obey or take a beating.

I didn't tell her I would not be beaten—nor did I point out that the only reason they kept me on was that they knew nothing about running the stable, and, while it would be easy to hire an indio to shovel manure, they would not easily find a master of horse-shoeing and animal doctor to replace me.

What grieved me most was the way Héctor cheated the horses, and their masters, with feed.

The owners wanted their fine horses fed corn. Héctor charged for it, but fed the horses cheaper grains, even buying feed at a bargain price that was dried out or mildewed and charging for the better feed.

I loved horses and would have put up with el diablo to work with them, and that was about how I felt about dealing with the new owners of the stable.

As I grew up working for Gomez, I had spread my wings to the outskirts of town, to the corrals where horses were traded and trained.

I watched fascinated as horse traders brought their horses to town to sell and barter with. So much fine horseflesh, so exciting to watch and learn as masters of the trade appraised horses and bargained over them as if their whole lives were at stake with each transaction.

And I watched as trainers broke horses to the saddle. It was not a gentle craft, nor were the horses usually completely broken before they were turned over to their owners.

The partial breaking was done by saddling up the horse for the first time and mounting it. Once the rider was aboard, the horse would go racing across the pasture galloping and bucking, the rider hanging on for dear life as people ran to get out of the way.

By the time the horse had gone to the end of the pasture and back, if the rider had hung on well enough, the animal was too tired to put up any fight and was turned over to its owner, who would take it home and continue the breaking and training process. Only merchants with a soft behind and older caballeros had the horses completely broken to the saddle.

Going to the corrals was the only relief from the stable, but my new masters even forbid that because they wanted to control my every waking moment.

I still managed to get away occasionally when a horse had to be taken to the corrals or brought back from there, and sometimes when it wasn't necessary for me to be at the stable, I simply left and went to the corrals, ignoring the venomous looks I would get from the swine husband.

Gomez only had a pair of mules he kept to pull his feed wagon, so it was at the corrals that I had learned to break, ride, and train horses, besides judging their monetary value.

Breaking a horse with a wild and crazy ride had risks besides the broken bones for the rider. Sometimes horses sprained muscles or even stepped into a gopher hole and broke a leg and had to be put down.

Owners of extremely valuable horses often hired me to do the breaking because my method was a little less violent. While I couldn't "talk" a horse into accepting a saddle, with my whispers and cooing I was able to convince most horses not to go into a full gallop even though I, too, had to hang on tight and occasionally got thrown because they were still powerful beasts full of energy and spirit.

Whether it was to treat a sick horse or break one

to the saddle, horse owners frequently made the arrangement with the stable owners. Gomez had always let me keep a bit of the money, but the new owners kept it all, although I got an occasional coin for work I picked up myself at the corrals and never told them about.

This morning a trader who knew me asked me to show a potential buyer a horse that I had trained. Besides the animal's physical condition, the horse buyer was interested in the horse's walk, pace, and gallop, which I put the horse through. The buyer, a young caballero, wanted a horse that he could parade in the small park called a paseo along the river to the admiration of the town's affluent señoritas.

I have been told that every town has a greenway where caballeros can parade in their fancy clothes and prance horses for admiring young women in open carriages, and that the paseo in Mexico City was so large that the entire town of Oaxaca could fit into it.

I had trained the horse in what caballeros considered to be a more elegant movement. Called the paso, in reference to the way the horse was taught to pace, the movement was different than the ordinary and simple trot.

When the horse performed the paso, it moved a bit side to side, with its two hooves on one side hitting the ground at the same time and then the two hooves on the other side doing the same thing.

The paso was used mostly for show, but it actually created a smooth, comfortable ride that a horse can maintain for long distances and is suited for mountain journeys.

Another movement I had to put the horse through—the rayar—was not of my liking. It was a fancy display of horsemanship that machismo riders used only on the paseo and was dangerous for the horse.

To perform it, the horse was taught at a gallop to suddenly put its forefeet straight out, similar to what a mule does to keep from sliding down a steep slope, and then to whirl around to face in the opposite direction.

To teach the maneuver, a line is placed on the ground where the horse is supposed to stop and turn. That line, the border where the horse stops to whirl, was called a rayar. It required strong hands and a good command of an already-trained horse to get the movement right.

I didn't like the trick and avoided training a horse to do it whenever I could because it damaged the horse's forefeet. But it was a favorite of the young men showing off on the paseo—prancing dandies is how I thought of them, endangering a horse to attract a woman.

I was a better horseman and fighter than any of them, but because of my blood curse, I shoveled manure while they pranced in fancy clothes and expensive horses.

While getting an admiring glance from a pretty señorita was worth some endangerment, the rider should be the one who's put in danger, not the mount.

I told myself that I would never be interested in horse tricks on the paseo even if I were a caballero, but sometimes when I saw the lovely women with their fancy gowns and grand carriages, the men with their clothes studded with leather and silver, the horses prancing proudly . . . I daydreamed a little and wondered what it would be like to have pure blood, to be in their position, and to be able to live and love and laugh—

That was sentimental nonsense, boyish fantasies

that were never meant to be. Besides, there were times working with horses that I truly felt exhilarated—when I saw that my treatment of a horse's malady had brought it back to its feet, when I was able to take a horse at a full gallop to test the animal's speed and stamina, feeling free with the wind in my face and a powerful animal under my control.

Eh, at the end of those moments of being as free as the wind, when I had to turn the horse and go back to where I was still just a lépero and stable boy, I fought a temptation to keep going, to leave Oaxaca in the dust behind me.

Sí, I had a wanderlust, probably created by endless hours at night listening to Gomez as he sucked on a jug of wine and told tales of his travels as a boy that took him across a great ocean from mother Spain to the colony and over mountain ranges and high plateaus before he settled in Oaxaca.

What was beyond the Valley of Oaxaca?

Other than the stories Gomez had told me, I knew only what I overheard on the streets: that Mexico City was the queen of cities, a place where the streets are so wide, carriages can travel six side by side; that in Guanajuato, a city so rich in silver, a mine owner once paved a street with silver for his daughter's wedding; that Vera Cruz and Acapulco were where the products of the colony flowed out and imported goods flowed in.

While the cities were just names and stories to me, sometimes when that wind was on my face and a powerful horse was galloping beneath me, I dreamed of riding into those places to experience the land, the people, and especially the women . . .

Ayyo! My daydream was smashed as a dirty little lépero street boy ran up to me.

"The stable owner says to get back and serve their customers."

He began to plead with me for a handout.

I threw the boy a copper to stop his whining.

TWENTY-FOUR

THE STAGE COACH to the capital and a gachupin's fancy coach were being hitched by their coachmen as I arrived back at the stable.

A group of Spaniards—several men and a woman—were nearby, waiting for the coaches.

I almost turned and ran in the opposite direction when I heard the woman speak to one of the men and then heard his reply.

The naked woman and her married lover!

Unable to resist the impulse, I glanced over. I had seen the woman only in pitch darkness and hadn't gotten a look at all at the man, but I knew their voices.

They stood farther apart than necessary even for strangers, keeping up the pretense that they didn't know each other as they spoke to the others in the group.

Once I got over the moment of panic, I chuckled over the notion of going up to them and asking what he did with the sheepskin sleeve he used to catch his male fluid.

My good humor lasted until I almost bumped into my new master as he staggered in the stable's main room and blew the stench of soured wine in my face.

"Get busy," Héctor growled.

"Doing what? The coachmen will handle the carriages."

"Work," he muttered, looking around confused for

a moment as he attempted to identify something to keep my idle hands occupied.

What I wanted to do was drag him to the pile of manure waiting to be hauled away and bury him in it, but I took my anger out at the anvil, shaping a horseshoe.

Héctor sauntered over to the cheating husband to fawn over him, but the gachupin waved him away, as he would to a fly buzzing around.

Apparently getting brushed off by the man was enough attention for Héctor to imagine that he had been rubbing shoulders with nobility.

"Don Carlos de Rueda is the brother-in-law of the marquis," he boasted when he came back. "He is in Oaxaca to celebrate the return of the marquis from Spain. He owns the finest horse in the colony, a stallion of the bloodline of the warhorse Cortés rode in the great battle against the Aztecs."

Héctor veered off to collect a fee from the stagecoach driver, or I would have pretended to be civil toward him and asked him more questions.

Not only was my own interest stimulated because the gachupin owned the most famous stallion in the colony, but he had made that puzzling statement to his lover last night:

"What you do for my stallion has kept me in gold so far, but as the animal grows older, suspicions will arise."

What could a woman do for his stallion that keeps him in gold?

Why would suspicions arise?

The two of them departed in their separate coaches, and I was left with another question.

Héctor said that the stallion owner was in town to celebrate the marquis's return from Spain. Had that other stallion owner, the one called El Mestizo, who was my benefactor, also returned from Europe?

I asked Héctor.

"Sí, the man is back with his brother." Héctor gave me an appraising look. "He sent a message that he is coming by the stable with a horse he wants boarded. He requested you be present to handle the horse."

My heart leaped.

"Listen, lépero, you must remember to tell El Mestizo how well we treat you. He is only the mixed-blood brother of the marquis, but some people say he has the marquis's ear."

"Only the mixed-blood brother? You phony little shit of a mouse, you would lick the sweat off his cojones if he let you!"

I don't know how the insult popped out of my mouth. Neither did Héctor. But the expression on my face must have been that of el diablo himself because the man backed away from me, gawking in fear, and fled to the house that he occupied with his wife.

I realized that it wasn't just the insult to my benefactor that had generated the slur to Héctor. Something in me had changed—my view of the world, and of myself.

When I was street trash, there was only me and other léperos at the bottom and the rest of the world above us. But I had now lived almost half of my life among pure-blooded Spaniards. I found some of them intelligent and brave; others, like Héctor, were spineless worms who would not have survived a night taking care of themselves on the streets.

Hearing Héctor demean El Mestizo, just one of many such slurs I'd heard from those with "pure blood" over the years about indios and mestizos, had finally snapped my patience. The drunken little weasel had cheap wine and indio beer in his veins while El Mestizo carried the blood of the great Cortés and the heroine Marina.

To hear that El Mestizo remembered me and wanted to show me a stallion made me giddy with joy.

I had always secretly hoped that someday he would return to Oaxaca so I could thank him for taking me off of the streets, and also show him the skills I had learned.

There was only one dark shadow that tempered my elation: I had greatly insulted Héctor.

If a gachupin had insulted him, he would have fallen to the ground and kissed the man's feet and licked his dirty toes. But hearing it come from me, someone he not only felt superior to, but the only person around that he could actually lord over because he was a spineless worm, made him dangerous.

To me.

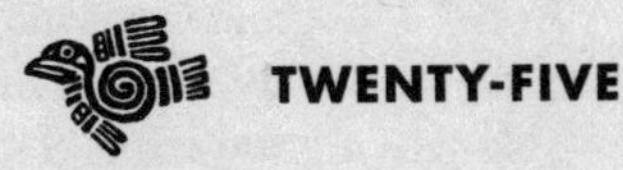

TWENTY-FIVE

WHEN EL MESTIZO arrived, he and his vaqueros had in tow a great black stallion.

I was awed at the sight of El Mestizo. All the saints of Christendom could have risen and come to me and I would not have been as affected as I was by the sight of my benefactor.

Nine years had not put any noticeable gray into his thick black hair. That was because of the indio in him, though a few gray specks had settled on the dark mat. That was the Spaniard in him. A few more wrinkles at the eye—perhaps because of the worries a gachupin carries. But otherwise, the Prince of Mestizos looked the same as he had when he took a mudlark off the street and made him a stable boy.

Héctor appeared suddenly, flying by me, fawning over El Mestizo as if the marquis himself had arrived. And in a sense he had for Héctor, because this was probably as close to the Marquis del Valle the drunken stable owner would ever get.

El Mestizo gave Héctor a polite nod, addressed him as señor when he said good day, and sidestepped him to approach me.

Like a fool, I awaited him as if my feet were planted in the ground. I was so in awe of him, so grateful for what he had done for me, I didn't know what to say or what to do.

"I heard many good things about you from Gomez

over the years. He wrote that you are not just a master of horses, but *the* grandmaster of horses in all Oaxaca."

Ayyo! The great man had kept track of my progress even halfway around the world.

"He was a good man," I said. "He treated me fairly and taught me a great deal. I miss him."

"So I have heard." He gave me an appraising look. "You are full-grown. Stronger than most, eh?"

"Perhaps." I gestured at the blacksmith's anvil and hammers. "Those are my swords and pistols."

"May you use them only in peace. Since I have been back, I have heard from others about you. Caballeros who trade and train horses say that you can make horses rise from the dead."

I laughed, embarrassed. "No, señor, but perhaps I have kept a few from going to horse heaven by asking them not to leave."

"I see you are still talking to them. And do the horses tell you where they hurt?"

"Sí, señor, they whisper it to me when no one else is listening. Do you have need of my services? A horse suffering a malady?"

"No, actually I just wanted to make sure my stallion is well cared for tonight in the stable. What do you think of my prize?"

I walked over to his horse to get a better look. The vaquero holding him warned me off. "He doesn't like it when people get close."

I ignored him and got close. The spirited stallion stomped his feet and neighed, and I hummed as I walked around him, running my hand along his flank and rear.

"He is temperamental, territorial, strong-willed. Sired by the stud that I shared a stall with."

"Yes," El Mestizo said, "and he inherited his arrogance."

"Is his bloodline good?" I asked.

"Almost the best. It runs back to one of the horses of the conquest."

"Cortés's warhorse?"

"One of them, though not the most prized of all."

I wondered if the "most prized of all" was the one owned by the man Héctor said was a brother-in-law of Cortés's sons.

I almost told him what I had overheard about the stallion bearing the most prized bloodline but didn't because it would involve a great many explanations, most of which I would be hanged for.

"Where is the sire?" I asked.

"Back in Spain, producing champion horses for caballeros who also prize the bloodline of the conquest. I didn't want to have him make the long sea journey. He is most happy with his mares and oats."

The stallion stopped fidgeting and gave me a nudge with its nose.

"There," El Mestizo said, "you have won the friendship of another of my horses. Perhaps someday you will come to my hacienda and meet all of my horses."

I was thrilled by the intimation that El Mestizo might have a job for me at his horse ranch.

Spaniards were coming up to the entrance to claim their horses.

"You have customers to attend to," El Mestizo said. "The stallion's name is Rojo. Take him to his stall and make him comfortable."

El Mestizo left, and I told the men who had arrived that I would be with them momentarily.

Red was an apt name for the stallion, both for its

temperament and its color. Like its sire, its color was the reddish-brown called chestnut, but it had more dark shades of red than I'd ever seen.

As I was leading the stallion to a stall, Héctor approached me, full of wine and bravado.

"Take care of the customers," he slurred. "I'll put the stallion away."

"El Mestizo wanted me—"

He jerked the reins from my hand and gave me a shove. "Get away, you lépero bastardo."

Héctor pulled at the reins and the stallion reared back, sending the stable owner stumbling into the coal brazier. Héctor yelped from pain as he brushed against the hot blazer, knocking it over, sending hot coals scattering on the ground.

"You filthy animal! I'll give you a lesson you'll never forget!" he yelled at the stallion. He grabbed the short-handled coal shovel and raised it, stepping up to the stallion.

"No!" I shouted.

I caught the shovel below the metal blade. Héctor pulled back on it and I hung on.

"Let it go!" I yelled.

He wouldn't let go and I had to wrestle the shovel out of his grip. He swung his fist at me, catching me on the side of the face. It wasn't much of a punch. I shoved him away from me, sending him stumbling backward to fall on his rear.

He snarled up at me, pulling his knife from its sheath as he rose. Once he was up on his feet, he charged at me.

He swung the blade at my face, and I caught his wrist and twisted it until he dropped the blade.

Jerking out of my grip, he stumbled again and

tripped, falling backward, hitting the back of his head on the anvil.

One of the Spaniards bending down beside Héctor looked up at me with disbelief.

"He's dead. You murdered him!"

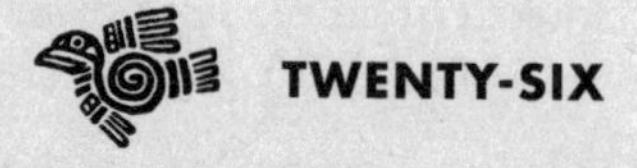

TWENTY-SIX

"I—I DIDN'T kill him, it—it was an accident," I stammered.

The Spaniard stared at me. "You murdered a Spaniard, you half-breed!"

"No—"

The commotion attracted other Spaniards into the stable from off the street, and I backed away from them as I saw their accusing faces.

"A lépero's killed a man!" one of them shouted.

El Mestizo pushed his way through the group that was forming. He looked at me and asked, "What happened?"

"I was attacked with a knife and I defended myself."

"He's just a stable boy and I saw him hit Héctor. He killed him," a man yelled at El Mestizo.

"I will take him to the constables and explain what happened," El Mestizo told the man.

"Constables, hell!" another Spaniard yelled. "Get a rope; we'll string him up right here."

"No!" El Mestizo stepped in front of the man, causing the man to back up. "There will be no lynching. It was an accident."

"He's a mestizo, too!" someone shouted. "Grab the lépero! I've got a rope!"

As the group of men came at me, the stallion spooked and reared, raising its powerful hooves, causing the men to collide with each other as they stumbled backward from a horse that weighed almost as much as ten of them put together.

I grabbed the rein as the stallion reared again and it jerked me back. I held on with both hands as it lunged forward, knocking aside men and sending others scattering as it burst out of the stable and onto the street.

Running head-on at an oncoming carriage, the stallion swerved. As it broke its stride, I hopped on the ground and pulled myself up with the reins.

"Go!" I shouted in Rojo's ear, and off he went, taking me down the street and out of town, the wind in my face, any pursuit behind me eating my dust.

TWENTY-SEVEN

I RODE WITH the wind in my face, but I had none of the exhilaration that I imagined I would experience when I broke out of the confines of Oaxaca and stepped into the unknown.

In my daydreaming I had imagined my journey would be one of adventure and discovery.

Instead, I rode from the only life I had ever known with the feeling that all the hounds of hell were snapping at my heels.

Rojo had taken me where the stallion wanted to go. I had just hung on, images of what had happened back at the stable burning in my head: Héctor going at the horse with a shovel, the blow that sent him down, Héctor coming back up with a knife to carve out my heart.

"It didn't happen!" I shouted to the wind.

When the big stallion paused to rest, I stared stupidly around, wondering where I was.

Looking at stone effigies, I realized where the stallion had carried me: Monte Albán, the ruins of the great Zapote civilization.

Dismounting, my stomach twisted in knots, I hid among the ghosts and silent edifices of the past.

I was no longer shaking, but my thoughts were jumbled, ricocheting like a musket ball bouncing off rocks—*I should return and explain to the chief constable that I did not mean to harm Héctor. Nothing will happen. God and El Mestizo are my witnesses—*

No! I'm a half-blood stable boy, a lépero with clean clothes. Héctor was Spanish and his widow would demand my blood.

Nor was there any certainty that I would even get to tell my side of the fight to the constable. Those who saw what happened wanted to hang me immediately. If men like that got their hands on me, my version would only be told to el diablo himself because I would be carted off to hell.

And I was a horse thief, too. El Mestizo's defense of me no doubt faded when I ran off with his prize stallion. Now he would probably even tighten the noose around my neck if he got the chance.

I was only a couple hours' walk, half an hour's ride on a good horse, from the town, but it was the farthest I had ever been away from home.

From here, where the only people were etched in stone, I had no idea which direction to go.

Had a search begun for me? It was only midday, but I knew on other searches that had been launched from Oaxaca that the constables were slow to get started and needed to gather provisions, mounts, and men, preferring to head out early in the morning.

The distance a wanted man put between him and the searchers mattered little because there were few places to go and ultimately word traveled faster than horses and there would be no place for the criminal to hide.

I knew the sun rose in the east and that the capital was somewhere to the northwest, but that told me as much as knowing that heaven was over my head and hell beneath my feet.

Rojo found grass to graze upon, but I had no food and no weapon to kill game with. When night fell I would have to sleep on the bare ground without covers.

Ayyo! I was confused. I didn't know what to do, where to turn. The only route that I knew was back to town, but my gut told me that would be sure death for me.

I walked around the ruins, my nerves raw, trying to get my thoughts in some sort of order. I knew a little about the ancient site, that Monte Albán was one of the great Zapote indio sites that existed before the conquest.

The priests at the cathedral in Oaxaca spoke many times about the site, not to praise it but to damn it as representing a religion that they called barbaric and godless.

But there were gods, not the same as the one the Spanish priests worshipped, but powerful indio gods that made the people of Monte Albán a great and mighty empire centuries before the child Jesus was born.

The might and power of these ancient gods was obvious to me as I walked hundreds of feet along what appeared to be the main square of the site.

I passed stone edifices of naked men in twisted poses, some of them with their manhood cut off; other carvings showed naked women, dwarves, and what appeared to be some sort of medical procedures, even drilling into people's heads.

I thought about my indio blood and the power of it in times of old as I walked among the shattered ruins.

Although there were sporadic uprisings, the indios so greatly outnumbered their masters that if they had rose as a whole, they could have driven the Spanish from what they once called the One-World. But even before the conquest the indios had no unity.

Before Cortés and his conquistadors defeated the Aztecs and ripped apart the fabric of indio society, the One-World had been divided into regions by language and customs—Aztecs, Zapotecs, Mixtec, Tarasca, Otomi, Maya, and a dozen other groups.

By the time the Spanish were landing at what came to be called Vera Cruz by Cortés, the Aztecs had already dominated over half of the One-World, rising to power about a hundred years before the arrival of the Spanish.

The Aztecs had been a savage northern desert tribe that slowly fought its way into the lush, wet garden now called the Valley of Mexico.

Once in the green valley, the barbaric horde first stole the culture of the peoples they fought and conquered, and then their treasures. While the indios never occupied a large part of the One-World, their legions moved swiftly and brutally to ravage kingdoms and force them to pay tribute.

Their domination was a brutal one in which the demanded tribute was not only treasure and women, but often thousands of slaves to be sacrificed.

Ayyo! Those were the days when indio gods demanded human blood to quench their thirst and refused to give the people rain and sunshine needed to grow food if their need was not satiated.

To the Aztecs who wanted to keep the good life they were enjoying, that meant sending a constant stream of sacrificial victims up the temple steps to have their hearts ripped out at the top.

The blood of the victims obtained as tribute fed the gods well, with the gods in turn giving the Aztecs victory in battle.

My own blood includes that of the proud Zapotec, a longtime enemy of the Aztecs. For sure my mother was indio, perhaps Zapotec or a mixture with Aztec, but I did not know my father's blood.

Because I am taller and fairer than most indios, it was assumed by the whores in the house where I was born that a Spaniard laid with my mother and that I am a half-breed mongrel.

A telling blow against the unity of the indios to resist was the way they permitted their masters to throw them all into the same pot.

Despite the many indio cultures that the Spanish found in the One-World, they called all indios Aztecs rather than referring to the individual ethnicity of the various nations. Even the name Aztec was a false one. The Aztecs had called themselves Mexica, but the Aztec name was applied to them because of a misinterpretation by the Spanish.

Not only was it simpler for the Spanish to call all indios by the same name, even if it was the wrong one, it also permitted the conquerors to show their disdain and to aid the indios in losing their individual identity.

That same planned contempt was also part of the Spanish scheme of complete conquest, which included the burning of the books containing indio history when they set fire to thousands of their codices, the dismantling of their temples where the Spanish said they had worshipped pagan gods, and, the final blow, the enslaving of indios until they were little more than farm animals working for Spanish masters.

The complete subjugation meant not only that the backs of millions of indios that occupied the lands were bloodied as the conquerors went on a bloodlust for wealth but also that the priests that followed them burned at the stake any indios who failed to worship the Spanish god—a deity that they assured the indio was all-loving, kind, understanding, and merciful.

But even though the ignorant Spanish referred to all indios as Aztecs, the truth was that there were many indio cultures, and a brave few of the indio groups were still resisting the terrible bondage the Spanish had enslaved them in. Every few years since the conquest in 1521, indios rose up in anger about the way they were treated.

In the Oaxaca region there were Zapotec and Mixtec, and each took a turn battling the Spanish, even up to now.

Ayyo! I didn't know what any of it meant, but the images did nothing to remove the gloom and doom I felt.

Finally, I rounded Rojo up, stroking his warm coat as I led him to a walled area where we would not be easily spotted if someone passed nearby. Like his sire, the chestnut stallion accepted me and permitted me to guide him with little effort.

As I lay shivering in the cool night, curled up in a fetal position to conserve heat, I wondered again what I would do.

New Spain was a big place, but it was controlled by the Spanish, and mestizos were not as plentiful as either indios or Spaniards.

That the search for me would be relentless was obvious. Killing a Spaniard was considered a greater crime than killing a hundred indios, though I hoped that the zeal of those in town who knew Héctor would be tempered by the fact that they knew he was a drunken swine.

I wondered how far I could get with Rojo. I had heard that the farther north one goes, past the silver mining towns, past the great deserts beyond the silver mountains, were green areas where there was freedom from Spanish rule and only small populations of indios.

I lay awake that night, wondering what it would be like to be free and not have to worry about the pursuit of men who wanted to take my life.

TWENTY-EIGHT

THE NEXT MORNING, from a high point on top of the Monte Albán ruins, I saw the posse coming from the south. They were still a couple of miles away, but moving fast up the slope.

Almost immediately the horsemen split into three parts, with the center group coming straight for the ancient site and the other two wings moving to approach from the sides.

Someone must have spotted me because they knew I was here—the posse had split up to trap me by covering the flanks. That only left one route they could not get to fast enough—directly to my rear. But, carefully scanning the hilly region, I spotted three constables on mules, moving faster than the rest of the posse that was saving the strength of its mounts as it came up the slope.

A mule was not as fast as a horse, but as the offspring of a male donkey and female horse, it inherited some of the best qualities of both and had more endurance than a similar-sized horse.

The posse's plan was obvious—they knew I would have to flee to the only way out, to the north, but even if I got past the three mule riders, those constables would continue to pursue me long after the volunteers and the rest of the constable's men returned to Oaxaca. No doubt the three were on the biggest mules in the chief constable's herd.

The objective would be to ride me to the ground, to keep up a relentless pursuit until my horse collapsed from exhaustion.

I knew their strategy from conversations with Gomez when we shoed the chief constable's herd.

"They run 'em to the ground using mules with the most endurance," Gomez said.

As they anticipated, I mounted Rojo and set out north, the only route open to me.

"You have to outlast them," I told the chestnut stallion.

The men on the mules would be made from the same mold as the cadre of constables: indios and mestizos with bellies pregnant from frijoles and indio beer. Their mules would also be carrying tack—saddle and harnesses—plus the men's bedrolls, food, water, muskets and balls.

Rojo was younger, bigger, and faster than the mules. I was lighter and carried no weapon, food, or water, and was riding bareback.

The mules would drop from exhaustion before Rojo did.

My life depended on it.

I set out, not knowing what lay over the next hill, not knowing where my next meal would come from, or where I would find blankets to cover myself with at night or a saddle and other tack so I could ride more comfortably.

My taste of freedom so far was bitter.

I had learned much over the years at the stable—I was a master horseshoer, horse doctor, and horse trainer—but none of those talents would help me because word would spread like wildfire about a mestizo wanted for killing a Spaniard. Wherever I went, working at a hacienda or in a town stable, the hunters would eventually catch me.

I had one talent ingrained in me that I knew would help me survive.

I was a thief.

TWENTY-NINE

THE MULE PURSUIT lasted only a day and a half. I suspect the men gave out before the animals.

Even when I was certain the hot pursuit was over, I kept going, northward first and then west. I chose the direction of travel without any real thought, but perhaps I turned west because I knew that the capital lay somewhere in that direction, a couple weeks' journey. A lot of people were in Mexico City, and perhaps I could hide among them.

I paid a visit to a hacienda stable late at night to get a saddle—one used for wrangling cattle on the range and not the kind to impress señoritas on the paseo—and kept myself in maize and fruit by picking them along the way.

I rubbed blackberry juice on the stallion's reddish coat, hoping that it would fool—at least at a distance—anyone who was looking for a stolen chestnut.

It was easy to avoid people and places: the land was wide open, and there were few fences anywhere in the colony and few roads except the dirt ones between towns and the narrower paths to villages off the main routes. Between the small towns and villages along the route, most of which were a day or two apart, were small clusters of indio shacks where women sold tortillas, water, and other fare to travelers.

I might have enjoyed quiet, relaxing days and seeing new territory if I didn't have to constantly look behind me to see if beer-bellied constables on sweaty mules were bearing down on me.

Eight days away from Oaxaca I had my first serious encounter with people—that is if you consider a gang of bandidos as human beings.

Five of them found me napping by a river. Rojo was grazing nearby. The horse's whinny had warned me that strangers were coming, and I watched with half-closed eyes as they approached.

I could have made a run for it, but I recognized immediately what they were—and wondered if there wasn't an advantage for me in their coming.

Ayyo! "Bandidos" was a compliment to the filthy, disgusting lépero trash that surrounded me. Four were armed with branches they used as clubs; the other I took to be the leader because he was the biggest and had a knife and a rusty pistola that looked more likely to burst its barrel than propel a ball.

They had a skinny mule that had a swollen ankle and two donkeys, all almost as dirty and skinny as they were.

The animals smelled better than the bandidos.

I got to my feet and leaned against a tree, leaving my knife sheathed, but keeping a limb within reach that I could use as a club.

"What are you worthless léperos doing so far away from where you can beg for food even a pig wouldn't eat?"

Insults were the only way to deal with this trash. Too stupid not to bite the hand that feeds them, they would take a pleasant greeting as a sign of weakness and jump on me like a pack of hungry dogs.

The leader pointed the rusty pistola at me. "We are rebels fighting the gachupins."

He had the square pug nose and mean eyes of a

swine and a name for him immediately popped into my head: Cerdo—pig.

I burst out with a guffaw I couldn't hold back. "Eh, Cerdo, you are rebels from soap and water."

The pistola shook in his hand, but he didn't attempt to pull the trigger, which was probably locked by rust.

Rojo neighed and stamped his hooves as one of the trash approached him.

I nodded at the horse.

"Amigo, you can have him if you can get in the saddle, but you won't be able to. As bad as you stink, the horse will treat you like vermin that needs to be stomped."

"Brave talk for a prisoner," Cerdo said. "I haven't killed you yet because I want to take time and have the pleasure of cutting out your liver to feed it to a dog. The horse is already mine because you will be dead when we leave here. Watch him," he told the others.

I doubted whether the bandido had ever been on any mount larger than the poor skinny mule he came in on. But fool that he was, he walked boldly up to Rojo yelling, "Snort at me you stupid animal and I'll—"

Rojo reared and brought his hooves down in front of the bandido, sending him stumbling backward onto his rump.

As Cerdo slid backward to distance himself from Rojo, I walked over and picked up the pistola where he had dropped it.

The bandido leader came off the ground with his knife charging me.

I swung around and hit his knife hand with the pistola, sending the knife flying, and swung back around, whacking Cerdo across the side of the head.

I could have smashed his brains with the blow—if he had any—but I deliberately only grazed him.

He dropped down to his knees, holding his bleeding head.

The others simply froze in place and stared at me. If I had said boo, they would have run.

They were outcasts, misfits, but I was also a misfit and an outcast and no doubt more wanted by the authorities than any of them.

I realized the only path for me was to be almost continuously on the road because I would never be safe in a town.

And that there would be strength in numbers if I could turn this rabble into a real gang of bandidos.

I gave Cerdo a long look and wondered if I should kill him because I had humiliated him. Someday he might get his revenge with a knife in my back.

But I was too soft to kill him, even though I was sure that I would live—or die—to regret it.

PART 4

VERA CRUZ ROAD, NEW SPAIN

A.D. 1566

Once a dumb lépero, always a dumb lépero.

THIRTY

AYYO! I'D SPENT months trying to turn hopelessly stupid and mean-spirited léperos into smart bandidos. My horse had more good sense than the pack of them.

We were too small and weak to attack a big hacienda, and I would not let them steal from small rancheros, so that left stopping coaches on the open road—but not just any coach. If there were two or more guards for the coach we didn't dare attempt to rob it because dealing with more than one musket carrier was too much for these fools.

I had made sure they were well mounted on the best mules we could steal and had pistolas that at least made a big bang even if they did not project a ball accurately. Mostly I relied upon the fact that because there were five of us and we made a lot of noise and looked fierce, the coachmen would give up immediately without a fight.

That was the entire purpose of organizing them into a gang of bandidos—intimidation by sheer number—because there was little behind the bravado except cowardly worms. But none of them had the brains of a worm.

Shouting and a fierce appearance had to make up for the fact they could not shoot straight—when they were lucky enough to load the pistolas with the right amount of powder to send balls flying but not exploding in their faces, which is how I lost one of the gang. Lost, but he was not missed.

I taught them to wear masks so they were not recognized, to search a coach more thoroughly than the passengers themselves because money and jewelry would be hidden the moment it became apparent that highwaymen were about, not to kill because the viceroy's constables worked much harder to catch killers—not to mention that it makes it much more difficult to get into heaven.

Finally, I drilled into them to turn and run if passengers in the carriage began shooting. I wasn't worried about my men getting killed, but I didn't want the innocent mules they were riding getting harmed.

I also taught them to ambush the carriage to be robbed, one of them firing a shot in the air to surprise and terrorize the victims so that they knew we were armed and dangerous while the others charged, shouting like demons with pistolas appearing ready to throw death at anyone who resisted.

Ayyo! It was inevitable we would have to shoot back at times, and I warned them that I would put a bullet in one dirty ear and out the other of the bandido who missed a man and hit a horse.

Mounted on stolen mules, carrying stolen pistols, and wearing stolen clothes that shined in comparison to the dirty rags they wore when I first met them, one would think they had developed into a workable gang. But they could be counted upon to make mistakes that even a jackass wouldn't.

As we waited for a coach with a driver and single guard to approach, I again drilled the attack strategy into their heads:

"We wait in hiding and charge out in ambush style just before the coach crests the hill, catching it at its slowest, when it's least likely to try to outrun attackers."

We would come from both sides of the road, shouting like maniacs.

One man would fire his pistola in the air. Because I could not trust them to load their weapons properly in the first place, I decided I would be the one to discharge the gun. I had a second pistola loaded and ready to use once I had fired.

We had staked out a spot on the road between Vera Cruz and Xalapa, the mountainous route from the high plateau called the Valley of Mexico down to the sea. The narrow mountain road was the lifeline of the colony because it was used for goods being shipped to and from Spain, handling many times the amount of goods that came to Acapulco on the west coast from the Far East.

More than ninety percent of the people and merchandise that entered or left the colony used the Vera Cruz route even though the steepest mountain sections were too narrow for coaches. Goods came by mule train, and women and other travelers unable to ride a horse or mule came by litters that were strung between a mule at the front and rear. At the top of the mountains, the passengers got into carriages for the final stage of the journey.

Shipments of goods were too well protected for our little force to attack, as were "caravans" of travelers and merchants who banded together, so we waited for the rare lone traveler or a coach that had had problems and could not keep up with the others.

I looked around at my little force as a carriage was coming up the hill, wondering what mistake would be made this time.

When the carriage was almost at the crest of the

hill, I yelled the command to charge out of hiding, and Rojo leaped forward as I fired my pistola in the air.

They all fired a shot in the air.

Eh, do you see the problem with everyone firing a warning shot when charging an armed carriage driver and guard? There is only one ball to a pistola. After it is fired, the bandido has to stop and go through the tedious process of reloading ball and powder. While that is being done, the would-be victims would shoot back, no?

Fortunately only two of the four pistolas fired—the other two misfired, leaving the people on the carriage with the impression that two of the weapons were still loaded. It was embarrassing that the sole reason the carriage driver and guard didn't blow the bunch of us away with their blunderbusses was the mistaken impression that my gang of street trash still had loaded weapons, when in fact I was the only one with a pistola that could be fired.

I was lucky they didn't shoot themselves or even something much more valuable—their mules—when they pulled their pistolas.

On this day, the good Lord's dark angel delivered unto us a plush carriage that had dropped back from a larger group because its rear axle had partially split. There was a single guard on the coach, and the driver had his hands full keeping the carriage on the road because of the narrow passage. Both the driver and guard leaped off the coach and ran as soon as we came riding up.

The coach was roofed, but I could see that only two women were inside, a young woman perhaps in her late teens and an older woman who took one look at my pistola and screamed and fainted as I rode up to the coach window.

I slipped off the stallion and jerked open the coach door and started in when I saw a redheaded señorita and the flash of a blade. I leaned back as the blade flashed by, and I felt the sting as it slit my right cheek.

Ayyo! I howled. A woman cutting me with a dagger! I'd run into a redheaded she-devil.

I pointed my pistola into a pretty face with emerald-green eyes, and she fell backward against the seat. I stuck my head in the coach and got the flash of white petticoats just before she kicked me in the chest with the heels of both shoes.

I went flying backward and down to the ground, landing flat on my back with a thump that took the breath from me.

Without a thought, I flipped back onto my feet, caught a quick breath, and jerked open the door as the young woman tried to hold it closed.

The blade flashed again, and I grabbed her by the wrist and twisted it out of her hand.

She yelped in pain, then kneed me in the stomach, and I flew off the coach but landed on my feet this time. I jerked the door open again. I saw another swirl of petticoats as her feet came at me like a pair of windmill blades.

I threw my weight on her legs and got ahold of her dress about thigh high and pulled as hard as I could as I stepped backward out of the coach. My boot heel caught, and I went down to the ground again, on my back with the girl on top of me.

We stared at each other for a pregnant moment. I was mesmerized by her startling green eyes.

She banged her forehead on my nose and I howled with pain and rage. What the hell did she think she was doing? I was a dangerous bandido.

I pushed her on the ground until I was on top of

her. Her hands and arms were flying at me, and I tried to grab them, but she was bucking like a wild and untamed stallion.

"Let me go," she yelled, pounding on my chest with her fists and kicking with her feet.

I tightened my grip on her. "You are acting like a wild animal."

"You're the animal."

She tried to squirm out of my grasp, but I finally managed to pin her arms behind her back.

She winced in pain and I immediately felt sorry for her. I had never handled a woman roughly before. Not having had a mother, a sister, or a wife, I knew little about women except that they were the weaker sex.

She spit in my face.

Ayyo! I wasn't about to release this she-devil—not just yet. She was attacking me like a ferocious animal, and I knew that she would put a dagger through my heart if she had a blade.

I looked into those sparkling liquid eyes that were on fire with rage and grinned.

"And what do you find so funny?" she hissed.

"You are like a wild horse that needs to be broken."

"And you are a filthy lépero who robs carriages and tortures innocent people."

"Hey, she is right, amigo," Cerdo said. "We are léperos who rob carriages and torture innocent people—but we are not filthy."

That got a howling laugh from the pack of bandidos who had been standing there watching us as we wrestled on the ground.

I grinned, too. I couldn't help myself. What a woman! Most women would have cowered in fear, and this one was ready to take on a whole gang of murderous thieves.

"Why don't you show her how you torture innocent women," Cerdo said, still laughing. "I'm sure she will like it. Then we will show her, too." He started to undo his breeches. That caused another howling laugh from the pack.

"Pull down your pants and I'll cut off your pene and stick it in your mouth." I turned back to the señorita. "Don't worry, no one will touch you; you are under my protection."

She spit in my face again. "You filthy animal!"

Such gratitude. I kept a tight grip on her. "We do not torture women." I looked into those fiery green eyes again.

"Sí, only men," Cerdo said, smiling.

She stared at me for a long moment. "You are hurting me now."

"I will release your arms if I have your word that you will not attack and spit on me."

Her face was not plastered with powder and lipstick like some of the other women but was soft, delicate, and innocent.

She lowered her eyes and said quietly, "You have my word."

I did not trust this wildcat of a woman—the anger still burned in her eyes—so I slowly released her arms.

"But you are still a filthy pig," she hissed as she dug sharp claws into my face.

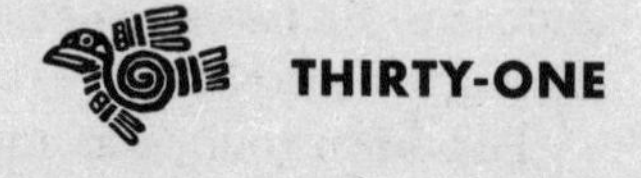

THIRTY-ONE

THE WILDCAT CLAWED at my eyes as the léperos pulled her off of me—she still managed to get in a kick.

I got on my feet. My mask had been pulled off my nose but still covered half of my face. She had laid my cheek open and my nose felt as if Rojo had kicked it.

And she stared at me, defiantly.

"Animal!" she yelled.

Ay, caramba! The wildcat thought *I* was the animal? This time I was the *victim*.

"Tie that she-demon up," I told Cerdo. "All of you help," I said, knowing the swine would not be able to handle the young woman by himself.

I opened the coach door to find the older woman, perhaps the girl's aunt, mother, or chaperone coming awake.

She opened her eyes, met my stare, gaped, uttered a faint cry, and swooned again.

I didn't know if her fainting spells were an act or a defensive move like a small animal faking death to fool prey, but as long as it left me free to ransack the coach without her coming after me like the younger woman, her swooning worked well.

The first place I looked was in the crack between the front and back of the seats, where people stick their money and jewels the moment they know highwaymen are about. Since it was the first place a thief like me looked, it was not the best hiding place.

I pulled out a gold brooch from the side where the girl had been seated and slipped it in my pocket.

Moving the old woman over a little so I could check the seat crack behind her, her eyes fluttered open, then popped wide when she saw me inches from her. She gasped and closed her eyes tight again. This time I knew she was faking.

The girl screamed and I swung around.

Ayyo! The lépero trash had pulled up her dress and Cerdo was pulling down her petticoats.

I flew out of the coach and knocked aside the first one of the gang who stood in my path, sending him sprawling, while two others quickly got out of my way.

I stuck my pistola against Cerdo's ear and said, "If you had any brains, I would blow them out."

"We want her."

"This is what you get for disobeying me." I hit him across the side of his head with the pistola, sending him over onto his side. Then I kicked him in the stomach.

I grabbed the girl by the arm and pulled her to her feet. She was wide-eyed from shock.

"Get back into the carriage and help the old woman. No harm will come to you."

I called for the driver and guard to come out of the bushes where they were hiding and get the coach moving. They hadn't gone far and they came out, slow and leery but hurried when I yelled at them to move faster.

As it rolled away, the girl stared gravely at me out the window.

I saluted her with my pistola and turned back to the léperos.

I watched the coach until it crested the hill. As it disappeared from my sight, I suddenly felt emotionally empty. I realized that for a brief moment I had experienced something special—besides the slash of a knife or the bump on my nose. I had looked into the eyes of this woman and felt a connection, something beyond the urge to make love that I usually felt when I saw a pretty señorita.

Ayyo . . . whatever I had felt, the source was gone, cresting not just the hill, but leaving me eating the dust of the coach wheels. There was nothing in the coach for a man like me whose closest connection to carriages besides robbing them was having been run over by one as I begged in the street.

With a little sigh for what might have been had the Lord not given me tainted blood, I turned back to the worms.

"Imbeciles. The whole lot of you combined don't have the brains of a slug. Didn't I tell you that killing and raping brings out the constables and army ten times more than just robbing? If you had raped that girl, her father would have put out a reward, and we would have been hunted down and crucified."

They said nothing. Just stared at me without any expression on their faces. Not even Cerdo showed any emotion.

The blank stares gave me the shivers.

Not because they hated me—I had known that since the day I teamed with them. And it wasn't just Cerdo who wanted my blood, even though he was the one who was the most frequent objective of my kicks because he was usually the one leading the others into folly. The whole pack of them hated me for good reasons—they knew I didn't respect them, that I treated them like the mangy dogs they were. But this was different. For the first time I felt that they would actually do something about it.

Maybe putting them in clean clothes and on decent mules and making them think they were really bandidos had deluded the soggy mush they used for brains into thinking they really were dangerous desperadoes, that they deserved some expression of respect from me.

If I stuck with them I knew I'd get a knife in me while I slept. No, I would get four knives in me because they lacked the courage to come at me alone and could only act as a pack—and only while I slept.

I was finished with them, too. Not only were they hopelessly stupid and untrustworthy, it was inevitable that they would get me killed or hanged even if they never got up the courage to attack me themselves.

Keeping my pistola trained on them, I gathered their guns, took the reins of the four mules, and mounted Rojo.

"What are you doing?" Cerdo asked.

"Going my own way."

"You're leaving us without guns and mules."

"I'm protecting you from shooting yourselves. Go back to begging on the streets; you're not worthy enough to be bandidos. *Vaya con el diablo, amigos.* May you rot in hell."

THIRTY-TWO

I FELT FREE as the wind as I rode away, the léperos shouting curses and death threats behind me.

They were dirty baggage that I no longer wanted to pack. Hopefully an army patrol would find them walking on the road and string them up at the nearest tree.

Before light fell I made camp by a river and took a bath, washing the stench of the léperos from my own body. I ate tortillas and salted beef and then lay on my bedroll and stared up at the stars, feeling the slash on my face.

The bleeding had stopped, but I would be left with a scar an inch or so long. It didn't bother me because even the sting I felt at the moment brought the young woman into my thoughts. She had left a mark on me, not just on my face but in my heart, that I would not forget. Her vivid green eyes still burned in my memory.

I looked at the brooch I had found in the seat where the wildcat had sat. Opening the clasp, it revealed an ivory cameo of a woman's face. I was certain it was her mother because of the resemblance.

The brooch's casing was gold and encrusted with gems, making it very valuable. But any instinct on my part to sell the brooch was quickly extinguished because it was unlikely that she would have carried a memento of her mother if the woman was still alive.

Not having had a mother and remembering her

only holding me against her warm, soft bosom, I knew the brooch must be very precious to her. If I could, I would return it to her.

I didn't know all the paths the good Lord had set out for me or that el diablo would trick me onto, but I knew I would never see the girl again because our worlds were too far apart. Even if I did, she'd quickly have the constables on me. The brooch would be my only memento of her, and I would not sell it, even to save my hide.

Putting it on a cord, I hung it around my neck.

Ahhh . . . As much as I wanted to think about the green-eyed young woman who had ignited in me feelings I had never experienced before, I had to put aside thoughts of her, daydreams and idle wishes that were as practical as imagining the king of Spain knighting me.

For the first time in my life I contemplated about what my life might be in the years to come.

I did not want to continue as a highwayman. The road between Vera Cruz on the coast and Xalapa on the plateau where the Valley of Mexico lies was well traveled and frequently patrolled. Inevitably, a bandido would someday fall into the hands of a patrol of soldiers who hang them or the vigilantes who crucify them.

Besides, I was tired of moving to a different campsite every night and never daring to go into any town for fear I would be recognized by someone I had robbed.

It had been a long time since I worried about being wanted in Oaxaca. The town was a month's journey and felt lifetimes away. I was no longer the stable boy who fled on a stolen horse. I now dressed like a vaquero and rode Rojo as if I was born to the saddle.

My first love was horses, and I dreamed of owning a small ranchero where I could raise and train them. The notion had been in my head from that day I met the léperos.

Eh, a small ranchero with a good stock of horses, a lovely señorita to share it with, what more could a man want?

There was only one problem. It took money to buy a ranchero. And I was not going to find it robbing people on the road.

For a certainty, although my heart was no longer in being a bandido, stealing was still going to be a part of my life because it was the only way I knew how to survive.

Pilfering from those who had too much in order to provide for myself who had so little didn't bother my conscience. But my heart was not in robbing people. At least not face-to-face.

I needed money to buy the land, build a house and corrals, and stock the ranchero with horses and cattle.

The solution was obvious to me. I would get the money the best way I knew how—by stealing horses.

I didn't really consider it stealing, anyway, because I would never have stolen a man's personal mount. But horses that are raised in pastures on big haciendas and sold to the highest bidder were another matter. They didn't care who owned them as long as they were fed well and not mistreated.

THIRTY-THREE

THE NEXT MORNING I sold the mules to the indios of a village, charging them only what they could afford because they existed under the harsh penalty of an encomienda tax.

Indios who were better off sometimes owned a donkey, but few had a mule, so they were happy to get the animals.

I would not have sold the mules to a Spaniard. As old as they were, the mules would have been packed with heavy loads until they dropped. I knew the indios would treat the animals as treasures, caring for them as well as they cared for themselves.

As I passed the horse pasture at the hacienda of the encomendero who collected an encomienda "tax" on the village, I saw a mare grazing away from the rest of the herd in a fenced pasture. She would have been set apart to keep her from getting pregnant because the owner had a particular stallion in mind, probably one that was better than any he owned.

She perked up when she saw Rojo, and I felt the stallion tense beneath me.

Mi Dios! The poor mare could be attacked by a jaguar or a pack of wolves. It was my Christian duty to protect her.

I started humming as I took down two log rails and led her out and left the rails on the ground so the hacendado would not know whether the mare was stolen or had wandered away.

Besides, his vaqueros will be busy rounding up the rest of the herd that would follow the mare out of the pasture. I didn't take more than one because that would have caused a major hunt to track them.

That night as I rubbed down Rojo and the mare I realized this was the beginning of my quest for a ranchero. Before I sacked out on my bedroll, I felt a little lightheaded and even blessed. Like a priest who had saved a soul.

VERA CRUZ

Believe me, amigos, when I tell you that Vera Cruz is a hot ember that has been kicked out of hell, a place where the fiery tropical sun and fierce *el norte* winds turned earth to sand that flayed the flesh from bones.

—Cristo the Bastardo
Gary Jennings, *Aztec Blood*

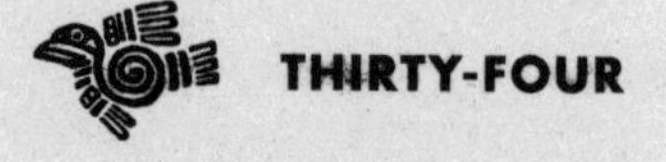

THIRTY-FOUR

MEXICO CITY WAS called the queen of New Spain and Vera Cruz the whore, but as a man selling stolen horses and seeking the loving arms of a woman—even paid affection was better than no affection—a Jezebel city was exactly what I needed. And being a harlot was not the worst thing that could be said about the colony's chief port.

Since ninety percent of what came and went from the entire colony passed through the town, including people whose business it was to relieve the weight of a man's purse with dishonest fingers, it was a busy whore.

While the merchants owned the boxes of goods, bales of cloth, and barrels of sugar that would be shipped to Spain, the streets belonged to prostitutes, smugglers, and gamblers—all of whom would have starved if there were not sailors and other fools like me who arrived in town with coins jingling in their pockets and eyes too filled with the sheer color and variety of people, clothing, and activity on the streets to perceive that there were thieves and scoundrels much more ruthless and talented than a backwater horse thief like me.

The many inns that served wine and beer and pulqueras with their cheap indio concoction had in common not only drunken patrons and games of chance, but a backroom or upstairs where sex was sold not by time with a woman but up to the ejection of a man's honey. After that, you were quickly hustled out the door to make room for the next customer.

Fortunately, a muleteer I'd camped with the night before I arrived in Vera Cruz told me the secret to get my money's worth. Demonstrating with a pumping action with his hand, he said, "Before you go in, give your own self pleasure."

But it wasn't just to take the edge off of my lust and the velvet off my pene that I had come to the city with a notorious reputation for being open to about anything.

Selling stolen horses was easier when you dealt with horse traders that didn't ask too many questions. Vera Cruz was the perfect place for that type of trader, though the one I was dealing with today was curious about why I sold so many young horses.

"How is it all the horses you sell are weanling foals?" a horse trader looking over my small herd asked. "You must have had a whole herd of pregnant mares."

A foal is a horse less than a year old, and a weanling foal is one that had recently been weaned from its mother's milk. And there was a simple reason I had so many weaned foals: I stole mares that were either pregnant or would be as soon as Rojo did his job.

Stealing mares and having Rojo impregnate them not only gave me fine-looking foals, but ones *without a brand*. With no mark of ownership and mixed-breed foals because I stole whichever ones I found available, it was impossible for even the finest judge of horseflesh to identify the foal's parents.

It had been a slow process because the gestation period for a mare is nearly a year, and it takes close to another five or six months for the foal to be weaned.

I had been at it for three years, stealing and breeding, selling a few foals or altering a brand on a grown horse to get enough money to keep myself in tortillas and my horses in grain until I had enough foals to take to Vera Cruz. I sold off the rest of the mares cheaply because of the brand problems and herded my foals to town.

The young horses were fine-looking animals all, and I sold them for the gold that jingled in my pocket.

Those dull yellow coins bearing the round features of our good king of Spain Philip II, master of the greatest empire in the world, were the price of the ranchero I dreamed of owning. So far I had worked with just a corral and small pasture hidden away in the mountains, but now I would be looking for a real piece of land where horses and a family can be raised.

It would not be a big hacienda, but I am now a master breeder and have a sire capable of turning out champions. When I left Vera Cruz I would be heading for the Nueva Galicia, where the town of Guadalajara has been established. A couple of weeks travel northwest of the capital, it is not only a long ways from Oaxaca, but because much of the region beyond Guadalajara is wide open and unsettled, its inhabitants are ready to welcome newcomers without asking questions.

Who knows—perhaps the itching in my feet for new territory will take me even farther, to that northern region beyond the great deserts where there were few Spanish and where horses were still magical beasts to indios?

Ayyo! A man with a small herd of good horses would be both a king and an esteemed teacher in such a place.

I would spend one more night in Vera Cruz, this one relaxing instead of bargaining, playing some cards, drinking some fine Jerez brandy, and rubbing down some flesh that is softer and smoother than the coats of horses that had occupied my time for the past several years.

I stabled Rojo in the best stall in town and warned the stable boy that I would cut off his ears if he did not feed Rojo the ripe corn, oats, and apples I selected. I left the saddle and other tack inside the stall with Rojo, knowing that it would be there when I came back to get the horse—along with the trampled body of anyone who tried to steal the silver-studded saddle and harness I bought for Rojo as his prize for performing his manly art so well.

For myself I rented a "stall" in an inn on the waterfront, choosing the place because I heard that it caught a little breeze after sundown, stirring the hot, heavy air in town that smelled like the breath of the dead.

After watching a card game and shaking off a couple of harlots who looked as if they had been providing pleasure to sailors since before I was born, I took my bedroll up to drop in my room so I could return and find myself a card game and a woman that appealed to me.

I kept the gold coins in my front pocket, where I could feel the reassuring weight of my "ranchero," then headed downstairs, where food, drink, cards, dice, and matters of the flesh were arranged.

Ordering Jerez brandy, when the bartender asked me how much, I pointed at a beer mug and said, "That much."

Ayyo! I only got down half the mug before I gasped, lost my breath, and fought back choking. The brandy hit me with the kick of a mule, burning all the way down my throat, sending a shock down to my toes, and coming back up to fry my brains.

I was used to pulque, the cheap, white-colored indio beer made from the tall, spiked maguey plant. Pulque tasted like sour milk; the Spanish brandy like sweet liquid fire.

I stood shaky for a moment, getting my breathing back, wiping the sweat on my forehead.

The bartender laughed at me. "Not used to the fine brandy gachupins drink, eh mestizo?"

That hit me more than the brandy. Locking my knees, I picked up the mug and swigged down the rest of the brandy. It went down easier because my throat was already fried. I wiped my mouth, smothering a cough as I did.

A sailor to my side leaned over and said, "Amigo, brandy is taken in little doses. Drinking it from a mug will blow your mind and knock you on your ass."

I tapped the side of my head. "I carry the blood of two great civilizations in me. Brandy would never take my mind." I slammed the mug down on the counter. "Another."

THIRTY-FIVE

I DOWNED THE brandy and slammed the half-empty mug back on the bar as a whore snuggled up close to me.

"Señor, let me show you pleasures like you have never experienced before," she sang in my ear.

The brandy I so proudly gulped down was hitting me. My face was stiff and my tongue knotted, but I had enough sense left to know that the hand being slipped into my front pocket wasn't searching for my cojones.

I grabbed her wrist and pulled the hand out. "I'm not a fool."

But of course I was a fool or I wouldn't be in a position where I could pass out and have my gold stolen. I had just enough sense to know I had acted with more bravado than brains. I had never been drunk before but I had watched men make themselves helpless and open to robbery because they drank too much. On more than one occasion on the streets of Oaxaca I had had my own hands searching for coins in the pockets of a drunk.

I pushed away from her and headed for the stairs. If I was going to be drunk on my ass, I knew I better do it in my own room, lying against the door to keep out the vultures who had guessed what the bulge in my pants represented and would slit my throat to get it.

They probably thought it was just silver. Had they

known it was gold, my throat would have already been cut.

My room was three floors up, on the top floor. As I came up the stairs to the third-floor landing a man was trying to push his way into a room while a woman was attempting to shut the door.

"Go away or I'll scream!" she yelled.

"I just want some loving for my money," he slurred.

I could see the woman was no whore. It was obvious from her gown, hair, and lovely features that she was a Spanish lady of fine breeding and quality.

The two backed away from the door and into the corridor grappling, the man holding on to the woman as she tried to pull away and get back into the room.

A drunk molesting an innocent woman! Not when Juan the Ranchero was present.

I came up behind the man and stuck my foot in the crook behind his knee, sending him off balance. As he stumbled backward, I grabbed him by the back of his coat and directed him to the stairway and gave him a hand falling backward down the stairs.

He tumbled and rolled over on his side. I hesitated on the landing, teetering a bit myself, wondering if I should step down and kick him in the head to make sure he didn't pull a knife and come back at me, but there was no fight in him. Instead, he started sliding down steps on his rear end without even looking back.

"Thank you, señor," the woman said, "I would have come to great harm if not for you."

"My pleasure." I attempted a sweeping bow and wave of my arm and fell forward a little. "Sorry, a little brandy."

"A man deserves a little relaxation," she said.

Her voice purred as soft as a kitten. I was instantly in love—or at least in lust.

"I worked hard and now I'm going to buy a ranchero."

I padded my pocket that had the bulging gold. It was safe boasting to such a lady, eh? This woman of quality would have had the price of a dozen rancheros in her jewelry box.

"You must come in before that terrible man comes back."

She took me by the arm and pulled me into her room. Being close enough to smell her fragrant scent added to my lightheadedness. No flower I had ever smelled had the intoxicating bouquet that she radiated. She smelled like a goddess, not of cheap wine like the women downstairs.

She poured brandy from a fancy ruby-red bottle into a fine goblet and handed it to me.

"You must join me in a toast of your courage. No knight of the realm acted with more courage and gallantry."

"I—I—" Telling her I had too much brandy already would make me look like a fool, so I took the goblet and raised the cup in a toast. "But you have none."

"A lady doesn't drink. I am the Countess Isabella del Castilla y Aragon, newly arrived from the court at Madrid."

Nobility! I had never spoken to a noblewoman, except for the time I told a marquesa to hand over her earrings when I was robbing her coach.

"I don't know what I would have done if you hadn't intervened. To tell you the truth, I believe the man was sent here by another man to threaten and rob me."

"Tell me the scoundrel's name, and I will cut out his heart."

"It's actually a former lover. There, I've shocked you, I know, but I feel I can tell you the truth. I am a widow. My dear departed husband owned a hacienda and silver mine, but I'm afraid he was so old that the only thing he could give me was everything that money could buy. But not that tender caress that every woman needs." She placed her hands demurely just below her throat. "Oh, my, you must think I am a terrible person, but I assure you, I was not this way before I was joined into marriage with an old man."

"I will cut out his heart, too." I realized he was already dead, but that was the brandy talking.

Her brandy didn't taste any stronger than the one I had had in the bar, but it seemed to affect me faster, making my tongue stick and my whole body numb almost as soon as I'd downed a swallow.

She came closer to me, so close I felt the warmth radiating from her red lips and her handsome bosom.

"My ex-lover could storm in here in a jealous rage. May I count on you, Sir Knight, to defend and protect me?"

I tried to say again that I would cut out his heart, but my tongue was so stiff it sounded like baby babble.

She steered me to the open window. I almost fell over before I got to it.

As she helped hold me up I tried to put my arms around her, but she pushed them aside.

She was becoming a blur to me and I tried to focus on her. My head was becoming heavy to hold up. I wanted to get to the bed and lie down and close my eyes.

"You need a good rest, my brave knight, because you will be jostling with another in the morning."

Her hand dug into my gold pocket.

"I'm going to keep this safe for you."

Some primeval instinct told me that a woman who would stick her hand in my front pants pocket to remove my gold was no lady, but I felt as if my hands were tied behind my back and my legs were stuck in place.

"Nooo—" came out of me, but she still came out of my pocket with my sack of gold coins.

I tried to grab it from her but my hands were clumsy and uncoordinated and she easily pushed them aside.

A jumble of words came off my tongue as I tried to tell her that she was taking my gold but she just kept whispering soothing things in my ear.

I started laughing, giggling. Nothing that was happening made any sense. I put my arms around her again, not tightly because I couldn't bend them, just flopping them onto her shoulders.

She leaned away as I put my weight against her and then she suddenly pushed me back.

I felt the window sill just below my buttocks and stared at her stupidly as she gave out a cry of exertion as she shoved me with both hands.

I went out the window backward, falling into a black void.

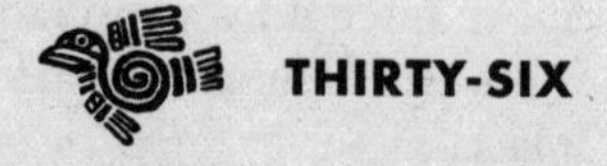

THIRTY-SIX

I CAME TO life with a seagull on my back and sand in my mouth.

Lying facedown on the sand behind the hotel, the tide was working its way up my legs. I got my eyes open just enough to recognize that it was bright day-light, and the glare hurt.

My head felt as if it had been lain on an anvil and pounded with a sledgehammer, my guts had a hole burned in them, and an ugly bile was working its way up my throat and into my mouth.

I wasn't sure if I was alive or if this was hell. Those were the only two choices for a horse thief.

I crawled a few feet and then got to my knees and started to stand up. Getting to my feet wasn't going to happen and I dropped back down, first to my knees and then pitching forward, flat on the sand again, and then I felt myself falling again, dropping into the black void even though I knew that I was on the ground.

I woke up to screams. It took a second to realize that it was the squawk of seagulls fighting over a fish while a couple of the city's ugly black vultures stood by pa-tiently as they waited for me to give up the ghost.

I rolled over to a blaze of blinding sun that felt like I'd been stabbed in the eyes. I tried to think, to get my thoughts in order about who I was and what had—

My gold! I reached for it and the pocket was flat. The sack was gone. Panic started pumping strength back into my limbs.

The bitch who called me her knight had drugged and robbed me before she shoved me out a window. The fact that my neck wasn't broken and I wasn't a feast for the vultures that were as common as flies in the town was nothing short of miraculous.

I would have been better off with a whore—at least I would have seen it coming.

The bitch had my ranchero money. My hard-earned money it had taken me so long to gather from the mares I stole. I thought she was a lady, but she was a common thief—no—no, I was a common thief; she was a woman and of the gachupin class and had no right to steal.

I dragged myself up, getting onto my feet, unsteady but burning with rage.

She'd give me back the money or I'd kill her.

Hell—I'll take back the money and kill her anyway.

THIRTY-SEVEN

"SHE'S GONE," THE india maid cleaning rooms on the top floor told me.

She didn't know where, so I went back downstairs and questioned the man who tended the bar and rented rooms.

"Gone," he said.

"I know she's gone and she's taken my money with her. Tell me where she went before I—"

He reached below the counter and brought up a machete.

"Just tell me where the countess went," I said, more civilly.

He howled. "Countess! She got past customs without the custom master realizing she's an actress and picaro bitch."

An actress and a picaro. An evil combination, worse than a common thief. I crossed myself. "Picaro" was the name Spaniards gave a type of traveling rogue, a vagabond who made their way by stealing, swindling, and cheating at gambling when they weren't taking advantage of women of means. But I had never heard of a female picaro.

And an actress! The woman was truly the daughter of el diablo. Actresses and actors conducted themselves with such wanton debauchery that they were not permitted burial in church cemeteries for fear they would contaminate consecrated ground.

"Tell me where the bitch went and I will bring back her head so it can be shipped to Spain."

He spit on the floor. "She hasn't gone far. She was arrested as she tried to leave the hotel in the middle of the night. She drugged and stole money from the governor's cousin. When he tried to get it back, she and a male accomplice attacked him and threw him down the stairs. They have her in the cell at the governor's palace and are searching for her partner."

He mimicked holding up a rope that was strangling him. "They're searching with a rope in their hands."

I cleared my dry throat and ordered a mug of pulque, not eager to go out onto the street. I wondered if I was going to be hanged for something I didn't do, rather than for the many crimes I committed. Well, I did throw him down the steps, but I had been tricked into doing it. More important, I wondered what happened to my gold after Isabella or whatever her name was had been arrested.

Was my gold seized by the governor? That seemed to be a real possibility. If it was seized, how would I claim it? No mestizo has that kind of money, except perhaps El Mestizo himself. Not that the governor would be in any hurry to return it. Whatever he seized, he sent a portion of it to the king in Madrid and kept the rest.

It was becoming more evident that the chances of meeting up with a hangman were growing the longer I stayed in Vera Cruz. If they didn't hang me for beating and robbing the governor's cousin or for my many crimes, they would do it simply because I was a halfblood who could only have come by that much money illegally. Which was not a bad assumption.

I had to make sure the governor had the gold because the countess might have hid it before she was grabbed. The woman had the liquid tongue of a lépero when it came to lying and deception. God only knows what she told the governor in his jail—or his bed.

She may even have a male partner who had it.

And there was one other very good possibility—*she may still have the gold on her.* I doubted that jailers would search a woman prisoner. Women in jail were rarer than mestizos with a pocketful of gold. There would be no reason to search her, and it was probably forbidden by the church anyway.

If she still had the money or had hid it, why would she tell where it was?

Giving that one some thought, I came up with what I considered a clever ploy. I would tell her that I'd give half of it to her—at least I'd lie and say I would. No—I'd tell her I would use half of it to buy her freedom.

Ayyo! What I'd do if I got the gold is slip a coin to the hangman so he tied the noose loosely so she suffered a long time.

When I got to the stable I discovered I didn't have the money to pay Rojo's stall bill. I had only a few coppers in my pocket. But I quickly came up with a solution. The silver-studded saddle and harness I bought the horse paid the bill and got me some silver pieces and plain tack after I bargained with the stable master. He got the better of the deal, but I wasn't in any position to complain.

I also overheard the stable master telling a customer that a posse had left town looking for the man who attacked the governor's cousin, heading down the road that led over the mountains to the capital. He thought that they wouldn't go far in the heat, that they were just making a show for the governor and would be back soon.

Not wanting to raise suspicion by asking questions,

I left the stable and slowly made my way up the street toward the center of town where the governor's palace was located.

I didn't know what a palace was supposed to look like, but I had been told that the house and administrative seat of the governor of Vera Cruz was not one of the grand palaces in the colony. Even though it was a block long, it was a simple wood structure, two stories high, with a wall that went around the building and the interior courtyard, which made it like most of the homes in the colony except that it was larger.

The structure was built to ward off pirate attacks, rather than for aesthetics, but from what I could see it lacked the solid-looking fortifications that the fortress on a small island in the bay had. The lower floor was part of the wall, and there were no windows at that level.

I didn't know if the building had a dungeon or above-ground jail cells.

When léperos came out begging, I spotted a boy that looked smarter than the rest of them. Street kids knew more than the mayor of a town, so I showed him a copper and asked what he had heard about the woman that had been arrested.

"They're holding her in a guardroom inside."

The boy explained that there was a freestanding guardhouse shack outside the walls at the entrance and another one inside the walls that was part of the building itself. It had barred windows. The bars were placed not to keep someone in, but to keep invaders out. So few women were ever arrested, there would be no regular cell for one.

The guardhouse next to the front gate was not there to defend the palace, but to collect a fee from those who wanted an audience with the governor. No defense of the palace or the town was needed unless suspicious ships were spotted.

"She pays for food to be passed to her through the bars."

That was typical—jail food was not provided and the prisoner either had some coins or sold a possession to get food.

Now I knew where she was, but the fact she was close to the guardhouse was a problem—I was a wanted man. It would be a little obvious if a mestizo paid her a visit.

I thought about dressing as a lépero and was sure I could pull it off—once a lépero, always a lépero. But I passed on the idea. The thought of buying the clothes off the back of one of the filthy, diseased creatures was too disgusting. Besides, if I had to make a fast getaway on Rojo, he might balk at the stench.

I smelled food as I passed an inn and it gave me an idea.

THIRTY-EIGHT

WEARING A LEATHER apron and a kitchen hat, and carrying a dish heaped with fish, string beans, and papaya, I walked across the square to the barred window on the wall of the governor's palace.

"Señorita, your food."

Her face popped up between the bars. She was beautiful, even imprisoned. Eh . . . the witch would probably share the governor's bed tonight and be free in the morning.

"I already got my—"

She stopped as she recognized me.

"You!"

"Sí, the man you stole from and tried to kill."

"I thought you were dead."

"The Lord Himself intervened."

"He'll change his mind when he finds out you're a horse thief."

That caught me by surprise.

"They know all about you." She said it as a taunt. "It didn't take long for them to figure out that you sold stolen horses."

The horses I sold in Vera Cruz were not stolen; it was their parents that were stolen, but I didn't bother to explain.

"Eh, woman, it was hard work—not like the quick, treacherous way you took a man's money."

"Why have you come here?"

"I want my gold back!"

She laughed. "Come in and get it."

"Hand it out and I will give you half of it when you get out. I'll use some of it to buy your freedom."

Ayyo! The lies were badly formed and spoken even worse. My lépero's liquid tongue had stiffened before an even better liar.

She stared at me and I knew what captured her attention—getting out. She didn't believe I would give her half; it was too farfetched that I would share my own money with her, but she was in and I was out and how she could use me to get her released was giving her thought.

"Tell me, mestizo, how would you get me out of here if I gave you back your money?"

"I would buy your freedom with it."

She shook her head. "That won't work. The governor would simply seize you and the money."

"I would break you out."

"How? The bars are steel."

I looked over the bars. They were steel, but were held in place by wood. And not strong wood at that. Vera Cruz was on the hot sandy coast and the nearest forests were on the mountains. It never got cold in the area so building materials were not substantial and dry-rotted quickly.

"I have a strong horse," I said. "I'll tie a rope around the bars and jerk them out. You lean out and I'll pull you out onto my horse. It's a big stallion that would carry us both as we were babes."

That plan seemed to give her some thought and I enlarged upon it.

"The outside guard post is left unmanned at dusk when visitors are no longer allowed in. We would be out of the city before any of the guards in the palace realized what had happened."

"And what do you get out of this?"

"My gold back. Half of it." I grinned with as much sincerity as I could muster when I wanted to reach through the bars and strangle her.

"You help me escape and it is all yours."

"You still have it?"

"Of course."

"Show it to me."

"Get me out of here and I will stick it back in your pocket on our way out of town."

I shook my head. "No, you have to show me the gold. I can't trust you after what you did."

"Oh! How it hurts to hear you say that; coming from a common horse thief, it wounds my heart."

"I'm going to leave you in there to rot."

"Be back with your horse and rope at dusk. I'll be waiting for you."

"I won't do it."

"Of course you will."

I glared at her, completely dumbfounded as to her logic. Did she think that I was a puppet on a string? That she merely wiggles a finger and I jump the way she wanted me to?

"Why do you think I will help you when you won't show me the gold?"

"Because you are a thief with no other options."

THIRTY-NINE

SHE WAS LYING about giving me back my money, of course. But she told the truth about one thing: I had no other options, at least none that got back the price of my ranchero. There was only a small chance that she had the gold, perhaps concealing it by sticking it down her dress into the crevice between her ample bosom, and even less of a chance that if that was true, she wouldn't stick a blade in me before we got out of town.

Assuming that by divine intervention I managed to avoid a dagger in my back as we rode off into the sunset with Rojo, I would probably end up being used by the governor's guards and posse as target practice.

Gritting my teeth, I got my horse and a strong rope and sat in the shade of a tree along the main street to keep myself in plain sight under the theory that no one would suspect I was a wanted man.

With the way my luck had been running, the rope would be used to hang me.

Falling light of dusk gave the city a golden look, hiding some of its ugliness, as I returned with a rope.

I rode Rojo slowly up the main street and into the central square, making my way with the horse at a walk. I was not in a hurry because I had no confidence in what I was doing. I had argued with my common sense and lost because desperation overrode my survival instincts.

As I got close to the window, I sat higher in the saddle and got the rope ready to loop it through the bars.

I was only a dozen feet away when I saw her, not at the barred window but suddenly appearing on a balcony above.

"That's the man who harmed the governor's cousin!" she cried out.

The ugly face of a man suddenly appeared at the barred window where she should have been, and a pistola slipped between the bars.

I ducked in the saddle and gave Rojo a kick and a shout at the same time the gun went off.

The bullet went wild and so did the horse as the gunshot startled him. He took off at a fast gallop as men with muskets suddenly appeared on the flat roof of the palace and began firing.

Rojo ran as if all the hounds of hell were snapping at his hooves.

I hung on, crouching down in the saddle, expecting a musket ball at any moment to end my miserable life or Rojo to catch one that sent him tumbling and smacking the ground with enough force to break all of my bones.

I turned the stallion as soon as I cleared the main square when a group of horsemen came down the street to cut me off.

The posse had come back and had gotten into position to cut me off from the main road out of town.

I kicked and yelled for Rojo to sprout wings if he had to and held on as the stallion went between buildings and jumped a fence and then another.

As night fell I no longer heard the sound of muskets or the hooves of a pursuit.

Miles out on the sandy road that led up the coast before turning inland toward the mountains, when I felt it was safe, I finally pulled up Rojo and let him walk.

She had betrayed me, no doubt for a reward and her freedom. Fool that I was, I anticipated she would and still walked into the trap.

The "countess" was truly a demon in a dress.

Only one thing, other than that I prayed she rotted in hell, came out of the trap set for me: it confirmed she didn't have the gold. The governor must have seized it because if she still had it, she would have let me help her escape.

I didn't have the gold, either.

PART 5

SIR KNIGHT TO THE RESCUE

FORTY

HEADING UP THE coast out of Vera Cruz, I was sure I left pursuit far behind as Rojo opened up his stride after I walked and then rested him.

A posse would not keep up the chase long once night had fallen and I was out of sight. Traveling at night was dangerous with a horse because the road was sandy and paved with ruts and potholes. Besides hoping your horse didn't break a leg, it was the time deadly snakes slithered around looking for something warm-blooded to bite.

I traveled through the entire night, dozing in the saddle, walking in front of Rojo when I couldn't see enough of the road in the moonlight to know if there were holes he had to avoid. The region was almost entirely unsettled except for a few indios who sold tortillas and brackish water from huts at several places along the twenty-mile stretch of sands and stinking swamps before the route to the Valley of Mexico started up the mountains.

One bit of luck in my favor was that the pursuit was on the hot, swampy, coastal plains where sunstroke would get you if the terrible contagion called black vomito didn't strike you down first.

The people of Vera Cruz, from the governor down to léperos on the streets, lacked the energy and determination in everyday life that was evident in Oaxaca and other places I'd been, and most say it's because the heat and foul conditions made working hard impossible.

During a short period of winter when snow fell on distant mountains, Vera Cruz cooled down to the point of being livable. But during most of the year the region was insufferably hot, and Vera Cruz became almost a ghost town because everyone who could left their homes on the coast when ships were not due in and stayed in their homes on the other side of the mountains where it was cooler.

I couldn't have slept on the ground even if I had taken the time to lay out my bedroll and share the ground with snakes, scorpions, and poisonous spiders—I was too angry at my own stupidity to rest.

Three years of work had been lost in an hour of being played a fool by a woman. She tickled my ego and took everything from me—my gold and my dream, leaving me just with my damaged pride.

I grit my teeth thinking about her. If I ever met up with that woman again . . . Ayyo! I crossed myself. Even I knew that burning her feet over a fire, a favorite torture of the Inquisition, was too harsh. Maybe just a little toasting would do. Or better yet, tying a rope to her neck and dragging her behind Rojo over a bed of cactus.

I amused myself for about two minutes with all the ways I would take revenge on the woman before I gave up the ghost on the subject because I knew in my heart I wasn't capable of any of them.

More important than revenge that I would never have the opportunity to take or the dark heart to administer, I had to make a decision now about what I was going to do. To start all over and go back into horse stealing, I needed money for food for myself and the horses and a new territory to work because word would be out about me.

The choice as to how I would make the needed money seemed obvious: the route from Vera Cruz over the mountains to the capital was the most traveled road in the colony and the most robber-infested.

I would go back to being a bandido.

There was good reason that the road was beloved by bandidos—not only did more people and merchandise flow on it than any other road in the colony, but the route itself was difficult for the army and constables to patrol because of its narrow paths and length, its numerous small bridges that could be burned to cut off pursuit, and its rocky terrain in which rockslides could be triggered to cut off a small group of travelers from caravans of heavily armed mule trains of merchandise and pursuits by law enforcers.

A sole traveler was the most vulnerable. As I started into the mountains, I hoped that bandidos would come after me. Two pistolas and a machete from my saddlebags were now ready to be used.

It was one of those days when killing someone would have been a pleasure.

I would not be in a position to rob until I got beyond the narrower parts of the mountain pass that led to Xalapa, the main stopping area before travelers proceeded onto the capital.

It was a four- to five-day trek from Vera Cruz to Xalapa during good weather and could take several times longer during the rainy season. At the speed I was going, I would make it in half the time.

Being a lone highwayman was fraught with much more danger than leading a band of dumb léperos.

Seeing one masked man charging at a carriage most likely would get the guard riding next to the coach driver to fire his harquebus rather than throw his hands up in surrender.

As I did with Cerdo and the gang of worms, once I reached the area on the mountain where the road widened and carriages were once again in use, I would stay away from the heavily guarded mule trains and passengers that tended to travel together as a caravan. I would wait and find a straggler or a carriage with problems, a not infrequent occurrence since the "road" at best was full of rocks and ruts.

Once I had passed beyond the mountain path suited for mules and goats and was well along the road to Xalapa on which carriages were in use, I left the road and moved slowly along a ridge just above it. The low ridge gave me a good view of movement on the road.

I saw a carriage in the distance and heard gunshots. Squinting to get a better look, I realized that a carriage was being attacked.

Two men on horses charged a carriage whose driver and guard were sitting in the shade of a tree eating their midday meal. One of the mules pulling the carriage went down as it was hit by the gunfire. The horsemen had deliberately shot the mule to keep the carriage from being driven away.

As the horsemen came up to them, the coachmen stood and raised their hands in surrender. The front rider stopped his horse next to a coachman and, without saying a word, swung down with a machete and split open the man's head as if cutting a melon.

The second coachman started to run, and the other bandido rode up behind him and hit the man behind the back of the neck with a machete, nearly severing the head.

Ayyo! It was unnecessary violence—the two coachmen had already surrendered.

I spotted a third man. He slipped out of the side of the carriage opposite to the highwaymen and ran.

A bandido spotted him and yelled, both kicking their horses to cut him off as he ran. From my vantage point, I could see that the man was running toward a deep river crevice without realizing it was not an escape route.

The man running appeared young, slender, and well dressed.

I slipped my bandana up over my nose, grabbed a pistola, and gave Rojo a kick.

To distract them from the running man, as I came off the ridge I shouted so the murderers would know I was coming.

That halted them fast, and they both turned toward me. I could see the confusion on their faces.

One of the men charged me while the other wheeled and went for the running young man.

The man came at me at a full gallop, a pistola in hand. He had already used his pistola to frighten the guards into surrender and had not had time to load, so he must have carried two pistols as I did.

I pulled Rojo to a stop and the other man took the movement to be one of fading courage on my part, but he was wrong. The way his horse was running, with him bouncing in the saddle, he would have to be nearly on top of me before he got close enough to get off an accurate shot.

Sitting calmly on Rojo, I waited until I had a good shot and raised my pistola. The man realized his mistake and got off a hurried shot that went wild. As he wheeled his horse to make a run for it, I went after him, giving Rojo his head, knowing the bandido would not get far on his much smaller mount.

I put the pistola back in its holster attached to the saddle and took out my machete.

As I came up behind the man, he turned and gave me a look of fright—the same look that had been on the face of the coachman he murdered in cold blood.

I made him a headless horseman and kept going, heading for the man who was running for the cliff with the other bandido behind him.

The man from the coach had reached the edge of the crevice and saw that he could go no farther. The rider bearing down on him fired, and the man stumbled backward and disappeared over the edge.

The highwayman had used both his pistolas. Unlike his companion who tried to outrun me, he took one look at my big stallion and stopped and held up his hands.

He was surrendering.

It caught me completely by surprise, but I realized what he had in mind. My mask said I was another bandido. He was right that I would permit some courtesy among thieves. But he was a murderer.

As I rode up to him I pulled out my pistola and shot him between the eyes.

"No quarter for murderers," I told his body as I galloped by.

A horse whinnied, and I looked farther along the ridge from the spot where I had come off. A man on a horse was there, watching—and wearing a mask even though the two bandidos who did the attack had not bothered to hide their faces. He wheeled his horse and was quickly out of sight.

Strange. It made no sense to me. For sure, he wasn't

like me, a thief who just happened along. Eh—there weren't that many lone bandidos on the road. He had to be with the other two, but had stood back, watching what was taking place. Waiting to pop out of hiding if his compadres needed the help? He would have seen that the coachmen had surrendered. Why didn't he come down then?

Whatever his motives for not taking part of the action, even with the quick glance I got, I learned something about him: he was riding a good horse, not the skinny nags the two other men were on, and his clothes were better than his two amigos wore. The dead men were dressed in well-worn work clothes, what a vaquero working with cattle and horses would wear. Pretty much what I was wearing.

The clothes of the man who fled were also the kind worn on haciendas, but his were of a better quality, what a majordomo or foreman who never got his hands dirty would wear.

Because of the mask he wore, I wouldn't recognize him if I passed him on the street . . . but I had more of an eye for horseflesh than most people and would know his mount if I saw it again.

I galloped to the edge of the crevice—a hundred-foot cliff down to river rapids. If the carriage passenger who went over was not already dead from being shot, he would not have survived the fall and rocky rapids below.

"*Vaya con dios, amigo,*" I said, crossing myself.

Two coachmen, one gachupin, all dead. Even one of the carriage mules was dead.

I got into the carriage to see what valuables I could find. The two horses of the bandidos had not gone far, and I would round them up later. I'd take them and the remaining mule with me.

The interior of the coach was not as grand as some, and that told me it was not the personal coach of the passenger but had been hired to transport him to the point where coaches could run again.

I ignored the trunks strapped to the back and top of the coach and went inside to go through what he would have carried close to him—other than what went over the cliff with him.

Rifling through the young Spaniard's bags in the coach, I discovered that he was a personage of wealth because his clothes and jewelry were expensive.

I slipped on a well-cut, soft leather doublet and put on his hat, laughing as I played the gachupin. Eh, I could get used to the soft life of a Spanish caballero with nothing to do but parade in the paseo all day and play with cards and women at night.

I took off the vestlike doublet and put on breeches and a waistcoat, then put the doublet back on and admired myself in a small mirror I found in the bag. I leaned out the open door.

"Eh, Rojo, meet Don Juan Lépero de Oaxaca."

He ignored me and I went back to rummaging.

"Antonio de los Rios" had a royal letter permitting his passage to the colony and a letter of introduction to the viceroy from an official in the colonial office. While I had not learned to read well enough to understand all the words in the documents, I had seen travel documents among the effects of people I robbed and recognized the names and seals of the officials.

"Antonio, you have friends in high places. Which means you are a personage of importance despite your young age."

I heard horses coming and stuck my head out the window of the coach. An army patrol was coming at a gallop from the direction of Xalapa.

Behind me coming up the road was a mule train.

A ridge was to my right and a sheer drop where I could join the young gachupin in a watery grave to my left.

Ayyo! I was boxed in and caught with dead men and not just loot in my hands—I was wearing stolen clothes.

While the rest of the army patrol came to a halt before the coach, an officer dismounted and approached on foot.

I stepped out of the carriage and removed the gachupin's hat, using it to make a sweeping bow.

"Antonio de los Rios, at your service, señor."

FORTY-ONE

"I'VE SEEN THE two bandidos before," the officer, a capitán in charge of the patrol, told me after he had looked around at the carnage. "Trash that hangs around pulquerias. They would slice their own mothers' throats for a real."

Since it took eight reales to equal a single piece of eight, about an ounce of silver, the capitán didn't think the dead men had valued their mothers much.

I merely nodded at his sage observation, too worried I would say something that revealed that I wasn't a Spanish gentleman. He was in awe of me for having dispatched two bandidos after my guards were killed without firing a shot, and I wanted to keep it that way. I would have given my valiant guards the credit for the kill, but it was obvious that their muskets had not been fired.

"It was pure luck and the hand of God," I said with great modesty. "I surprised them by fighting back."

"You say a stranger came to your aid?"

"Sí, as I said, sadly the man went over the cliff and was lost in the terrible rapids below."

The officer made the sign of the cross. "May God accept him for the hero he was. Is that his fine horse?" he asked of Rojo.

"No, his horse went over with him." I gave a quick answer to that one so the officer would not grab Rojo for himself. It was common on long trips to have a personal horse hitched to the rear of a coach.

"I brought the stallion over from Spain. I was about to ride it to the nearest settlement to get help and have my possessions transported. I have urgent business in the capital."

I made sure my chest swelled a bit when I added the last bit.

"Of course, from your travel documents, it is obvious that your business in the capital is most important."

The moment the capitán saw my papers, he began to fawn over me. Eh, I was a peninsulare from Madrid and he was a low-ranking officer in the colonial militia, which did little except patrol the Vera Cruz–Xalapa trade route.

He shouted orders for my trunks to be loaded on mules.

"I will leave men here to clean up this mess and bury the dead while I escort you to Xalapa."

Ayyo! The last thing I needed was to be taken to a city where I would have endless chances of being exposed as a highwayman and imposter.

"That won't be necessary. I would be remiss if I took you away from your urgent duties of protecting the many travelers along this treacherous route. I will just ride my horse to Xalapa—"

"Oh no, Señor Rios, that would not be possible. I would be broken down in rank and sent to the northern desert to fight the savage Chichimeca if I did not personally deliver you to Don Riego."

I cleared my throat and pretended I was trying to remember. "Ah, Don Riego . . ."

"Sí, Don Domingo del Riego, the viceroy's aide. He is waiting for you at Xalapa."

"Waiting for me," I repeated.

"Of course, señor. The mail packet from Madrid brought word of your coming a week ago. We were told to be on the lookout for you and take you to Señor Riego when we found you."

My brain was freezing up as I tried to keep up the pretense, but what he said got through loud and clear: he was taking me to the viceroy's aide—who was expecting me.

Oh shit. I smelled doom.

So far I had avoided exposure as a fraud because I had Antonio's possessions. Nor was my olive complexion a problem—Spaniards come in many shades, and mine was similar to the southern Mediterranean skin color of many of them. But sooner or later I would say something that would reveal my complete ignorance at being a Spaniard fresh off the boat from . . . from . . . *from where*?

I had seen the word "Madrid" on the travel documents, and that was where the court and other high officials were located, but I didn't know if Antonio was also from there.

There were many cities in Spain and many ports, and, while I had heard of many of them, I didn't know which port I was supposed to have departed from. Madrid, perhaps?

Sí, that was it. If I was asked which port I had boarded ship at, I would say Madrid. It had to be the biggest and most important port in Spain since the king was there.

The officer paused for a moment to inspect the way "my" carriage trunks were being loaded on mules and then returned to escort me to my horse.

"This is not a privilege, of course, that we extend to all bearing letters of introduction from Madrid.

But your situation being unique, it is one the viceroy considers to be of utmost importance."

I didn't dare ask what was unique about my situation.

I should have burned Antonio de los Rios's papers rather than use them to identify myself.

Or eaten them.

FORTY-TWO

"YOU WILL FIND that the social life in Mexico City lacks the sheer magnitude of that in Madrid, Don Antonio, but not the brilliance," Don Domingo said. "The largest and richest city in all the Americas, Mexico is the queen of the New World and a glittering gem in our mighty king's possessions."

Señor Domingo del Riego leaned over and gave me a wink and a smirk. "As the heir to one of the largest fortunes in the colony, many an artful mother will be parading daughters for you at the ball that the viceroy will hold in your honor."

I smiled, but beneath my pleasant exterior I was burning with pure animal panic. I could barely restrain myself from running to the nearest hole and hiding.

Ayyo! Juan the Lépero, horse thief, bandido, and only God knows my many other sins, sat in a carriage with one of the most powerful men in the colony—and on his way to the biggest and richest city in the Americas where *the* most powerful man in the colony wants to entertain him.

This miserable lépero in a gachupin's clothes was one lucky devil, no? But I didn't feel lucky. I was certain that following the ball, I would be hanged as an imposter.

If I had seen a hole big enough to hide in, I would

have squeezed into it. Ayyo! I would rather face a test of my shooting skills than my social manners.

Since meeting Señor Riego I had managed to keep from being exposed as an imposter and fraud through sheer luck and the fact that I was such a lying bastardo. I didn't know how my artful verbal dancing was going to conceal that I knew so little about so much. So far I had mostly smiled a lot, nodded my head repeatedly, and made brilliant listening responses such as "hum" and "aah" while I found out tiny pieces about who I was—or at least pretending to be. Fortunately, the man loved to talk, words gushing from him like water rushing over rapids.

I had learned that I was the nephew and heir of a deceased sword and dagger merchant who greatly increased his wealth a few months before he died by financing a muleteer who claimed to have received the location of a silver lode from an indio whose tribe had kept the site a secret.

"I've heard he roasted the informant over a campfire until the man gave up the spot," Don Domingo said with a chuckle.

I suspected the indio whose feet got roasted wasn't as amused. However the muleteer got the location, the silver was there, and the fortunes of "my" uncle, Ramos de los Rios, climbed.

The good part was that even though I had met Uncle Ramos once in Spain before he came to the New World seeking a fortune, he was now dead. Had his ghost been in the carriage with us, I would have kissed his feet for having conveniently gone to the hereafter before I arrived claiming to be his heir.

A second piece of luck was that my relatives in the capital were cousins who had never met me. Eh, but there was another bullet to dodge—I had an elderly uncle in Guadalajara who had met me in Spain and was expected to come to Mexico City for a visit. Perhaps he would be in the city waiting as the coach pulled up. I kept that nightmare tucked behind the stiff smile I had painted on my face as I tried to hide my ignorance behind the hums and aahs.

"Although you have not met your cousin Don Carlos de Rueda, I am sure you are aware of his position in the colony," the viceroy's aide said.

"Naturally," I muttered, wondering what the hell was his position. Spanish upper-class men added the honorific "don" to their names, so that told me nothing except that he was rich.

"His wife died, of course, a fine lady. Did you meet any of her family while you lived in Madrid?"

"Hum," I muttered, giving the matter great thought as I stalled and wondered what the right answer would be.

"Of course," Don Domingo said, "the name Cortés, while famous in Spain, lacks the incredible power it has in the colony."

I was so surprised I couldn't manage a listening response.

"Being married to a daughter of the conqueror had many benefits for Carlos."

That would make Carlos's wife a sister of El Mestizo. Whose horse, which I stole, was hitched to the back of Riego's coach at the moment.

"Had she had children before she died, they would have shared the Cortés bloodline and Carlos could have relied upon her family, the richest in the colony, for support when he suffered his losses trying to manipulate the price of maize. Don't you agree, Antonio?"

"Hum," I nodded. It wasn't just a question. Riego had a sly look when he tossed it out. What was he getting at?

"I'm certain that your cousin Carlos is most pleased and gracious about the fact that your uncle chose you as his heir rather than him."

"Aah." I got it. Riego was telling me that this Carlos was royally pissed that the uncle had cut him out and put me in. Even a lépero understands that when you're broke, you're going to hate the person who got rich at your expense.

"I'm sure my dear cousin Carlos will light a candle at the cathedral to celebrate my miraculous escape from death," I intoned, giving the statement as much sincerity as I could but conveying just a hint of facetiousness because I was getting the feeling cousin Carlos was not an amigo of the viceroy's aide.

I detected the hint of a chuckle under Riego's breath.

"Amigo," he said, "you will hear gossip in the capital that I am angry at your cousin for selling me a lame horse, but that is nonsense. As a gentleman, I know for certain Carlos would never deliberately cheat me."

"Aah." So that was why Riego was doing a not-too-subtle character assassination of Carlos, a horse deal that went sour because Carlos misrepresented the quality or condition of a horse—a not uncommon occurrence in horse trading, a business only slightly more ethical than robbing coaches. But you could cheat a man at cards or steal his mistress and be less likely to be called out onto the field of honor than you would if you cheated him in a horse trade, because all men, from fat merchants to léperos like me, thought of ourselves as caballeros and thus experts at horses.

Not that Riego was the type to settle the matter in

a duel. He appeared more likely to use his quill and ink on paper to extract his revenge.

"I bought the animal with the understanding that a horse in the bloodline of the conqueror's own warhorse would have the strongest possible limbs. For it to have turned lame after a short time was unacceptable. Don't you agree, Antonio?"

"Absolutely." I actually did agree with him. Everyone in the colony had heard of El Reye, the most magnificent stallion in all New Spain.

Something Riego had said was ringing a bell in my head, but I had so many strange things coming at me that I couldn't quite put my finger on it.

FORTY-THREE

I KEPT THE conversation on horses, a subject I knew more about than the viceroy's aide.

"The stud fees on a horse carrying the bloodline of the conqueror's own warhorse must be extremely high," I said, not volunteering that the stallion hitched to the carriage also had the bloodline of the conquest warhorses, though not the coveted lineage of the horse Cortés rode at the battle of Otumba.

"For a certainty. El Reye is the most valuable horse in New Spain, perhaps in the world. I suspect there are none more valuable even in the king's stable in Madrid. The stallion not only carries the bloodline, but has the grace, stamina, and lines of a great horse."

"Sí, such a horse would be very valuable," I said.

"Worth as much as a good-sized hacienda. And Carlos needs all the stud fees he can get now that he lost so much money."

Riego explained that Carlos had attempted to make an enormous profit on maize by buying large quantities of the grain and holding it back from sale, thereby creating a shortage.

"Merchants had made large amounts of money manipulating the price in that manner before, but this was the first time a caballero who was considered part of the aristocracy of the colony attempted it. It would have worked except that poor people who starved the moment the price rose rioted and the viceroy allowed the emergency maize reserve to be sold, thus bringing down the price to less than what Carlos had paid."

I only half-listened to Riego as he yanked on somewhat jealously about speculators in maize, beef, and other commodities who were able to make profits by manipulating the supplies, but what incredible arrogance Carlos had displayed in believing he was capable of the same.

I had a more important subject on my mind, remembering the conversation in a room at the inn in Oaxaca nearly four years ago about a problem with a prize horse and something Héctor had said:

"Don Carlos de Rueda is the brother-in-law of the marquis," Héctor had boasted.

Ayyo! Life was a circle, and I had gone full circle around and come back to face someone I saw in Oaxaca years ago.

I turned my features away from the viceroy's aide so he couldn't read the consternation I'm sure my expression was exposing. It was unlikely that Carlos would recognize me as the stable boy who had served him. No—it was impossible. He was a gachupin—a low-caste stable boy would no more remain in his memory than the street trash his carriage rumbled over.

He would not see me as I was that day—a worker dressed in clothes one step from rags and wearing sandals that left me little more than barefoot—but as I was now dressed, in clothes of silk and fine wool.

I was uncomfortable in the clothes not only because of the richness of the materials and tightness of the fit—Antonio was my height though less solidly built—but because of the style. These were the clothes of the wealthy merchant class who rode almost always in carriages, not of caballeros who wore clothing suitable for riding a horse even if the men only rode on the paseo in the hopes of attracting the attention of señoritas.

To the indios and mestizos, the word "gachupin" simply referred to a Spaniard who metaphorically raked their backs with sharp spurs by taking the food from their mouths while working them hard and paying little. But the original wearers of spurs were the conquistadors, men who earned their spurs in battle. That was the kind of gachupin I wanted to be.

Ayyo! In the merchant's garb, I felt like a wolf wrapped in silk.

I also worried that my smell would expose me as a lépero to the viceroy's aide. A thousand times I've heard gachupins say that we of the lower classes smelled worse than pigs as they covered their nostrils with nosegays to block out the stench.

In the hope that it would hide my lépero odor, I had put on perfume I found in Antonio's toilette box. I also discovered that Antonio's clothes in his trunks smelled from rose petals and cinnamon and other herbs in little pouches laid among them.

The gachupins were so concerned about their smell that they even gave their clothes a scent. I suppose they thought that their excrement smelled sweeter than everyone else's, too.

I was getting more nervous and antsy as the man rambled about things I knew nothing about, but escape wasn't possible. At least, not at the moment because the aide's coach was escorted by a dozen soldiers, each armed with a harquebus.

"When we near the capital, I will send a speedy messenger ahead to let your relatives know you are arriving. They will want to gather at your uncle's home—your home now—to welcome you."

"Excellent," I thought, really excellent—another chance to be exposed, another nail in my coffin.

Ayyo! The first chance I had, I would jump on Rojo and leave my relatives and Mexico City in my dust.

Another problem perhaps even more urgent than whether I would be hanged as an imposter throbbed in my head, one that had my finely honed survival instincts screaming that I had better watch my back.

Cousin Carlos had money problems. He had not only failed at manipulating the price of maize, Riego told me, but had tried to recover his losses at cards, a sure disaster for a desperate man.

Carlos had big money problems in a society where failing to pay debts resulted not only in loss of social stature but debtor's prison. And he was next in line to inherit a fortune that would save him from the mire he appeared to be drowning in.

To avoid humiliation and possible imprisonment, would Carlos resort to murder?

I had met the man in circumstances that revealed his true character. Hiding behind the drapes, I had quickly learned that he was deceitful to his wife, her family, and to horse buyers, which in my eyes made him a step lower than the swine I tried to turn into a respectable gang of bandidos.

I had already deduced that the bandidos that attacked Antonio de los Rios's carriage had set out not just to rob, but to kill—shooting coachmen that had not even bothered to raise their weapons, and not wearing masks, showed that they did not intend to leave anyone alive. The target had to be Antonio and not just his possessions because there was no reason to kill—the man was running away from his possessions when he was shot.

The killings had not made sense to me on the road

to Vera Cruz when my blood was still hot and my machete bloody, but rocking back and forth in the gachupin carriage it made great sense to me now because I knew Carlos had the motive to hire assassins to kill Antonio.

I had only a vague impression as to what Carlos had looked like when I saw him in Oaxaca and had not seen him mounted on a horse, but I had noted that the man riding away from the massacre on the Vera Cruz road had been dressed better than the bandidos.

One thing was wrong with connecting Carlos to the killing of Antonio—the man watching the attack from the ridge was not Carlos. I am better than most at judging not only horses but a man on one, and I am certain that Carlos was a bigger man than the horseman on the ridge.

But that didn't alter my belief that what I witnessed was a deliberate murder rather than just a robbery. What had the officer told me about the bandidos—he had seen them before, that they were the sort of trash that would slice a throat for a piece of silver?

I knew the type well from my own time spent hanging around pulquerias, listening to the talk, watching the scum that could be hired to kill, steal, or do anything else except a day's labor.

I also knew the type well enough to know that they were too smart to kill someone unnecessarily—as I repeatedly told my lépero highwaymen, killing caused more trouble than it was worth.

For sure, the two bandidos who attacked the coach of Rios were not so stupid to have wantonly killed just to rob. The only reason to have made murder the goal was that they had been paid to do so. Even if the third man was not Carlos, an important gachupin like Carlos could have sent an emissary to hire killers.

Ayyo! Once one's conscience has been whetted from bloodletting, spilling more blood would not be as difficult as the first time. Besides, the killer can always cast off the sin by going to confession and doing penance, along with giving a nice gift to the priest who granted it.

I had a burning question that I wanted to ask the viceroy's aide, a man who seemed to know everybody and everything about the colony by the way he babbled nonstop about who was making or losing money or having love affairs: Who else would want to murder Antonio besides a money-hungry relative? Was there a line of people who wanted the man dead? Perhaps because of some old blood feud or because Antonio had stuck his pene into someone else's woman?

Did I step into the shoes of a dead man only to join the man in the grave?

PART 6

MEXICO CITY, NEW SPAIN

A.D. 1569

FEAST OF THE CONQUERORS

Conquistador Bernal Diaz del Castillo in his account of the Conquest wrote that following the final battle against the Aztecs, Cortés' soldiers held a drunken celebration in which conquistadores got up on table tops and boasted of the great wealth they had grabbed.

Some said they would only buy gold saddles for their horses, while the crossbowmen boasted they would now use golden arrows.

Full of wine and bravado, the men then raped the Aztec women who had been captured in the battle.

—Bernal Díaz del Castillo, *Historia verdadera de la conquista de la Nueva España*

FORTY-FOUR

WHEN WE CAME out of the foothills, I saw Mexico City spread out on an expanse of water and was awed. Oaxaca, Vera Cruz, and Xalapa, the biggest cities I had been in, were villages compared to the sprawling city posed on a vast lake.

"I'm happy to see you're impressed," the viceroy's aide said. "It is said that the capital is the most European city in the Americas, that because of the canals, it's like Venice. Have you been to Venice, señor?"

"Hum," I said, as if I was trying to remember whether I'd been there. I thought it was a planet.

Riego dived right in to talking about the city's history without pinning me down to whether I'd been in Venice.

"You know, of course, that the city's built on the bones of the Aztec capital called Tenochtitlán. After the conquest, Cortés had the pagan temples and the great palaces of Montezuma and his high nobles razed and used the stone blocks for building the city."

"Which is why the streets are so straight?"

"Exactly. Unlike other cities that spread out in different directions without any planning, Cortés had the city laid out. He insisted it be the capital for a number of reasons, including its prestige as the largest city in the Americas before the conquest. Also because the conquistadors were quite fascinated with the city from the moment they saw it, probably from about the same spot you observed it today. Enchanting, they called it, an island crowded with great towers and temples rising from the lake. They wondered if the city was real or whether it was a dream."

About the same feeling I had, except for me the city was poised to be a nightmare.

"The soil is so saturated with water, no one can be buried belowground in the city," Riego said. "The island it sits on was much smaller when the Aztecs first made it their capital. They increased the size of it with floating gardens called chinampas that eventually became landfills.

"The city worked well for the Aztecs because they had only their own feet and small boats in which to move people and goods. Surrounded by water and having no beasts of burden, it was supplied by foot over the causeways and with thousands of canoes. But as you know, Don Antonio, we are a nation of horses, mules, carts, and carriages that require hard-packed soil, hardly the ingredients of a city on an island laced with canals and frequently subject to flooding."

Eh, I was beginning to like the sound of being called Don Antonio. It had a nice ring to it, no?

"But the great conqueror, the Marquis del Valle," he said, "recognized that there was a compelling reason why the Aztec capital should become the center of the new colonial government. The city evoked both fear and obedience among the indios. They were used to obeying the commands issued from it.

"Cortés was even wise enough to use a name that keeps the Aztec mystique alive. Some suggested giving the city a Spanish name, as Cortés did with the very first city he created, Vera Cruz, or even calling it New Madrid. But the clever conqueror called it

Mexico, because, although we use the name Aztec, that breed of indio called themselves the Mexica."

I knew much of what he told me from the tales told of the conquest. What I needed more was a lesson on being a Spaniard.

"I must warn you, Don Antonio," the aide said, "you will find some resentment among criollos in general because you are a peninsulare."

"Why is that, Don Domingo?" I asked, taking a pinch of snuff he offered.

"These colonials hate those of us who come over from Spain to serve the king in this distant place but plan to return home. When the previous viceroy died, they even had the imprudence to petition the king and ask that he permit them to govern themselves. Can you imagine the howls of laughter and ridicule the request created in Madrid?" He leaned closer and spoke in a confidential tone. "It's the weather, you understand."

"The weather?"

"The warm climate makes the colonials lazy and . . ."

I could have told him that I already knew that the hotter it got, the lazier people got, but I only half-listened as he droned on about the inability of the colonials to govern themselves and their ignorance about the state of the world and struggles for empires. The struggle I was having was to keep from breaking out into an open sweat the nearer we got to the city. Eh, if he thought criollos were ignorant about the world, what was he going to think when I tripped myself up with my lack of knowledge and manners?

After Riego had finished raking the criollos over

the coals, he started in on how ungrateful the indios were for not appreciating all that the king was doing for them.

"The indios would be in dire straits, indeed," he said, "if we permitted the criollos to exploit them as much as the criollos tried."

He was too uninformed about indios to know that they didn't distinguish between the injustices they suffered at the hands of criollos and the ones they suffered from peninsulares; that all Spanish were gachupins to them, wearers of sharp spurs; and that while the temples of their bloodthirsty gods of yore were gone, their beating hearts were still being ripped out in sacrificial rites as the Spanish gorged themselves on riches created by their labor.

"Colonials boast that anything found in Madrid could be found in the city, except for the king," Riego said.

He went on to describe the Spanish ingenuity and prowess in building the city, speaking as if Cortés himself had rolled up his sleeves and had begun dismantling the great stone edifices of the Aztec empire and packing them on his back to build his palace and the city around it.

Eh—there is an indio way of looking at the world and a Spanish way, with my mixed blood permitting me to peek at a bit of each.

That Spanish image of how the city was built left out the fact that the invaders rounded up tens of thousands of indios to work as slaves to build the new city from the rubble of the old one, driving them with fear and the whip much the same way Sunday school priests say that the pharaohs of Egypt built their great monuments.

The churches were built the same way, by thousands

of indios the priests called converts and the indios called slaves being forced to dismantle the temples of their defeated gods and use the stone to build churches.

It didn't disturb the priests that the great blocks of stone from the pyramid dedicated to Huitzilopochtli, the Aztec war god, which stood in what is now the Zócalo, were used as the foundation for the city's main cathedral despite the fact that they had been stained with the blood of sacrifice victims.

The indios knew that they had not shared in the prosperity and grandeur of the city that was the largest and richest in the "New World."

While the conquerors lived in grand houses and palaces, many only staying long enough in the colony to get rich, city-dwelling indios worked as servants and laborers and lived in squalid shacks, mostly made out of wood and cornstalks, although a few were of adobe.

I was used to hearing the Spanish of Oaxaca speak of indios as if they were farm animals, but the tone of Riego was different. The aide's "experience" with indios was limited to seeing them carrying merchandise on the streets and working as household servants. He did not see them as beasts of burden but had the mentality that indios were child-like and had to be protected even from themselves.

He finally got around to something close to my heart.

"The worst plague in the city is not constant flooding or the stench from the excrement that pours into the lake, but the dirty, disgusting, blood-tainted léperos." He shook his head, in wonderment. "You have never seen anything like these creatures in Madrid or anywhere else. They loudly beseech for a coin for food and then use it for indio beer at a pulqueria. They eat little but multiply faster than their brother rats and lice. Truly creatures damned by God."

"And stupid, too," I added. "From what I saw of the creatures in Vera Cruz."

MEXICO: A PROUD, RICH, AND FLAMBOYANT CITY

It is a byword that at Mexico there are four things fair . . . the women, the apparel, the horses, and the streets . . .

The streets are very broad, in the narrowest three coaches may go, and in the broader six may go in the breadth of them, which makes the city seem a great deal bigger than it is.

The people are so proud and rich that half the city was judged to keep coaches, for it was a most credible report that in Mexico in my time there were above fifteen thousand coaches . . .

The coaches exceed in cost the best of the Court of Madrid and other parts of Christendom; for they spare no silver, nor gold, nor precious stones, nor cloth of gold . . . for their horses there are bridles and shoes of silver.

Both men and women are excessive in their apparel, using more silks than stuffs and cloth. Precious stones and pearls further this their vain ostentation; a hat-band and rose made of diamonds in a gentleman's hat is common, and a hat-band of pearls is common in a tradesman.

—Thomas Gage, *Travels in the New World*
[circa A.D. 1625]

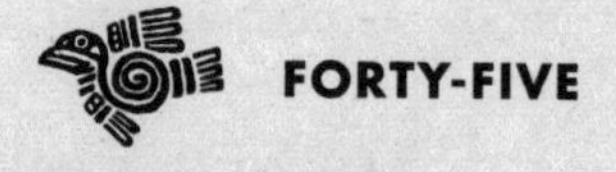

FORTY-FIVE

THE CARRIAGE RUMBLED along a long causeway, carrying us across the lake to where we would enter city streets. The bridge was crowded with people, pack mules, carts, carriages, horsemen, and even small herds of goats, sheep, and cattle on the way to be butchered.

Just as in Aztec days, the most common "pack animals" were indios, who were capable of carrying large bundles, as much as half their own weight, for great distances.

"Less expensive than mules," Riego said, "and they eat less."

The lake and canals flowing into the city were almost as pressed with people as the causeway, on which swarms of watercraft, hundreds, perhaps even thousands of canoes piled high with vegetables, fish, firewood, and cloth, were bringing items to marketplaces.

Señor Riego waved his hand at the waterline of the city as we got near the end of the causeway.

"Now there is something that would be rare indeed in mother Spain or the rest of Europe, amigo. You see that there are no defensive walls around the city or around our government buildings as there are on the coast."

"The city is an island and easy to defend?"

"True, but also because the only threat is an attack from the sea, and we are far from the coastline. No other nation besides Spain has a large enough settlement in the Americas to be a threat by land. Even though we have indio problems up north and occasionally even small uprisings in other areas, the indios are no real danger to the might and power of the king's army and the colonial militia."

I didn't ask him why, if Spain's military might is so great, fighting of indios has been going on for over forty years with no end in sight. And how come the viceroy couldn't make the Vera Cruz and Acapulco trade routes safe.

"Are those of mixed blood a threat?" I asked, curious as to what he would say.

"Flea bites, amigo, that is all the mestizos are capable of."

The city streets were as densely packed as the causeway, with Spaniards on horseback and in carriages joining the throngs that came in on the causeway. And Riego told me that there were other land bridges over the lake to the city.

I had never seen so many people at one time in my life. Riego told me that there were more people entering and leaving the city across the causeways in the morning than there were in the entire city of Vera Cruz even when a fleet was in.

"Most of the indio goods end up in the Tlatelolco, the largest of the native markets, one that dates back to Aztec times. Only servants and the lower classes shop there."

"Naturalmente," I offered, "the common people must eat, too, no?" I made it sound like I regretted they had to be fed. Eh, I was not only dressed like a gachupin, I was beginning to talk and think like one.

Riego pointed out a prominent structure near the entrance to the marketplace: gallows. Three bodies were swaying in the breeze.

"In the time of the Aztecs," he said, "their temples had racks of human skulls from heads that had once sat on the shoulders of sacrifice victims. It was a reminder not only to their false gods of the sacrifices they had made for them, but what would happen to themselves if they disobeyed the commands of the Aztec emperor."

He smirked. "Our gallows is a reminder to the indios that our justice is even swifter."

Despite my blood getting hotter the more I listened to the arrogant Spaniard boasting about the prowess of his people when I knew that, despite his boasts, compared to me *he* was a flea *I* could swat aside, I was stunned and awed at seeing the city.

I already knew from my first view of it from a great distance that no city I had been in came anywhere close to the size and magnificence of the capital. But to see the streets, to be on them, *ay di mio!*—the major thoroughfares of Mexico City were as wide as the main square in most of the cities I had been in.

I realized that Mexico City truly deserved its title as the queen and very heart of New Spain, a gem that has been polished with the wealth of the colony.

To have heard homes described as "palaces" had little meaning to me until we rumbled by huge stone structures that the wealthy encomenderos, big hacienda owners, and silver-mine owners had built. Palaces were the size of city blocks in Oaxaca and Vera Cruz and were not made from flimsy materials as they were in most other cities.

"It's been over forty years since the conquest, and there are even still a few of the original conquistadors living," Riego said. "The old warriors are treated with the respect given to popes and ghosts."

As soon as our carriage wheels began rumbling

down city streets, we were besieged by filthy, ragged, disgusting léperos. They beseeched us in the most agonizing, pitiful, and heartrending terms, even claiming that charity to them would be blessed by God.

They were the most vile and insufferable pack of thieves and beggars that I had ever seen. At their most obnoxious, the léperos of Oaxaca, Vera Cruz, and other cities I had been in paled in comparison to these demons of beggardom. I alone had had the whine and intonation in my best days to match these beggars.

As they were beaten back by the guards, the viceroy's aide used a rose-scented nosegay to block their stench.

"Did I lie to you about these howling devils, Don Antonio?" he asked.

"Truly creatures damned by God, Don Domingo," I said, accepting a nosegay offered by the man.

What horrible whining! What vile stench these creatures emitted! I took a pinch of snuff to relieve my poor nose.

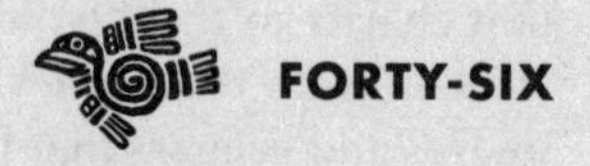

FORTY-SIX

"I SHALL GET out here," Riego said as the carriage pulled up to the viceroy's palace. "The carriage will deliver you to your new home, where your loving relatives await you."

With knives, guns, and poisons, no doubt.

I sat back in the carriage and gritted my teeth and rubbed my pistola with the itchy palm of my hand. I would have preferred to jump on Rojo, who was being pulled behind the carriage, and gallop away, but I had discovered a couple of things since I blundered into the attack on Antonio de los Rios.

First, being a gachupin was an interesting change of habit for me.

For the first time, I had gotten a true dose of what léperos were like from the point of view of respectable people. I had been a lépero, and in other cities I had had léperos whine and beg from me, but here, in the guise of a gachupin, I had truly experienced what these creatures were really like.

Whew! They stunk.

Second, I was actually intrigued by the murder of my namesake. Why was the real Antonio murdered? Greed? Jealousy? Vengeance?

I knew I could ride away from it, but stepping into his shoes had made the killing of him personal to me. Not just because I was the next intended victim, but because I had fought for him, seen him die, worn his clothes, and used his name.

For a certainty it wasn't from a sense of honor that I decided to carry forth as Juan the Gachupin. Maybe I really had become a gachupin in a short time.

Or maybe the fact that I had just inherited a business of fine blades— swords and knives—had a certain appeal to a man of my persuasion. I had always stolen whatever was handy and sold the loot for a fraction of its value because a mestizo could not have possessed things of value.

But I was no longer a half blood. I was a gachupin. Which was the most important reason I was not running.

Now I could steal things of greater value.

FORTY-SEVEN

BEING TRANSPORTED AS a person of quality in my carriage to my home, I wondered just how many houses I owned. And whether I had a hacienda. With fine horses?

Most gachupins had a house in Mexico City even if their business of mining, hacienda, or merchandise required some care elsewhere in the colony. At the very least, wealthy gachupins spent more than half the year socializing in the capital.

I wondered if I now had a hacienda that I could leave the city and stay at without raising suspicion.

Of course, before I did that, today I had to face a host of relatives at my city dwelling. And tomorrow perhaps the hangman at that gallows Riego was so proud of.

As the carriage pulled up to the grand house that I was master of, I tensed, wondering what the chances were that the elderly uncle from Guadalajara had arrived unexpectedly. It was too late to flee because people had gathered to greet me at the open gate to the house. Men, women, young, old, at least two dozen of them.

At the head of the greeting line was Carlos de Rueda.

The naked woman who pawed me in Oaxaca wasn't with him.

As I stepped down from the carriage, my knees

shaking as they sensed "Imposter!" would soon be shouted, I put on a brave grin as they clapped and yelled "El héroe!"

Carlos stepped forward. "Welcome, cousin. You have cheated death and slain dragons, and we honor you as a hero and conqueror."

He saluted me with a wide sweep of his hat.

A matron stepped in front of him, pulling a teenage girl with her.

"My daughter, your second cousin, twice removed. You must come to a party at our house, where you can get to know her better."

Ayyo! I've known horses I'd rather bed with.

FORTY-EIGHT

IT BECAME A blur of names that I would never remember, faces with smiles that I found more insincere than a beggar's whine, marriageable daughters whose sole interest in me was the size of my fortune rather than my cojones, and questions I hated answering about how I managed to kill two bandidos when I had been employed in Spain as a keeper of a merchant's accounts and once considered the priesthood.

"God guided my hand," I said, repeatedly.

Carlos pulled me away from the mob and pointed at Rojo as the horse was being led into the stable by a servant.

"I recognize your horse."

I froze, and my hand touched the pistola I had under my coat. I didn't know what to say and gave him a stupid smile.

"The bloodline, were you aware it's colonial?" he asked.

"Ahh," was all I could manage.

"They love our horses in Spain, eh. You could have saved the expense of bringing it over. I breed the finest horses in all of New Spain from a champion stud that carries the bloodline of the conqueror's warhorse. Naturally, since you are family, the price would be insignificant compared to the value of you owning a horse with a royal bloodline."

"Gracias," you lying bastard. I believed him as

much as I did card cheats, picaro women, street beggars, and horse thieves.

Perhaps it was my imagination ignited by suspicions and the fact that I knew from Oaxaca that he was a man of deceit, but I sensed animosity toward me from Carlos. No doubt I would have felt the same if I had lost out on a fortune during a time of great need because of the miraculous survival of someone else.

Despite his pretense at civility, Carlos quickly let me know that he was of higher social rank than me and my other relatives, having been married to a member of the first family of the colony, the Cortéses.

His sheer arrogance was enough to tempt me to ask if he had tried to have me killed because the rich, powerful family he married into was not bailing him out of his financial problems. I held my tongue, of course, but while he could get away with acting arrogant to Juan the Lépero, I, as a newly ordained gachupin, was tempted to cut him off at the knees.

After having daughters pushed at me more blatantly than I've been solicited by whores, and broad hints from newfound relatives that I could make a great deal of money with an investment in a certain silver mine or a shipment of this or that goods from the mother country, I recognized pretense and pretentious motives.

I would not have survived life on the streets if I was not an exceptional judge of bad character and evil motives, not to mention a practitioner of such traits myself.

I had discovered a great deal about gachupins now that I was one of them: they were the same as street people, indios, muleteers, and about everyone else I had ever met.

The only difference between these people and the

people I rubbed elbows with my entire life was that the gachupins hid the fact that they were no different than the rest of us by the silk on their backs, a thin layer of perfume, and sharp spurs to rack us with.

The bunch of them was gone in an hour, with Carlos the last to leave, but it was the longest hour in my life. When I finally gave a phony smile to Carlos, along with a lying promise that I would soon be around to look over his horses, I met the servants and got a tour of the house.

The servants were two married couples—the majordomo and the housemaid, the stableman and the cook—plus the unmarried gardener and the unmarried serving girl.

My house was not the biggest or the smallest of fine homes but was laid out as almost all were: two-storied and flat-roofed, it had the interior courtyard with an obligatory fountain surrounded by lush greenery and a stable for the horses and carriage of the owner.

To my eyes, it was a palace!

As darkness fell and my "loving" relatives were long gone, and as the majordomo began his round of locking up the front gate and lighting the lamp on the wall next to it—"to help the street's night watchman spot thieving léperos," he said—I sat in a high-back chair.

With my feet up, a shiny pistola from my new collection of expensive dueling pistolas on my lap, a fine Toledo sword leaning against the side of my leg, and a glass of aged brandy in my hand . . . I threw back my head and gave a great laugh as I thought about what the majordomo's expression would be if he knew that the most thieving lépero in the colony was drinking the house's best brandy.

I suddenly choked and blew out a mouthful of brandy and stared at the glass.

The last brandy that had passed my lips had cost me a ranchero.

What if one of my jealous relatives had spiked the brandy with a bit of poison?

FORTY-NINE

"LIE TO ME and I'll kill you," Carlos de Rueda said. He tapped the end of the quirt he was holding against a corral post so Diego, his lead horse trainer, could hear the sound of the lead balls braided into the leather at the end tips. It wasn't a weapon to be used on a horse but on a wild animal. Or an enemy.

Diego didn't miss the signal that he was in danger of getting a beating that would leave him dead or crippled. And what would Carlos tell the authorities? That his horse trainer got kicked and trampled by a horse and they buried him before the hot sun rotted the body.

"You told me you saw him go over a high cliff," Carlos said, "but I saw him today at his house and he didn't have a scratch on him."

"There must have been a ledge where he fell," Diego said. "That has to be the only explanation."

"The only explanation I can think of is that you are a stupid bungler who failed to make sure he was dead."

"I told you a man intervened—"

"And killed your assassins; with you hiding so far away, you didn't get a look at him."

"I told you, señor, he had a mask."

"You tell me a masked man kills your two bandidos. But Don Domingo del Riego, second to the viceroy himself, says that Antonio killed the men. An army patrol heard the gunshots and was on the scene while the pistolas were still hot."

"But I know what I saw and the devil take my tongue if I am lying."

"The devil will take your soul and your body soon enough. Either you are lying or my dear cousin has no shame in taking credit and basking in the glory of having killed two men."

Carlos struck a pottery water jug with the quirt, breaking it. Diego stepped back, wondering if his head was next.

"Are you certain that the man in the carriage was Antonio? My cousin has a fine mount he brought over from Spain. Could he have been on the horse when the carriage was attacked and you saw a coachman go over the cliff?"

"I don't know, señor, but I tell you with God's truth that I am sure the man who did the killing was wearing a mask."

It made no sense, Carlos thought. Who was the man that Diego had seen? *If* he had seen another man. He knew from experience that the man was capable of lying to cover his mistakes.

He used the horse trainer because he followed orders and wasn't timid about killing if that's what he was told to do. But he didn't trust Diego for the most fundamental of all reasons: if he could buy Diego cheap for dirty work, so could anyone else, including Antonio.

"You're a coward," Carlos said. "You should have killed the man who intervened and then finished off Antonio."

"I held back while the two men I hired made the attack because you told me not to be seen," Diego said.

"How can I be sure you weren't seen?" Carlos asked.

"I had a mask on and was far away, far enough so that the man who came to the rescue of your cousin would not be able to identify me if he saw me again."

"You hung back and everything went wrong—then you fled."

"Sí, señor, and it is a good thing I returned to the hacienda instead of being dead at the scene of the robbery. If I had been found to be one of the attackers of your cousin . . ."

No explanation was needed that the crime would have been traced back to Carlos if Diego had been caught or killed. And Diego was stupid enough to point out the fact that he could turn into a liability for Carlos.

Carlos would have killed him on the spot, but he was not finished using him.

"If you say there was another man at the scene with a mask, then find him."

"Find him, señor? He may be a bandido. How would I—"

"Go to Xalapa, down to Vera Cruz if necessary, stopping at militia posts along the way. They will have bandidos and other vermin ready to be hanged or to be sold to labor gangs. Talk to the officers and soldiers who happened along moments after the fight. Bartenders in the pulquerias. If someone did help Antonio, find him. I have questions to ask him."

He didn't tell Diego, but one of the questions he wanted to ask the man was if he could identify Diego as the horseman who fled. Another question was why he would permit Antonio to take credit for the kills. If he could prove Antonio a liar and discredit him with the viceroy, perhaps he could also convince the viceroy to deny Antonio the inheritance.

FIFTY

AN ESCAPE ROUTE is what I needed. And I would not go as I came, with my pockets empty.

Such thoughts dribbled in my head the next morning. I dropped my fork onto the floor at breakfast and bent down to pick it up, nearly bumping heads with the servant girl.

Rising back up and remembering my manners, I carefully wiped the fork on the side of my pants before I stuck it into a plate of eggs and chili, showing I had manners. But she nearly ran as she raced out of the room with a shocked expression on her face.

Ayyo! I had to remember I was the master and a master never stoops to pick up anything a servant can get. It wasn't the first mistake I had made—that had been thanking the stableman for feeding Rojo last night. And I had gotten a surprised glance from the stableman when I spoke to Rojo before seeing him to his stall.

I had to stop making mistakes or I would expose myself as being *common*.

The thoughts went through my head as I was burning Antonio's clothes in the fireplace of the great room, right when the majordomo walked in and stared at me, openmouthed.

"They stink of ocean," I said, "I don't like smelling like a fish. How soon can you get a tailor to fit me with a new wardrobe?"

"I will go immediately to the place of the cloth sewers and bring one back with a selection of cloths."

"Make sure he is good. The most expensive will be the best. And the finest cloth, mind you."

I sounded as arrogant and as unappreciative as I could, the tone I had heard many a gachupin use when making a demand.

He left in a hurry, and I went back to burning clothes. The clothes smelled better than me but didn't fit well. They were all a little too snug and the shoes were longer and narrower than my feet.

I burned them all because of the threat of exposure and because I knew I was rich. Not that I had any money—yet. The viceroy's aide told me that all the gold and silver coins in the house had been seized for safekeeping by the viceroy after *my* uncle Ramos—that was how I thought of him now—died and would be given back as soon as the viceroy checked the papers of inheritance I had brought from Spain.

"In the meantime, your credit is good with any merchant in the colony," Riego had said. "The size of your inheritance is well known to the merchants, as well as to their wives and daughters."

Even the size of my feet was probably well known to everyone in the colony by now, considering how the viceroy's aide gossiped.

Hearing that I would soon have enough gold to stuff each of my pockets, I decided I would hop on Rojo and leave the city in my dust as soon as I had the price of a ranchero—or two—and a few of the other luxuries I was experiencing.

I had already been collecting a few items that I wanted from the house—starting with the best pistolas and swords my uncle had. I would buy a couple of pack mules when the time came and load them. Just two. I shouldn't let my greed be too obvious, eh. Unlike Cortés's men who died because they were carrying too much treasure on their backs when the indios were attacking, I wouldn't take so much that it slowed me down.

The one expensive item of my uncle's that didn't appeal to me was his horse tack. He had the gaudy saddles and bridles inlaid heavily with silver and semiprecious gems. Oversized, heavier than necessary, with stiff leather made to be polished rather than for the comfort of the rider and horse, my uncle's horse gear was that of a rich merchant.

My own tastes were more akin to being a caballero, but one that had rode the range rather than just the paseo.

"Pedro!" I shouted at the stable man, "have saddle makers bring me their wares. Gear for horsemen, mind you, not for merchants with soft asses."

I went down to check on Rojo when I heard pounding and found the groom had taken a shoe off of my stallion and was working it cold on the anvil.

"I noticed the shoe was a little bent, señor," he said.

"That's not the way you unbend it." I took the hammer from him and began to work the shoe. "This will do for now, but I want him completely shoed by a blacksmith. The best, mind you; if I find one nail that didn't go into Rojo's hooves straight, I will shoe the blacksmith himself."

I looked up from my hammering and saw that the stableman was staring at me wide-eyed, his jaw hanging down.

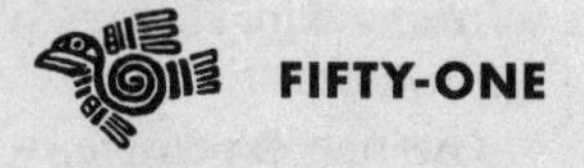

FIFTY-ONE

IT WAS TIME to find that escape route out of the city that I had been thinking about.

I had spent the last three days without leaving the house, being outfitted in a wardrobe, most of which I would not wear—thin silk leggings and pointed-toe shoes with high heels were not for me.

The first morning in my new home the majordomo came to me with messages on a silver tray. The first time he did so, with as much arrogance as I could muster, I told him to read them to me. There were all social invitations. And many more followed.

I had him reply to each that I was still recovering from my battle with the bandidos but would cherish their invitation in my heart until I was well enough to grace their house. Or something like that. I rattled off the idea and told him to polish it up.

Smart of me, no? Not only did I avoid gatherings where I risked exposure, but I didn't reveal to the servant that I couldn't read and write.

As I shaved, I reminded myself that I had to plan my escape because I could not continue to avoid social gatherings without making myself more of an object of attention than I already was. And there was always that threat of the uncle from Guadalajara coming for a visit.

Maybe I should hire bandidos to ambush him, eh?

Looking at myself in the mirror, it was obvious to

me that few of the many eligible daughters would be eager for my courtship if I was not rich, though I hoped that some women liked a man with a bit of the rogue in him. Perhaps that would be my saving grace someday when I found a woman to share my bed and fix my tortillas.

The dagger scar on the side of my face had not improved my looks. I was told once by a whore that it made me look dangerous, like a bandido. What can I say? God made my face ugly and that wildcat of a young woman carved it a little bit uglier.

I had two more surprises for my stableman—I told him to saddle Rojo because I wanted to take a ride.

"You will enjoy the paseo, señor. It is grande."

"I'm not going there. I want to see what the city itself looks like."

"But then you must take the carriage. I would have one hand on the reins and one hand on the whip to drive off the street vermin. On a horse you will be pawed—"

"Keeping filthy léperos away is why God gave caballeros boots and a quirt."

I didn't volunteer that I once was ran over by a carriage when I was a beggar boy.

He got his second surprise when I made an adjustment to the way he had hitched the saddle.

What is it about gachupins, I wondered? Are they incapable of doing anything for themselves?

My meandering after I left the house took me near the paseo, and with a chuckle I decided Rojo and I would take a little stroll along it just so I could satisfy my curiosity about whether paseo caballeros were true horsemen or just dandies showing off with fancy clothes and tack.

Coming off the city street, I passed through a crop

of trees and then onto the miles long, wide dirt path that went the length and width of the park—and into another world.

Ayyo! It was everything I imagined and much more than I expected.

I gawked as beautiful señoritas in elegant gowns and sparkling jewels paraded in one direction in fancy carriages, while moving in the opposite direction were young caballeros on horseback, wearing the most colorful and flamboyant jackets lined with pearls and jade, silk leggings, boots of calfskin as soft as a baby's ass, and hats with colorful plumes that would have made Aztec chiefs envious.

I stared at them—*they stared at me*.

I took a deep breath, wheeled Rojo and left at a gallop, going back through the forest, having Rojo jump a stone wall to get us back onto the streets in a hurry.

Only then did I breathe easier.

What I had seen in the paseo that caused me to panic had not been the devil, but the devil in myself.

Madre de Maria de Dios! Maria Mother of God!

I had seen paseos at Oaxaca and in Vera Cruz, but the men and women in those humble parks were nothing like I had come face-to-face with today.

The sheer magnificence of what I had seen, the carriages that looked like the conveyances of angels, the astonishing horseflesh—every one of them sired by a champion—

Even though I didn't respect the caballeros as fighters or horsemen, in my ignorance they looked like knights parading in fine clothes.

The women . . . mi Dios . . . even the ugly ones

looked like princesses waving down from castle towers.

And me? What had I seen in the reflection of the eyes of the caballeros and señoritas on the paseo? A bandido lépero with dirt between his toes.

Sí. For a moment I saw myself for what I was and what I wasn't.

I'm not a gachupin. My blood is not just tainted by a mixture of blood at birth, it is colored by the life I led on the streets and on the roads.

Moreover, now that I had seen what gachupins were like, that they were no more worthy of raking us with their spurs than we would be worthy of harming others and that such actions resulted from a sense of greed and ruthless exercise of power, I did not want to be one.

I was more certain than ever that I felt more comfortable among horses and other four-footed animals than I did with beasts that stepped on others with their two feet and grabbed what they could with both hands.

I knew I had to get out of Mexico City before I drew a pistola or knife and killed some bastardo of a gachupin who was beating a horse or a beggar.

And the city—Ayyo! What a stench! Unlike Oaxaca, which had clean air, or the putrid air of Vera Cruz, which at least got washed by an occasional sea breeze, Mexico City sat in a lake that was fouled and stunk as badly as a Vera Cruz coast swamp. And the air went nowhere except into my lungs, and what I breathed was heavy with the foulest excrements of man and beast.

No wonder the gachupins used nosegays. They should have cut off their noses instead.

Oh, Antonio de los Rios, whether you are singing with the angels or burning in hell, I wish you had not gone over that ledge and gotten killed.

I would be much happier and much safer now had I simply been able to have robbed you after I finished off the two bandidos.

FIFTY-TWO

TLALOC RIVER

The indio looked down at the man he had found lying facedown on the bank of the river.

Aztec by birth, the indio's name was Mazatl, and it meant "deer" in his native Nahuatl.

Mazatl had lived the entire twenty-five years of his life along the banks of the river, not traveling more than a couple hours in each direction. Those trips were only to get to the church at the nearest village to have his baby baptized so it would be accepted by the god of the white masters who ruled everything under the sky.

Less than an hour upriver the water flowed by a road that Mazatl knew many Spaniards traveled on, often with animals carrying loads, but he had never climbed the steep cliffs to walk on the road.

The hut where his wife suckled their babes and made their tortillas was not far from the river, alongside six other huts. They led a simple life, raising maize, fishing, doing a little hunting.

Too poor and too remote for even encomienda status, the small group lived simple lives.

At first he had been frightened by the white man's presence, wondering where he had come from. The river for sure, but there were no white settlements up or down the river as far as Mazatl had walked except for a church with a Spanish priest a half a day's walk from where Mazatl lived with his family.

He knew what a Spaniard was, had seen them on occasion, although the only one he had ever spoken to was the priest who spoke his indio language at the village church.

He recognized that the man he discovered near the river was a Spaniard from his skin color and that the man did not wear the same clothes as a priest. The man was young, perhaps in his middle twenties.

At first Mazatl thought the man was dead, but then he heard him groan and saw him stir. It was obvious that the man had crawled out of the water and onto the embankment after spending some time floating downstream.

Along the way, the man had been battered and bruised—from the way his left leg at the knee was twisted, it appeared broken to Mazatl.

The man was helpless and would die if he was left alone, abandoned on the embankment.

At first Mazatl tried to help him to his feet so he could get him back to the half dozen huts that the indio settlement was composed of, but the man was too weak and in too much pain to stand.

He told the man in Nahautl that he was going back to his people to get help carrying him.

The Spaniard didn't understand a word Mazatl had said. He thought he was being abandoned when the indio disappeared into the bushes.

He tried to get to his knees as he shouted, "Come back! For the love of God, don't leave me!" but collapsed back to the ground.

Antonio de los Rios sobbed, certain that he would die.

FIFTY-THREE

BACK ON THE street, I got back my composure, cursing myself for being a victim of my own fears. Getting myself into a better mood, I wasn't even annoyed when a howling pack of léperos descended on me.

They came at me like a pack of hungry wolfhounds from hell. The sheer number of them was daunting. The wails that came from their mouths would have even driven el diablo to tears.

I threw coins over their heads and kept going, unmolested as the beggars ran back and fought to get to the money.

There but for the grace of God go I. In a strange twist of human fate, it took blood on my hands to change me first from a stable boy to a bandido and then to a gachupin.

And I was certain the killing wasn't over. Carlos or whoever killed Antonio had to have been desperate. Sooner or later the killer would come after me and I would have to fight for my life. Or my fraud would be exposed and I'd have to shoot my way out of the city.

Either way, more blood was waiting to be poured and some of it might be mine.

I gave some serious thought to the difficulty of getting out of the city if I needed to in a hurry and with constables on my tail. Surrounded by water, with only a few causeways leading off the city-island, I had a feeling of being closed in, even without a posse after me.

Cortés must have had even stronger feelings when he was trapped in the city and had to get out before the Aztecs made him an evening meal. He found out that getting off an island isn't easy, especially when your men are loaded to the gills with stolen treasure and there are thousands of angry warriors on your tail.

I had heard the story from Gomez, the stable owner who cared for me and again from the viceroy's aide on the way to the capital.

The Spanish called it *La Noche Triste,* the Night of Sorrows, and had it gone just slightly differently, the city would still be called Tenochtitlán and my indio ancestors would be eating gachupins rather than serving them.

Cortés had managed to bluff all the way to the Aztec capital and into Montezuma's palace, holding the indecisive Aztec emperor a prisoner in his own house.

While Cortés was in the city, news came from the coast that the governor of Cuba had sent a force to arrest Cortés for "insubordination." Eh, the other Spaniard wasn't concerned about whether Cortés was following orders but had gotten wind of Cortés's incredible find of indio empires ripe for looting and wanted to grab them for himself.

Cortés left the capital with much of his force and met and defeated the opposing Spanish contingent on the coast. True to his daring style of leadership, Cortés convinced the defeated Spaniards to join his army by telling them of the fantastic city of gold that awaited them.

Before Cortés got back to Tenochtitlán, the officer

he left in command, Pedro de Alvarado, was told that there was a plot brewing by Aztec nobility to rid the city of the Spanish. Being both impetuous and a lover of violence, Alvarado had his men ambush the cream of the indio nobility during ceremonies at the main temple, slaughtering hundreds of them.

Shortly after Cortés arrived, the Aztecs attacked and the Spanish holed up in the emperor's palace. When Cortés sent Montezuma onto a balcony to speak to the indios, rocks were thrown, one of them striking the emperor, a blow that caused his death a few days later.

Of course, that was the Spanish version of the emperor's death. The indios believed the Spanish had killed him because he was going to rouse the entire empire against them.

Cortés made a decision to abandon the city, but not the enormous treasures in gold and gems his men had gathered, a fateful decision that would make fleeing the city more difficult.

As Cortés led his force onto a causeway to get out of the city, the Aztecs attacked, literally surrounding the conquistadors by attacking at both ends while warriors in hundreds of canoes attacked from the sides, hurtling spears and sending arrows until death was raining from the sky.

Cortés lost 154 Spaniards, about a quarter of his small army, and his indio allies suffered casualties of about two thousand. A brutal reality about how the Aztecs and other indios conducted wars was that they fought to wound and capture the enemy rather than outright killing them, so the prisoners could be sacrificed and eaten after the battle.

The strategy was a double triumph for the winning side because the prisoners could be sacrificed, thus pleasing the gods and ensuring more victories, and the victorious warrior could eat the heart of the foe he captured and gain even more strength.

The indio strategy of capture rather than kill would ultimately be one of the causes of their defeat by Cortés at the battle of Otumba, but it worked well enough on the Night of Sorrows for the Spaniards to look back at the city and see their captured comrades taking their turn up the steps of the temple where their hearts would be cut out.

Such a defeat would have spelled the end for any commander less daring and utterly determined than Cortés, but he soon defeated the Aztec army at Otumba, saying he managed it because he personally killed the indio's commander, a feat that created panic and confusion in the indio ranks.

The Night of Sorrows was no doubt made even more sorrowful than the mere loss of men by the fact that a great deal of the treasure the Spanish had gathered was also lost.

I didn't want to suffer the loss of either my life or my newfound fortune, so I needed to find a quick way off the island city. To scout out the routes, I started at one side of the city and began to make my way around, keeping close to the lake as I checked out each of the three causeways.

During Aztec times, the city was laced with canals so that most places in the city could be reached by either foot or canoe. A large number of those canals still existed with bridges over them.

As I rode around the city, what I had first concluded about an escape route proved true—there was no easy path.

The fastest route was over one of the three causeways, but that was also the quickest and easiest way constables could stop an escape. The posts for collecting tolls were maintained day and night, and there was one at the city side of each causeway.

Although the purpose of the posts wasn't to protect the city, but to collect tax on goods coming and going, they also served as guard posts to stop all movement on the causeways when the bells of the cathedral rang an alarm.

The only way I would make it over the causeway was if I went before the alarm was sounded. And that meant moving quickly—and not with a posse on my tail.

The other escape route was interesting, but had its drawbacks: escaping over the water.

Pausing on a bridge over a canal, I thought about a canoe escape as I watched dozens of the small craft being paddled and poled up and down the canal.

As I watched, a carriage came up beside me and stopped. Two things immediately struck me about the carriage—unlike most of the city carriages, the passenger section was fully enclosed, like the coaches that carried travelers between cities, and it was black with just modest silver trim. The passenger window curtain closest to me was slightly parted.

Taller in the saddle than the passenger space, I bent down to look in the window and give a friendly greeting, but the carriage pulled away as I spoke.

The incident made me uneasy, because I wondered if the occupant had recognized me.

Thinking about escaping by water, I could easily have indios with a canoe standing by at all times to take me out of the city on short notice, but it would mean leaving Rojo behind. I wouldn't do that, but I thought about having the stallion stabled outside the city so I was free to leave by canoe—and rejected the idea. Canoes were not as swift as the stallion, and a canoe would be easily observed from land, permitting a posse to be waiting for me on shore.

Another escape route was swimming—not by me, but Rojo, pulling me along with him as I floated and hung on to the saddle. I had broken the stallion into swimming for the times I would need to cross a river with constables on my heels.

The stallion was strong and would probably carry me to land, especially since the lake was not very deep for a good distance from shore, but it was a method I would use only in case of the most dire circumstances, since it meant I could only take treasure that could be stuffed into my pockets. It also meant swimming in waters that stank worse than a lépero.

No matter how I tried it, getting out of the city in a hurry with mules loaded with treasure was very likely to end with me in the viceroy's dungeon rather than a ranchero.

I was preoccupied, chewing over the fact that, like the conquistadors, I had planned to be weighed down with cumbersome treasure when I fled, in my case two loaded mules that would cut Rojo's speed in half, when I saw a woman that sent a shock through me.

FIFTY-FOUR

PONDERING THE INJUSTICE of the gachupins in making it difficult for me to acquire a dishonest fortune, I spotted a mop of red hair and a pair of startling green eyes in a passing carriage.

I froze in my saddle as stiffly as I would have had a constable stuck a pistola in my face.

Ayyo! It was her—the redheaded she-demon, the wildcat who came at me with dagger, claws, feet, and fists, and that beautiful mouth full of such demeaning remarks about my character.

She had left me with not only a scar to remember her by, but a wounded heart that would never heal—eh, what a poet I am.

I was sure it was her, in a carriage sitting next to another young woman and facing two more gachupin belles, no doubt on their way to the paseo to parade their beauty and throw flirtatious smiles at toy caballeros on prancing horses.

She passed, looking up at me, laughing about something as the carriage rumbled past me, going in the opposite direction.

Stunned, I foolishly turned in the saddle to see if she had also looked back and was about to begin screaming "bandido!" but she didn't turn her head. She had been looking toward me as we passed, but we never made eye contact.

I kept going, resisting the temptation to turn and look back again or, worse, to wheel Rojo and pursue her. In truth, the redheaded wildcat had been in my thoughts a thousand times since we tangled.

She could not have gotten more than a quick glance as I passed. Would she recognize me as the bandido if I approached and tipped my hat? I pondered that question.

She had pulled my mask down below my nose, but it still left half of my face covered.

I touched my cheekbone. She had left her mark there as sure as if she had carved her initials into a tree. I don't scar easily, so the mark was narrow and faint, but it was still obvious to anyone looking at my ugly face.

"But many men have scars," I told Rojo. And I am not a bandido; I am a gachupin, a man of great wealth and pure blood. When she looked at me, she would see the Spaniard in me, not the mestizo.

Right now I could race back to the carriage and ride alongside, flirting with her as if I was a caballero on my way to the paseo. And all she would do is act shy and giggle—

No, she would start screaming for the constables, too, with her friends joining the chorus. Seeing me on a big stallion instead of a paseo pony and not dressed as a caballero dandy would stimulate a memory of being manhandled and robbed by me.

Despite my feelings, I had to keep out of her sight. That would not be difficult, not only because Mexico was a big city but also because women of quality led very sheltered lives. It was improbable that I would ever pass her on foot on the street, and there was only a slightly better chance of her seeing me on horseback.

Sí, I was perfectly safe. But that didn't mean that I couldn't satisfy my curiosity and at least find out what the hellcat's name was.

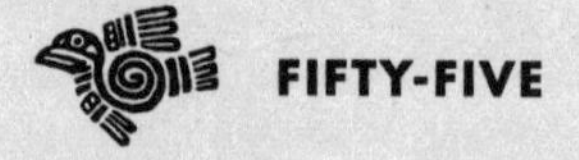

FIFTY-FIVE

"I WANT TO know the señorita's name," I told my majordomo. "And I don't want anyone to know that I'm seeking it. She may be married, spoken for; I'm new to the city and don't want to be meeting at dawn at the field of honor until I know the lay of the land."

"Sí, señor, I will be very discreet."

I described the carriage to him, and he asked about a coat of arms.

I shook my head. "No coat of arms."

"Then none of the señoritas were of the nobility," he said. "Young women of titled families generally do not socialize on the paseo with the girls of the merchant class."

"You're saying she's a merchant's daughter."

"That is the likely conclusion, señor. The young women tend naturally to also socialize with others of the same financial status. Your description of the coach suggests that it is a very fine one; thus she is probably very wealthy."

"She could have been the daughter of a rich hacienda owner," I threw in to show off my own knowledge.

"Of course, señor, of course. But . . ."

He paused and gave me a cautious look. It was the expression he used when he feared he might offend me.

"As with the merchants and nobility," he said, "not

only do the daughters of hacendados go to the paseo together, but most haciendas have been given a name by their owners and an emblem on their carriage doors similar to a coat of arms."

He added that the carriages of the rich silver-mine owners were so decorated with the precious metal that they were also easy to spot.

"Where was she seated in the carriage?" he asked.

The question puzzled me, but I told him she had been seated closest to the center of the road, facing me as we passed.

"Then her family owns the carriage. That is the seat closest to a caballero who would pause his horse and speak to the young women aboard. It is occupied by the coach owner."

This time I shook my head in amazement. The majordomo, who was an indio, as were the other servants, would have made a fine bandido with his ability to assess people.

"Your uncle, señor, told me that is how coaches are occupied in Spain also. Is that not true?"

Eh, I could have told him that he knew more about what happens in Spain than I did, but I only confirmed my uncle's information.

"Find her," I told him.

"With your permission, señor, I will start at the marketplace."

"The marketplace? A young woman of good breeding would hardly be found picking through ears of maize."

"No, señor, but her servants would. Servants gather and gossip about their masters."

"Excellent, then she should be easy to identify. Ask about a redhead with a temper as fiery as her hair."

It was his turn to be puzzled, and I realized I had

slipped and said something about her that I shouldn't have known.

"All redheaded women have fiery tempers," I said. "God made them that way."

Daughter of a rich merchant. A señorita with a temper as hot as her flaming red hair. Mexico was a big city, but that would reduce the odds a bit, though red hair was not uncommon among the Spanish.

The next morning I waited impatiently for the majordomo to come back from the marketplace. When he returned to the house, I kept myself from pouncing on him and hid my eagerness as he went about his duties.

I had already made too many mistakes around the house in terms of acting like a gachupin; it made me wonder what the marketplace gossip was about me.

"There is a young woman named Mercedes, the daughter of a rich cloth merchant, Bartoleme de la Cruz. With great respect, señor, the servants of her house say she is a fine young woman, pretty, but is quick to lose her temper."

"And her eyes?"

"Bright green, and she has a coach that matches the description of the carriage you saw."

Ayyo!

The majordomo told me the location of the merchant's house, and I immediately went to the stable and saddled Rojo, ignoring the look the stableman gave me as I once again did the work of a servant.

As I came out the gate, a carriage carrying the viceroy's aide pulled up and Riego hailed me.

"I have come to personally deliver an invitation," he said.

"Excellent," was all I could manage.

He eyed me narrowly and shook his head. "You

have gained a reputation as being unsociable, no doubt disappointing many a mother with unmarried daughters."

"I'm sorry, Don Domingo, my wounds . . ."

"Wounds? You didn't tell me you were shot in the battle with the bandidos."

"Not shot," I said, cursing myself for letting my tongue put me into a pile of manure up to my neck. "But I am a bit traumatized by all the excitement."

"Well, you look surprisingly healthy and vigorous for having such feelings. But this is an invitation you would dare not fail to accept. The viceroy is giving a costume ball in three days to welcome a new bishop. Everyone of importance will be there, including the Marquis del Valle, so it would be well for you to attend." He eyed me again. "It would also aid you when you plead your case about the inheritance to the viceroy."

I nodded as if I understood what he meant and was left sitting on Rojo, wondering, as the carriage pulled away. It finally got through my thick head, though. He was telling me that I had better show up at the ball and pay my respects to the viceroy because I would have to go before him to get money released.

That was reason enough to attend a gathering where I might be recognized. But there was also another very good reason.

"Everyone of importance" must include the daughter of a rich merchant, no?

I just hoped that it also didn't include the uncle from Guadalajara who could instantly disrobe me as a fraud.

The viceroy's aide had also said the Marquis del Valle would be there. Did that mean his older brother, El Mestizo, would attend, too? If so, that made it three people who could expose me as a fraud just with a glance in my direction.

The thought of going back into the house and throwing whatever valuables I could find into a bag tempted me for a moment, but I calmed myself down as I touched the locket that hung from a simple cord around my neck. Inside was a cameo of the young woman's likeness reflected by the carving of her mother's in ivory.

Was it worth taking such a great risk just to look into those lovely green eyes again?

PART 7

ONCE A LÉPERO, ALWAYS A LÉPERO.

FIFTY-SIX

A *COSTUME BALL.* I rubbed my jaw and thought some more. I knew the gachupins sometimes dressed up in costumes for their celebrations, because many times in Oaxaca I would see them in carriages on the way to such an event, but I couldn't envision what people did at a ball. Or what I was supposed to wear. And I didn't dare ask the majordomo—not directly at least. So I broached the subject indirectly.

"I was not fond of such affairs in Spain and I'm not enthused about attending one here in the colony. What did my uncle say about these affairs?"

"He enjoyed the music, dancing, women in their beautiful gowns, and spirited conversation over fine wine and brandy."

Ah, I got it, it was like a night at a whorehouse, except the drinks were more expensive.

"What costume did my uncle prefer?"

"A bandido."

I couldn't keep a straight face.

"We still have the costume if you would care to wear it," the majordomo said, misinterpreting my reaction as enthusiasm.

"No—no, it would bring back too many memories."

"Of course, señor, forgive me for my ignorance."

I went to the stable to brush Rojo down and talk it over with him. Not that I had any intention of showing up at the ball dressed as a highwayman. Eh, not only would the redheaded Mercedes recognize me, but there would probably be other gachupins at the ball whose gold I had taken after shoving a pistola in their face.

"What do you think?" I asked Rojo, not speaking the threat out loud but mentally pondering the possibility not only that I could meet up with the three people I've identified as being a threat to my life and freedom but also that at the party there could be someone I had robbed.

A few times when the opportunity arose and I had to act fast, I had pulled out my dagger or pistola and took a man's purse without having a mask on, but that was rare. Still, I would hate to come face-to-face with someone whose throat I had kept a knife on while I rifled their pockets.

Eh—if eyes are windows to the soul as the poets say, what were the chances of someone looking into mine and seeing a thief?

"It's not fair," I told Rojo, certain that he understood what I meant even though I couldn't speak the unfairness aloud for fear that the stable man would hear me.

All my past sins seemed to be coming back to haunt me just when I was on the verge of amassing a gachupin's fortune.

The majordomo interrupted my thoughts as he cleared his throat to let his presence be known.

"Sorry, señor, but I forgot to tell you. Many of the guests do not wear a full costume to the ball, but just an eye mask."

Ah . . . perfect. An eye mask would hide the part of my face Mercedes had seen.

My cleverness is only exceeded by my brilliance.

FIFTY-SEVEN

AS I EYED myself in the mirror, I couldn't keep an expression of disgust off my face at the look of the clothes the tailor had selected for me to wear to the costume ball.

"All the men will be dressed in a similar fashion except the clergy," he said, when he saw my look. "I realize we are only imitating what is being worn in Madrid and Caldez, Señor Rios, but I will do my best to ensure that your outfit will not embarrass you."

He misinterpreted my feelings. He thought I wanted to be more fashionable. Ayyo! I hated the clothes male gachupins wore to parties. They dressed as peacocks, not men.

Mind you, this was not a costume, but the typical clothes worn by a gachupin to a social gathering, to which I planned to add only an eye mask.

The tailor had outfitted me in a small, narrow black hat with a tall red feather sticking up, a ruffled collar of white silk that strangled me, and a short, waist-length jacket made of layers of black silk sown with gold thread and patterned with tiny, semiprecious stones.

Bad enough that the top half of my body was clothed in materials only a woman should wear, the worst was below my waist. Ballooning, baglike breeches came from the waist down almost to my knees. From the knees, tight gray hose covered my legs.

The pointed-toed shoes squeezing my flat, wide feet were little more than slippers.

Eh, I have gone barefooted, worn sandals made from the hard maguey plant, and gotten my first pair of leather boots off the feet of a caballero at gunpoint. I felt like a fop in slippers.

With the breeches ballooning out from my waist to knees and tight silk stockings covering my legs like another layer of skin, I looked like a fat man on sticks.

The one thing I did not object to was a medallion of St. Dominic hanging from a heavy silver chain around my neck. The saint was the founder of the church order that had dominated the Inquisition since the bloodthirsty Torquemada started burning nonbelievers at the stake. I chose it from my uncle's collection because the new bishop was a Dominican and in charge of the Inquisition for the colony.

Paying homage to the Inquisition seemed a very smart move, I thought, since I might someday taste its whips and chains.

Looking in the mirror, all I could do was give a sad sigh, after which I calmed the tailor because he once again thought the clothes were not fashionable enough.

Sí, I looked like a rich gachupin, dressed in clothes that even Cortés the conqueror had worn when he went to a ball, but gachupins grew up wearing these ridiculous outfits.

Dressing as a caballero, even with the fancy trim that was displayed on the paseo, would have suited me fine, but while a horseman's outfit was a "costume" to me, it was ordinary male daytime clothing to most gachupins.

My common blood also boiled because these were not the clothes of a man who had worked with his hands, even if the past few years my hands had held pistolas during working hours.

Since I was going to wear a black eye mask, I considered for about one second dressing as I did when I was a highwayman—clothes worn by hacienda vaqueros. I immediately put aside the thought as stupid since that was the way I was dressed when I robbed Mercedes—and many others.

One costume I could think of that would guarantee that no one recognized me was to come as an Inquisition torturer with a hood over my head. But I didn't think the new bishop would be amused if I portrayed a character that everyone knew existed but only whispered about for fear that the ears of the church—which were everywhere—would hear them.

The tailor left, insulted that I hadn't judged his clothes as fashionable as those found in Madrid. I took off the fancy ball clothes, put on the worn leather shirt and pants I preferred when working with Rojo, and went down to the stable to brush him and think about how I would manage to look perfectly natural in clothes in which I felt like a clown.

My street life still affected me. I had adapted well to vaqueros' clothes, even the finer ones worn by hacienda owners when they rode out to watch cattle or horses being herded, but I felt ridiculous dressed in silk stockings with a ruffled collar around my neck and a big red feather sticking up like a flag out of a small hat.

"You'd give me a good kick if you saw me," I told Rojo.

The problem wasn't just a matter of clothing but whether I would feel natural at the party. If I came across as not comfortable in my skin, a perceptive person would see through to my lépero blood.

The solution to my costume dilemma dawned on me as I stroked the stallion's chest.

"That's it," I told Rojo.

I realized that the one costume that would not expose me as a fraudulent gachupin was the very one I had worn for so long and still was not able to get out of my blood after many years.

I whispered the word in the stallion's ear.

"What do you think, Rojo?"

The stallion gave me a loud neigh and shook his head with approval.

FIFTY-EIGHT

COSTUMED IN CLOTHES I felt comfortable wearing, I still felt more like a prisoner on the way to the gallows than an honored guest going to a ball.

The feeling of being trapped was heightened by the fact that I was in a carriage rather than on my stallion. I would be better off running away on foot and jumping into the lake to swim from the city than trying to make a quick escape in a coach.

Not that my carriage wasn't a handsome thing. Made of oak and cedar, it was trimmed with a great deal of silver plate from the mine Uncle Ramos had had an interest in. The interior was plush green velvet and rich leather, with gleaming gold fittings.

The carriage's tack was just as richly decorated, heavy with gold lace and silver trim on the harnesses of the two carriage horses. Their black legs were trimmed with silk stockings down to their ankles.

I felt sorry for them. Though they were both gilded, they were embarrassed having to wear silk stockings. Even more ridiculous was that *their horseshoes were made of silver*. Meshed with a bit of iron to increase hardness, the silver shoes would still only last for the trip to the ball and back home.

Horseshoes worn once just so another gachupin might catch the sight of the expensive shoes as the horses lifted their legs . . . Ayyo! Many of the indios and mestizos in the colony went to bed hungry so vain gachupins could have their horses prance in silver horseshoes.

Looking at the gold fittings and abundant silver plating, my bandido mentality immediately began calculating that I could buy a good-sized ranchero and a herd of horses by just stealing the precious metals from the carriage—and it wouldn't be stealing, eh? Antonio is dead, and I deserve payment for avenging in blood his murder.

I am certain that the good Lord wanted me rewarded for my good deeds and would sanction my taking anything I could get my hands on. Which I intended to do as soon as I was able.

The viceroy's aide said I would be able to get the great man's ear tonight. I would convince him to release my money even if I had to cut his ears off.

Feeling like a trapped animal on the way to slaughter as my carriage carried me along city streets to the viceroy's ball, my anxiety level took a giant leap as the carriage pulled up in front of the palace.

"Señor Antonio de los Rios, guest of the viceroy," my coachman-groom announced as he brought the carriage to a halt.

A guardsman opened my carriage door.

"Welcome, señor—huh?"

He stammered and froze as he stared at me.

FIFTY-NINE

WORD ABOUT ME passed quickly up the line of guards as I made my way to the ballroom. After the first stares and gapes, I was greeted with grins and laughter.

I was tempted to ask them—eh, amigos, have you never seen a lépero before?

Tomorrow I would be the subject of raging gossip at the marketplace. I was a scandal, of course, not at the ball, because I hadn't entered the ballroom yet, but back at my house, where my servants had stood by wide-eyed and openmouthed as I demanded dirty clothes from the stable man.

"He's about my size," I told the majordomo.

Unable to face the world as a gachupin with skin-tight silk stockings, I fell back on a role that came natural to me: lépero.

"No clean clothes, mind you," I instructed the majordomo. "Bring me the clothes he was wearing earlier when he cleaned the stable."

Insanity. I saw it in the faces of my servants as I sent them scurrying to gather what I needed to make me a filthy beggar again.

Hair messed, clothes and face with soot on them, my face and feet almost black from soot, a little smell of manure . . . I could well pass for a lépero. I have to admit, even the smell felt natural to me.

It wasn't until I approached the doorway into the

ballroom that my heart began beating in my throat as I wondered whether a dozen people were going to start shouting "bandido!" and accuse me of having stolen their gold and jewels.

The doors swept open as if by magic, and, with my mind numb, I heard the announcement: *"Señor Don Antonio de los Rios!"*

Ayyo! For a moment I wondered who the hell that was.

SIXTY

TIME STOOD STILL. A moment in my life paused as I entered, and every eye in the room, from the aristocratic viceroy from Spain who ruled the colony with the power of a king to two hundred of the richest, most powerful, and most prestigious citizens of New Spain, turned to me.

I heard gasps. Exclamations. A *mi Dios* or two or three.

My heart plugged my throat, and I stood at the top of the entrance stairs and stared down as hundreds of eyes stared up at me.

Suddenly a man with a white beard, a red slash across his chest full of medals and honors, and the tallest peacock feather in the room in his hat stepped toward me. From his clothes I guessed who he was: His Excellency Don Gastón Carrillo de Peralta y Bosquete, 3rd Marquis de Falces, by the grace of God and His Majesty the King, Viceroy of New Spain.

"Bravo, Señor Rios, you have caught the true spirit of the lépero of the colony in your clothing. But—" He shook a finger at me. "Can you beg like one?"

"*Akkkk!*" I don't know where it came from; it wasn't a human sound but a howl that had escaped the deepest bowels of hell. I exploded with it as I came off the stairs groveling, whining, pleading to God, to the saints—*all of them*—and to the charity in the hearts of every Christian person for a simple handout, a bit of food or a coin.

No lépero, not even the lowest, foulest, most voracious had ever reached the pinnacles of whining and pleading that I burst out with.

The viceroy's jaw dropped, and he stumbled back as I came at him launching a begging attack that would have brought any street swine to a jealous rage had he heard it.

A woman screamed, another fainted, a man grabbed his sword as I got hold of the viceroy's leg and stared up at him with the most pathetic face. "A copper, your lordship, a copper so I can feed my children . . . or buy some pulque," I added.

He gaped down at me, and then it started in his well-rounded stomach and moved upward, a rumble that came up his throat and out his mouth as a great laugh.

For another moment time stood still in the ballroom, and then the laughter started, becoming guffaws and howls as the crowd imitated the viceroy's bellows.

Still on my knees, I let my muscles relax, feeling the tension drain out of them as I stared down at the floor and took a deep breath.

I had decided that the best place to hide was in plain sight.

As myself.

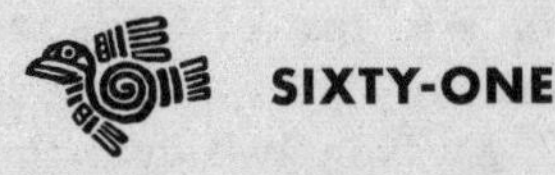

SIXTY-ONE

ANOTHER ANNOUNCEMENT WAS made, and I was instantly forgotten as the most important personage in the colony entered.

I had heard about the younger Martín Cortés ever since I could remember and had been raised in a region where he reigned with royal prerogatives. Seeing him now in the flesh, it was the differences between him and his brother that were most apparent to me.

Don Martín Cortés y Zuniga, 2nd Marquis del Valle de Oaxaca, was in his late thirties, a decade younger than his mestizo brother. Not only was the difference in their age and physique apparent, but so were the bloodlines. The marquis was pale white, tall and slender, with features that most women would find handsome, while El Mestizo was shorter, darker, heavier framed, and carried the extra ten years as an added burden.

But the biggest difference was in countenance. No gachupin I had ever seen, not even those with the bloodiest spurs, carried as much sheer arrogance and contempt for whomever his gaze fell upon as did the chosen heir of the conqueror. There was no question that he felt superior to everyone in the room, including the viceroy, who not only had an equal title of nobility, but was endowed in the colony with the powers of a monarch.

Though the Marquis del Valle lacked political

power, he was true colonial royalty, while the viceroy was just a powerful administrator. In the colony, criollos' adoration of Cortés the conqueror was second only to that of God, and his son wore an invisible crown.

I was in awe, even though I had already met one son of Cortés and had in fact stolen his horse.

I faded back into the crowd, expecting El Mestizo to be announced next, when I heard a woman whisper to another than the Marquis del Valle was always the last to arrive. The reason was obvious—the adoration of him would not be disturbed by the arrival of others.

Was El Mestizo not in the city? Or does his mixed blood keep him from being invited? I didn't know the reason El Mestizo wasn't at the ball, but it was a relief.

Carlos was suddenly beside me.

His presence instantly rankled me. I cringed a bit as I experienced the sensation of a snake siding up to me.

"An unforgettable entrance, cousin. Theatrical but risky. I give you credit because you carried off the masquerade without offending the viceroy. But it would have gone bad had he not found your choice of costume amusing."

His tone carried contempt for me and the stunt. I suddenly felt a complete lack of tolerance for the man. He was the type that went through life getting what he wanted because the people he pushed folded. The first lesson of the streets is that you go for the jugular when someone pushes you.

"Being able to carry off a pretense runs in our family, does it not, cousin?"

Leaving Carlos puzzled over my statement, perhaps pondering the inner meaning, I wandered around, getting my thoughts in order, really seeing the people and ballroom for the first time. Up to now I had been in a haze.

The ballroom was the largest and most incredible room I had ever been in. It was brightly lit with sparkling glass chandeliers and had beautiful cut flowers in vases placed in openings along the walls, while the wall themselves were lined with garlands of green branches and fragrant flowers.

Elegant, well-cushioned chairs made of the finest muslin and workmanship were placed where women could rest and cool themselves with fans that complemented their fashionable clothing.

Costumes were not as prevalent as I thought they would be. Most people simply added an eye mask to their clothes, although the ones that came in costumes were quite clever. I saw jaguars, a wolf, several Montezumas, a fairy, a Roman gladiator, and others.

It didn't take much for me to understand why most of the women wore a simple eye mask rather than a full costume: their evening gowns were dazzling—and the women didn't want anything to distract from the sheer elegance of their exquisite attire.

The gowns were of the finest silk, lace, and velvet material; their skirts were full and round, in soft shades of violet, green, and gray and adorned with gold and silver thread and sparkling gems. They wore necklaces of pear-shaped pearls.

Smells of sweet jasmine, bougainvillea, and roses permeated in the great ballroom, as well as the powders and perfumes that both sexes wore to hide the smell of any unpleasant odors on themselves. I was the exception, of course, but at the look on my majordomo's face I had at least not rolled in manure to make my costume even more authentic.

I paused and watched a pompous administrator newly arrived from Spain demonstrate a mechanical clock that told time. I had seen sun clocks tell time by the way a shadow fell across the numbers, but this drum-shaped timepiece, several inches thick and tall, hung on a chain from around the man's neck.

The timepiece had an hour hand, and the man moved it to show how it would strike the number of the hour. The time was not accurate, but no one cared.

As I turned to move away from the novel demonstration, I came face-to-face with dazzling green eyes.

I froze.

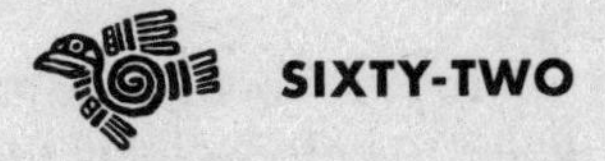

SIXTY-TWO

W*ILL SHE SCREAM?*

I hoped the question wasn't written on my face.

"Good evening, señorita," I croaked, instantly panicking that she would recognize my voice.

She looked past me and fluttered her fan for a moment, very ladylike, before giving me a smile that made my knees weak.

"I hope you're not going to beg for money, Señor Lépero. I'm afraid I have none."

I gave her a little bow. "A smile from you would enrich me more than all the gold in the realm."

The fan fluttered a bit faster, and she turned to an older woman who came up beside us.

"If you could make an introduction, Tía Beatriz, perhaps I could give this beggar what he requested?"

"My niece, Señorita Mercedes de la Cruz, daughter of Don Bartoleme de la Cruz. Would you honor us with your name?"

I gave another small bow. "Antonio de los Rios."

"I am pleased to meet you, Señor Rios," Mercedes said, giving me the promised smile—then she turned and left, maneuvering through the crowd with the elderly aunt in tow behind her.

Aah, gachupin etiquette—her aunt for a chaperone, on first acquaintance a mere smile. But I had survived our first meeting with a smile rather than a scream and now we were introduced, leaving an opening. Not that I knew the courting ritual for the upper classes.

Riego, the viceroy's aide, motioned for me to join him.

"You are about to be paid an honor. The viceroy is going to introduce you to the Marquis del Valle."

"Is this the right time to ask the viceroy to release my money?"

He gave me a shocked look. "At a ball? Of course not. Send a request to me later in the week."

"How long do you think it will take to get my inheritance released?"

He shrugged. "It will be done with much haste, señor, much haste, you can rely upon that."

His tone smacked of bureaucratic mire.

He gave me an encouraging grin. "But don't worry, your credit is good everywhere."

Sí. Until my creditors find out I'm an imposter and rip me to pieces.

"Señor Rios," the viceroy said, introducing me to Martín Cortés and his wife, Doña Bernaldina, and the bishop who was assuming command over the Inquisition in the colony, "defended himself with his sword after his coachmen had fallen. He fought off a gang of bandidos, killing two of them before the others fled."

The tale had grown a bit.

"God defended me," I said.

"Bless you and the sword you wielded like the angel Miguel defending the gates of heaven," the bishop said.

"Valor and a sharp sword are what my father and his conquistadors used to create this empire," Don Martín said.

"With help from the hand of God," the bishop said.

"Of course." The marquis gave him a slight nod.

"You will attend the ball celebrating our return to the colony," Doña Bernaldina told me. "I'm certain there will be a number of young señoritas who would enjoy hearing about your daring adventure."

Her husband turned to say something to the viceroy, and the viceroy's aide gave me a jerk of his head that told me I was dismissed.

Not ignored, but *dismissed,* as if I were a child that they were done being amused by. Me, the hero of the hour.

As I walked away it struck me that Doña Bernaldina had not given me an invitation to a ball, but a command. "You will attend," she had said.

That was confirmed by the viceroy's aide, who sidled up to me for a moment.

"You're lucky to get the invitation. The viceroy will be impressed if you are able to get a friendly message to him from Don Martín concerning the release of your inheritance."

As he moved away, a strong hand grabbed me, and I was swung around to face a matron.

"You must meet my daughter."

SIXTY-THREE

CARLOS SIPPED COLD wine and watched Mercedes as she talked with other young women on the patio outside the ballroom.

Mercedes had a reputation for a quick temper and a sharp tongue, and he wondered if she carried that temperament to the bedroom.

It wasn't just an idle thought because Carlos was certain he would soon find out the answer. He had been in negotiation with her father for weeks over a dowry that she would bring to their wedding bed. Once the amount was settled upon, a wedding date would be set.

Marrying the daughter of a merchant, even one of the richest merchants in the colony, as Mercedes's father had an interest in a silver mine, was grating to Carlos.

Carlos didn't have a title of nobility, but he was the second son of an hidalgo, a person of low nobility with no significant estate. That made him of the noble class because of birth. Hernán Cortés himself had been an hidalgo before the conquest and his elevation to the rank of marquis.

Carlos was expected to marry from the same class and had done so admirably when he married a daughter of the conqueror. But that had been at a time when he had significant wealth. His wife had passed and his gold had vanished, leaving him deep in debt and with no prospect of marrying a woman of moneyed nobility.

To Mercedes's father, his daughter's marriage to Carlos would be a coup, an elevation of social status for herself and her descendants.

Carlos had heard from gossip generated by the young woman's aunt that Mercedes had objected to the marriage because he was twenty years older than she, but that didn't matter. She would have no say in the selection of a husband. The only issue that mattered to Carlos was whether he could squeeze more dowry out of her father than he could get from another merchant with a marriageable daughter.

He approached Mercedes after he saw her staring at his cousin Antonio. Watching Antonio being hailed as a hero by his brother-in-law, Don Martín, and the viceroy while Antonio was claiming the inheritance Carlos so desperately needed put him in a barely suppressed rage. The fact that he was no longer a welcome guest at the Cortés parties and Antonio now was did nothing to soothe his foul mood.

"I see you were staring at my cousin," he said to Mercedes. "I hope you are not planning to throw aside my affections for a younger man. He, of course, is from the side of the family without a claim to nobility."

"No, Señor Rueda, I can assure you that I was not looking at him as a marriage prospect. Actually, I am considering taking vows to be wed to our Savior."

He chuckled and leaned closer. "From what I have heard of your temper, sweet Mercedes, you would spend most of your time as a nun taking beatings from the mother superior."

She edged away from him, unconsciously showing that she wasn't comfortable being close to him.

"I realized who Don Antonio looks like," she said. "Your brother-in-law, the marquis."

"What?" Carlos turned around and gave both men a look. "You're right, he does look a little like Don Martín, but I can assure you he isn't related to them."

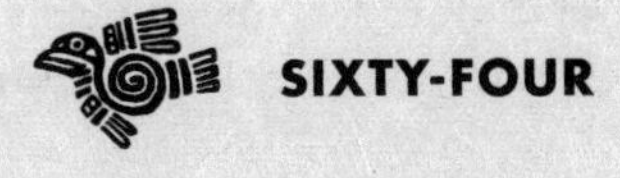

SIXTY-FOUR

I UNTANGLED MYSELF from the third mother who wanted the city's newest rich bachelor to meet her daughters and wandered away, heading for the patio, where I saw Mercedes was seated.

I passed her aunt-chaperone sleeping seated on a bench and found Mercedes examining the leaves of a lilac bush.

She turned as I approached.

"The viceroy's gardener needs to tend to this," she said. "Worms are eating holes in the leaves."

"Worms have to eat, too," I said.

She stared at me for a long moment, as if she was puzzled—as if she was looking for someone else behind the soot on my face. Finally, she said, "That was profound."

It was? I was referring to street trash and didn't understand what deep meaning she had attributed to my words.

The music began playing. She looked at the whirling dancers and then back to me.

"Are you going to ask me to dance, señor?"

I cleared my throat. "A wound to my leg . . ." and to my pride, I could have added, since I didn't know how to dance.

"Oh, you poor thing. It must have been a nightmare for you, fighting those bandidos."

"Sí, a nightmare."

"I was once attacked by highwaymen."

"No!"

"Yes. I fought and gave the leader a"—she stopped and stared at me intently. "Why, señor, I gave the leader a cut on his cheek about the same place you have been scarred."

"Amazing coincidence. I commend you for fighting back. But tell me, was this leader of robbers—"

"A beast is what he was, a bloodthirsty animal with a gang of—of worms, señor, slimy creatures who eat beautiful things that belong to others."

I made the sign of the cross. "Thank God you were not ravaged. The creature will never see the gates of heaven, that is for sure."

"He will never see the rope put around his neck on the gallows if I find him first because I will gouge out his eyes."

Ayyo!

Mercedes suddenly grew silent and stared at me with such wide-eyed intensity I caught my breath, expecting to be exposed.

"What's the matter?" I asked, not wanting to hear the answer.

"I—I don't know, you remind me of someone. A moment ago I thought it was the Marquis del Valle—you do have a resemblance—but when I looked into your eyes, I suddenly—" She gasped and clutched her throat. "Forgive me, good brave man that you are, God forgive me for the evil thought I have just had."

I heard a pronounced clearing of a throat behind me and turned.

Tía Beatriz, the watchdog, had come to the maiden's rescue. And mine.

"I'm sorry, señor—" Mercedes started.

"Antonio." I smiled.

She stared at me again, with those startling green eyes. "Señor Rios. I must leave. I have a terrible headache."

She swept by me.

I stood silently and watched her leave with her aunt.

Ayyo. She had seen the bandido behind the lépero.

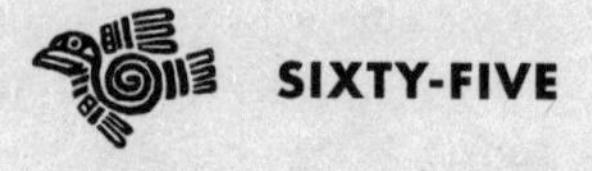

SIXTY-FIVE

I LEFT THE ball. I didn't know if I was supposed to take my leave of the viceroy, kiss his feet or a part of his anatomy that was a bit higher, or whatever the protocol was among gachupins for currying the favor of those in authority.

I was angry. Angry at Antonio de los Rios for dying and putting me in a position where I had finally gotten a view of happiness and knew it was forbidden fruit. Angry at myself for not listening to the lépero in me and throwing whatever I could find of the uncle's prized possessions in a sack and heading out with Rojo for a place where I wouldn't have to look over my shoulder—or worry when I looked into a woman's eyes that she would recognize the thieving bandido in me.

Angry at God for giving me despised blood.

How could blood be tainted? I wondered.

I have bled and I've seen gachupins, indios, africanos bleed. The blood all looked the same. I was tempted to cut some Spaniards and ask them how the color of their blood differed from mine.

When I reached the house, I bathed and dressed in the street clothes of a caballero and left on Rojo.

I knew the house of the Cruz family. I had ridden by it on several nights to see if I could spot Mercedes in a window.

She was right about me—I was an animal who had

led a gang of worms. Fine. That meant I no longer needed to concern myself with the rigid dance of social manners that characterized a relationship between a Spanish man and woman.

I was a beast and could act as one.

Dogs. The bane of the city. The packs came out late at night after the léperos tucked themselves away in the gutters.

Like Oaxaca, the city had two types of dogs—the barking ones that every homeowner had to warn of intruders and the hungry, growling, snapping ones that belonged to packs that roamed the streets at night looking for food.

If anything was going to give my presence away, it would be the dogs.

I was certain I knew the location of Mercedes's room because last night I had seen her closing the glass doors on a balcony. Such doors were usually left open to catch the breeze, as they were this night.

When the lights were out in the entire house, I made my move.

I woke up the street's night watchman, who was sleeping on the ground, and gave him a coin and a chunk of meat I'd taken from my house.

"The meat is for the dog," I said, after I told him I had a romantic rendezvous in the Cruz house. "It'll poison you if you eat it." That wasn't true, but I added the comment to make sure it got to the dog and not the watchman's own stomach.

As soon as I knew he had distracted the dog, I edged Rojo close to the wall, stood on the saddle, and dropped over, into the bushes. Making my way through the bushes, I got to the vine-covered trellis that grew up the wall to the roof. It was a path to the balcony doors I'd seen Mercedes shut—one for a human fly, but I was a lot heavier than when I played this game as a street boy. And there was no guarantee that the trellis was stronger than bare vines.

I had come too far to turn back. It was risky. No, it was insane. No man of reason would attempt such a thing. At the very least, Mercedes would welcome me with a scream that would awaken the entire household, if not the city's chief constable and his army of policemen.

That it could get me hanged had not kept me from doing things even more foolhardy, so I did what I had always done in these situations—I closed my mind to the danger and went forward. Foolishly.

Getting a handful of the wood frame and vines, I started up, making so much noise I was certain I'd soon see lamps in every room go on and her father with a musket.

Coming over the top of the balcony wall, I tried to sound less like a herd of stampeding cattle than I had been.

Crouching down below the rail because I was sure I could be seen from the street in the moonlight, I kept still for a moment, listening to the night for sounds that meant I awoke someone in the house. All I heard was snoring. Mercedes had a harsh, ratcheting, up-and-down snore. Oh well, maybe I snored, too, eh?

Taking soft steps, I crept quietly into the room, light from the full moon coming through the double doors and showing the path to the bed. The head of the bed was against the wall directly in front of me, with the foot pointed toward the balcony doors.

My heart beat faster as I saw her form under the covers.

Getting up to the bed, I whispered, "Mercedes."

The form under the blankets stirred, and I gently whispered her name again.

As she sat up, the moonlight caught her face, and I gasped and stepped back. The stern countenance and braided hair made her a Medusa with a head of snakes.

Tía Beatriz.

The first scream came before I had taken a single step for the balcony doors.

By the time I reached the railing, I was certain her long, bloodcurdling howl had awoken the entire city.

I leaped over the balcony, realizing as I was falling that I didn't know exactly what was on the ground at that spot. My feet came down in a thorny bush, and I hit hard, pitching forward, going facedown and slamming into the ground.

My breath was knocked out of me, but I reared up until I was on my knees, then on my feet and running, up and over the wall, still hearing her screams as if she was being ravaged by demons from the underworld.

That she had awoken every constable in the city was readily apparent to me, but as I rode Rojo at full gallop with a pack of wild dogs yapping at his heels, it was not only obvious that every mongrel in the area was chasing me but also that every guard dog for miles was howling.

If I had any sense, I would have just kept going, across a causeway and onto the road north. But I would have left with empty pockets.

Like those retreating Spanish, I was doomed to go down with treasure on my back.

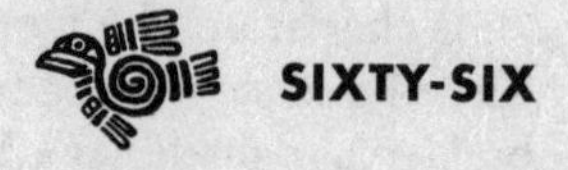

SIXTY-SIX

HIDING MY HEAD in the house for the next two days, I worked in the stable grooming Rojo, mending tack, and concocting a salve for a sore that a carriage horse had developed.

Not wanting the stableman around to wonder about me, I sent him on frequent errands to pick up supplies for the horses.

I was sewing a harness, reinforcing it with stronger thread, when the gardener came in. He stared at the big needle and thread I was repairing a harness with.

"What is it?" I demanded.

"My apology, señor, but a man wishes to speak to you."

"Who is he?"

"I don't know, señor, a gachupin in a carriage."

Ah, the viceroy's aide, no doubt with news about the release of my inheritance. After my performance at the ball, the viceroy must have decided to give me what I had coming.

I hurried out the gate and came to a sudden stop. It wasn't Don Riego's carriage, but a black enclosed one. The same black carriage that had pulled up beside me and paused on the bridge—with the curtains drawn.

I stared at the carriage, undecided about whether I should get my pistola—and my horse.

The carriage door opened and a man showed himself.

"Come aboard, Juan," El Mestizo said.

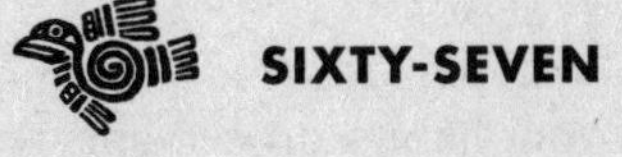

SIXTY-SEVEN

"How?"

The question of how he had found me hung between us—unanswered—as the black carriage rolled down the street.

Taking his time, El Mestizo lit a tobacco twist and blew out a steam of smoke. He offered me a leaf, but I shook my head. And I didn't repeat the question. He had heard it.

"Not so much *how,*" he said, "but more importantly, *what*? Once I knew, I had to decide what I was to do."

I kept my tongue. The "whats" were obvious—turn me over to the constables or let me make a run for it.

He had already made up his mind, and the only clue I had that I wasn't going to be immediately turned over to the constables was that he had come to get me rather than them. That meant he was probably going to give me a chance to run. Without my—his—horse. And with my pockets empty.

"But as to how, I believed I recognized you on the bridge, but I was far from certain. You have changed from the street child and stable boy I had seen. You are a gachupin, for sure. When I learned of your strange behavior at home, I became more suspicious."

"What strange behavior? You spied on me in my house?"

"*Your house?*" He leaned forward. "Is that something like . . . *your horse?*"

I shrugged. "I earned it in battle, señor. The house, at least."

"That you did—both of them. As for knowing your habits, my servants reported marketplace gossip about a wealthy young peninsulare who knew more about horseshoes than most blacksmiths."

"Aah, doomed not by the gossip of servants, but by my own stupidity in showing off my skills."

"You were doomed when you were conceived by a Spaniard lying with an india," he said, looking out the window. "Often it was by force."

He was talking about both of us, though I had never heard that his mother Marina had been forced to bed the conqueror.

Turning back to me, he said, "When my sister-in-law, Doña Bernaldina, told me about the lépero act you put on at the ball, I realized it might be a performance inspired by real life."

"A notion of hiding in plain sight that didn't work."

"Actually, you did well with it. The guests found it highly entertaining and accepted you without question as Antonio de los Rios." He blew smoke in my direction and peered at me with half-closed eyes. "Did Antonio suffer greatly when you murdered him?"

I realized we were pulling up to the building that housed the chief constable. My first thought was for escape, but his veiled stare kept me pinned to my seat.

"I didn't touch him. Had I gotten there a moment sooner, he would still be alive—less his purse, of course. He went over the cliff before I could bring down the killers."

He tapped the roof of the carriage, and I lurched back as it picked up speed. We rode in silence, each of us staring out a window, and I could tell he was fighting his own demons, ones no doubt I had inadvertently created.

"I believe you," he said. "When you accidentally killed that stable owner, I saw compassion on your face even though I'd heard that the man was a swine who'd cheated you out of an inheritance. Tell me about the fight on the Vera Cruz road . . ." He suddenly grinned. "And how you became a gachupin."

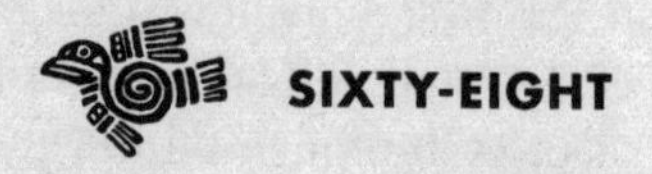

SIXTY-EIGHT

El mestizo dropped me off back at the house an hour later, after we talked about many things. I told him about my suspicions of Carlos, the brother of his late sister, and was told Carlos was barely tolerated by the Cortés brothers' family because of his inattention to their sister during her last days.

"He struck her once. Unforgivable. Had they not been married, I would have met him on the field of honor—not that he would have accepted a challenge from a mestizo."

El Mestizo was a man of mystery, something I had not realized. His coach was part of the mystique. It was enclosed to conceal the occupants, had no coat of arms, and was a color not commonly used, features that gave some anonymity to the owner—yet, by its very nature, the fact that it was unusual made it all the more distinct.

Why would he ride concealed but let the world know that it was him in the coach?

My guess was that he felt the world rejected him because of his mixed blood, and he wanted both to hide his head and strike back. The unique coach offered a refuge from their stares but told any Spaniard who saw it that this was a mestizo who bore the name and blood of the conqueror.

As I was stepping out of the coach, he made a puzzling statement about my presence in the city. "It's

God's will," he said. "Your destiny is intertwined with the people here. You did not come here by your own choice—you were guided here to avenge a wrong."

My first thought was that he was referring to avenging Antonio's death, but something about the grave way he looked at me when I stepped down gave me a shiver and sealed my lips from inquiring.

I started to walk away and he said, "Do not forget that you are invited to the ball at my brother's."

After the carriage rolled away, I stood for a long moment and watched it. Strange, but now I had encountered two people who could recognize me, one did, perhaps even the other, and I still was not in the hands of the constables.

A subject that had not been discussed was my future. I didn't volunteer that I was planning to run with as much as I could stuff into my pockets as soon as I had the opportunity—and he didn't ask. Nor had he demanded back his fine stallion.

I'm sure he knew it was not possible for me to keep up the Antonio pretense forever. Not only was there an uncle from Guadalajara who might unmask me at any time, but eventually someone who knew Antonio would step off ship at Vera Cruz and arrive in the capital. A constant influx of people came to the colony from Spain, and, no matter what their final destination, they all passed through Mexico City before moving on.

Besides getting the viceroy to release my gold, I had one other urgent need: to meet with Mercedes again before I left the city.

For what purpose? I didn't know—at least there was no purpose that I could define clearly. She was a gachupin; I was a bandido: it was hardly a heavenly match, nor was it one with a future. My own lifeline was most likely to be the end of a rope strung from a gallows—and it was just a matter of time and place.

El Mestizo had told me something that made a meeting with Mercedes urgent. In talking about Carlos, he mentioned that the man was pursuing a merchant's daughter for a large dowry—and I hid my surprise when he told me it was Mercedes.

She had to be warned about the man's evil nature. It might take some convincing if I was the source.

In the meantime, just like the avenger's destiny that El Mestizo said had propelled me to the city, fate appears to have given my heart to a redheaded gachupin, and I couldn't leave the city without it.

As I demonstrated climbing into the balcony at the Cruz house, knowing the madness of my acts had never kept me from doing them. My next move with Mercedes was going to be no exception.

In the morning I saddled up a carriage horse using the plainest tack, puzzling the groom at my choice, of course, and left the house. En route to my destination, I pulled a poncho over my upper body, put a scarf around the top of my head that came down over my forehead, donned a vaquero's well-worn hat, and darkened my face with the dye from tree roots I used on Rojo.

Looking very much like any other of the hundreds of wranglers who had brought horses or cattle into the city each day, I was waiting down the street when Mercedes came out of the Cruz compound in her carriage, on her way to pick up her women friends for their paseo socializing.

I went up the street as the carriage was coming down it. As it passed me, I dropped the locket bearing her mother's image into her lap.

I heard her exclamation and then a shout of "stop,"

but I kept going at an even pace, quickening the horse into a slow gallop after I went around a corner in case she ordered her carriage driver to turn and give chase.

What did I intend to prove by this act of utter foolishness?

Was there any doubt that she would know whom the locket came from? Any doubt that she would have the constables at my door as soon as she got her wits about her? Or talked to her father? Or her betrothed, Carlo the Murderous Bastardo, about the bandido that has come back into her life?

I resisted the strong temptation to load up mules and leave the city.

Only time would tell whether my next performance would be as a screaming lépero on a torture rack in the viceroy's dungeon.

A surprise came for me late in the afternoon.

An india servant girl came with a note she held on to tightly and refused to give to my servants, insisting that she had to hand it to me.

When I asked who sent her, she shook her head and stared at me, wide-eyed. She probably had never refused to answer a gachupin's demand in her life. I could have frightened the answer out of her, but I let her go because the note was plain enough and I was able to read it:

Our Lady of Assumption, Chapultepec mañana

Chapultepec was a hill outside the city where the Aztec emperors once had a palace and now there was a nunnery.

Mercedes wouldn't be planning to turn me over to the constables if she was arranging to have me meet her at a convent in the morning.

The message was unsigned. Perhaps it was a trap—a test to see if I would know it was she who sent it, thus confirming that I was the horseman who dropped the locket in her lap.

By going to the rendezvous, I would be revealing myself as a bandido. She could have told Carlos about the locket and her suspicions about me, and he could set a trap for me.

Regardless of the insanity of my act, the die had been cast when I gave her back the locket. Now I was in the hands of the fates, who had not handled my life gently in the past. And a señorita with a red-hot temper.

SIXTY-NINE

STILL UNSURE WHETHER I was running into a trap set by Carlos or the viceroy, I was grim in the morning when I set out for Chapultepec.

What had she said at the ball about what she would do to the bandido who attacked her? Gouge out his eyes out so that he didn't see the rope that went around his neck on the gallows? After wrestling with the woman, I was certain she was capable of it, so it may be that my fear of her handing me over to Carlos or the viceroy was misplaced—I should be worrying about what she personally planned to do to me.

I was making my way toward the causeway and coming up to the best inn in the city when I spotted someone from my past getting out of a carriage in front of the place of lodging.

The woman from Vera Cruz.

What did that picaro bitch of el diablo call herself? Countess Isabella del Castilla y Aragon. The name pounded in my head. Like a sledgehammer striking an anvil. Fire blew out of my ears, and I reached for my pistola—mentally.

I did sit upright in the saddle and glare, sorely tempted to run her down with Rojo, trampling her under his big hooves, then to head for the causeway and just keep on going. But I simply watched with no recourse as she went from the carriage to the inn with a man fawning over her.

The man was rich, of course, his clothing revealed that, and the carriage was of the ostentatious style of excessive silver trim preferred by the city's wealthier citizens.

He was flushed with excitement. No doubt the "countess" had stroked more than his ego during the ride, eh.

Obviously, the man was a dupe like me who thought more with his cojones than his brains when it came to women. He'd soon get his purse emptied.

It ate at me that I couldn't confront her and demand my money back—better yet, murder the slut of el diablo, getting my hands around her neck and squeezing till her eyes popped and her tongue hung out as she tried to beg me for mercy . . . or maybe I'd put a rope around her neck and drag her behind Rojo over a bed of cactus.

The mere thought of throttling the bitch roused my blood and gave my spirits a lift.

The money she stole was no longer important to me. I could throw enough gold candleholders in a bag from Ramos's house to buy a ranchero. But her making a fool out of me and stealing my hard-earned money deserved to be avenged.

Perhaps with an anonymous note written by a hired scribe, I would let the viceroy's aide know that a female picaro had come to town. And maybe a note to the Inquisition bishop, letting him know about the witchcraft she practiced, no?

SEVENTY

THE CONVENT AT Chapultepec, with its white-washed walls and red tiled roof, was nestled in a copse of trees with a sparkling stream gurgling nearby.

I saw her open carriage near the entrance, with her driver taking a siesta in the shade beneath it. Another carriage was also nearby, a closed coach much like El Mestizo's, but this one was red and the trim had an overly generous amount of gold.

When I got close enough I recognized the viceroy's coat of arms on the side of the red coach.

What I didn't see right away were the four constables sitting under a tree, their mules tied nearby as they played a dice game and ate the traditional midmorning light meal.

My heart leaped into my throat and I was ready to bolt, but the fact that they just glanced my way before turning back to the gaming kept my feet going straight ahead.

A nun greeted me at the gate with a stern look that appeared to be permanently carved onto her features as opposed to disapproval of just me.

"Señorita Cruz?" I asked.

She nodded at a collection box set on the wall beside the gate. I dropped in a piece of eight and she remained frozen in place. Another silver piece in the box and she turned and I followed her.

Ayyo . . . I had spent my life as a thief in the wrong business.

The nun led me into a small garden area, where Mercedes was on her knees trimming a rosebush. She stood when we approached and thanked the nun for looking after me. As soon as the nun was gone, Mercedes gave me a look that could have shriveled the thorny bush she had been working on.

"You disgusting bandido, did you think you won my favor by first putting me into danger and then saving me after you threw me to those creatures? I will have the viceroy drag you back to the city behind his carriage with a rope around your neck."

Had she read my thoughts about the countess?

"I'm happy to see you, too."

She stepped up to me and put the sharp tip of her cutting tool under my throat.

"Tell me how you murdered Antonio de los Rios."

I gently pulled her hand to get the sharp point away from my throat.

"You don't believe that or you would have sicced the constables on me already." I nodded at the locket she was wearing. "I kept it safe for you."

"And I should thank you for stealing it in the first place?" She hefted the cutting tool in her hand as if she was making up her mind to use it again. "You should be on your knees begging forgiveness."

I dropped to my knees. "I beg pardon, señorita, for forcing you to scar my face, making me even uglier than I already was, and for risking my freedom and life to return the locket that I kept close to my heart."

"I—I—"

Ayyo. Her face was red and she appeared to be wavering between shoveling the cutting tool in my gullet or giving a good scream.

I motioned her with my hands to stay quiet. "Stab me if you like, but don't scream," I said. "The viceroy's men will hear you."

"Get off your knees. You look ridiculous."

I got up and brushed off my knees.

"Tell me what happened to Antonio."

"Your betrothed had him murdered."

I expected her to take the accusation like a slap in the face, perhaps staggering back, swaying dizzily so I had to catch her as she collapsed from a terrible shock. But she just stared at me quietly for a moment before asking another question.

"Why do you say that?"

I described what happened. "It was an assassination, not a robbery. They were paid to kill; stealing would have been a bonus."

She again became quiet, pursing her lips, staring beyond me as she digested my accusation.

"That's why you didn't turn me in," I said.

She met my eye for a second and turned away again.

"Ah . . . sí," I said, nodding, as a revelation exploded in my head. "I thought you had the same feelings I had, that you fell in love with me when—"

"When—what? When you attacked me? Tried to—"

"I didn't try anything; I saved you."

"You—"

"Shut up."

"What?"

"Shut up or I'm going to turn you over my knee and spank you. Ay di mio, you are a mean-tempered shrew. If you don't start talking to me as a woman speaks to a man, I won't be your lover."

"I—I—"

She was speechless, but from the way she held the

bush cutter I still wasn't sure if she planned to use it on me.

"Why do you suspect Carlos," I asked.

She took a deep breath, let it out slowly, then walked around, pausing to examine a rosebud. Finally, she turned back to me with a grave but polite expression.

"Did you know that Ramos de los Rios was murdered?"

It was my turn to be shocked. I thought he had died of old age or one of the pestilences that periodically come back and hurry people to their graves.

"He was hit over the head as he walked home from an evening Mass. The killer was never found."

"And?"

"A niece of Carlos shares a carriage with me on the paseo. Carlos had approached Ramos for money after his business scheme cost him dearly. Soon after Ramos was killed, it was revealed that Antonio was his heir, not Carlos. She said that when Carlos found out he wasn't going to inherit, he flew into a terrible rage because he desperately needed the money. His wife said something to him that he took offense to about the matter, and he struck her."

"Perhaps asking if he had murdered his uncle," I mused.

"I don't know. But he is an evil person to strike his wife when she was sick, even if he didn't kill Ramos. And . . ."

"And?"

"I have always felt there was something . . . I don't know, deceptive, perhaps, dishonorable about him. I don't know—it's just a feeling."

"Did the niece say anything more?"

"No. But now that Carlos has approached my father to marry me, I'm horrified both at marrying a man who would hit a sick woman and troubled by my suspicions."

"What does your father say?"

"That I am finding reasons to avoid marrying Carlos because he is more than twice my age and I don't find him attractive. I find him both pompous and mean-spirited. My father is so enthralled that Carlos is a hidalgo and was related to Cortés by marriage that he's blind to everything else about the man."

"Are you looking for reasons?"

"Yes, but that doesn't leave aside my suspicion about Ramos's death. Don Ramos was a friend of my family. He treated me very kindly. He often spoke of his handsome nephew in Spain and would joke and tease that he was going to bring him over here to marry me."

She has another in line for her affections besides Carlos and me—and he is dead.

"Robberies are common," I said. "What makes you suspicious that Carlos was involved? Besides his need for money?"

"From the way Ramos's head was crushed in, he was hit more than once, but his purse was not taken. It wasn't necessary to beat him to death. He was old and rather frail; he could have been robbed with little violence. You are a bandido—have you ever murdered someone without robbing them afterward?"

"I'm a thief, not a murderer," I pointed out. But she had made a connection with Carlos and the crimes in my mind. "Murder, not robbery, was the motive for both. And Carlos stood to profit from both killings."

"For certain."

I shrugged. "There are no witnesses. He'll never be brought to justice."

"Exactly. That is why you must kill him."

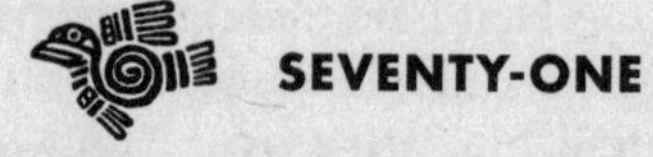

SEVENTY-ONE

ANTONIO DE LOS Rios managed to stagger to the river, grunting and grimacing with pain all of the way. The indio, Mazatl, had braced Antonio's left leg with sticks and a cord made from vines. It made the leg stiff and difficult to walk on, but he could at least hobble lamely. The alternative was to crawl to civilization, as he had been crawling for calls of nature before the indio had wrapped his leg.

He had set out for the river as a matter of desperation. He knew that somewhere upstream was the road that went between Vera Cruz and Xalapa. While he had managed some crude communication with the indio, he had not been able to find out how far the road or even how far upstream Mazatl had found him, but he doubted that he could have floated down the river for a great distance after falling from the road.

The second option was to go downstream, where, he had deduced from using sign language with the indio, there was a bigger village than the one he was in and a church.

As best he could tell, the village with the church was at least a half day's walk.

He knew from his crude linguistic communications with the indios that they didn't use canoes to get to the village because the river was too rocky and wild.

He suspected it would be easier to walk downriver than upriver because of the grade, but was convinced that the road upstream was much closer than the church.

The best alternative would have been to have waited where he was, convalescing until he was able to get help from a message the indios would carry down to the church. The next best alternative would be having the indios carry him on a makeshift stretcher to civilizaation, but either he was unable to communicate his desire to the indios or they were unwilling to accommodate his wishes.

He believed he had managed to get across the need to bring the priest or take him to the priest by drawing in the dirt a cross, a church steeple, and a stick man walking, but they just stared at him and shook their heads.

Antonio realized the indios were kind people, that Mazatl and the other villagers had saved his life, fed him, and tried to patch him, but they were extremely primitive, and he wondered if they avoided carrying him to the larger village out of fear.

Evil fortune, he thought, first to be attacked by bandidos who killed as well as robbed and then to need help from people who were isolated from society and didn't speak his language.

That he had been shot at close range and went over a steep cliff but survived showed that God had favored him. The lead ball from the pistola had brushed his clothes and had not even grazed him. He had gone over the cliff because he stumbled, not because he was shot.

As he lay day and night with nothing to think about but the pain and the fact that he had avoided being killed by bandidos by the bountiful mercy of God, he had convinced himself that the road was not a great distance from where he was.

Besides the walk on a bad leg and the many smaller injuries that had not completely healed, he realized that he would have to climb a steep slope to get from the river to the road. Climbing up at the spot he fell wouldn't be possible because it was sheer cliff, but as the road and river both meandered around the mountain, he was certain there had to be a spot he could crawl up.

And crawl he was willing to do. A life of leisure and luxury was awaiting him as soon as he got to Mexico City and claimed his rightful inheritance.

SEVENTY-TWO

DIEGO MADE HIS way along the road to Vera Cruz with Xalapa behind him, knowing that he could not return to Carlos's horse ranch near Mexico City if he didn't have information that pleased the man. Where he would go and hide from one of the most powerful men in the colony, he didn't know. But, for certain, Carlos would be relentless about having him hunted down and killed, if for no other reason than he knew too much.

He was unsure what information he could get that would please his employer. That the bandidos he had hired failed to kill the man Carlos wanted murdered was not going to change, though Diego had a hard time reconciling how he could have seen the man get shot and go over a cliff but the man was still alive.

He didn't blame Carlos for his disbelief and anger. He replayed the shoot-out over and over in his mind, and Rios's surviving didn't make sense.

Diego was puzzled by the fact that Rios was still alive and had the impudence to claim he had killed the bandidos.

"I know what I saw," Diego said, aloud, as he rode.

If he could find the bandido and use him to discredit Rios, he would be back in the favor of his employer. He wanted to return to where the ambush took place and look the terrain over.

There had to be a ledge just below the cliff, he thought. That was the only way Rios could have survived the fall.

To puzzle it out, he had to see the cliff himself.

SEVENTY-THREE

"MURDER CARLOS?" I was disappointed. "I'm not a murderer. You think I'm no better than Carlos."

"No—I'm—I'm sorry." She lowered her eyes and bit her lip.

"I was a thief. That's what happens to men who grow up on the streets. They steal first for food to survive and then it becomes the only way of life they know. The women who grew up with us become whores because that is the way they earn their tortillas."

"That's horrible."

"No, señorita, that's life. I don't have a false shine on me that was put on by stealing the food from indios and working servants as slaves." I gave her a sweeping salute with my hat. "Good day."

"I could call the viceroy, have his guards arrest you."

"That would be your privilege." I started to walk away, angry. I didn't want to leave; I wanted her in my arms, but my pride was hurt.

"Wait. You're—you're right."

"About what? Carlos?"

"About me. I don't want to marry Carlos. And I lied when I said I never thought about you except as a monster. I've never forgotten the man whose warm eyes I looked into before he saved me from those creatures of the night."

* * *

We left the convent to take a walk along the little river. She wanted to show me the flowers that grew along the stream.

She said she had set up the meeting at the convent because it was the one place she could go without her aunt as a chaperone or other young women as companions, as on the paseo. "A nun here is my cousin."

The viceroy's presence was a coincidence. She told me he came to the convent to get away from the city and tend a small garden.

Before we went through the gate, she instructed me to make a donation and didn't care when I said that I already had.

I went to drop in a silver coin and she said, "Gold."

I shrugged. It was stolen, anyway.

We walked and talked, and I saw in her the warm and lovely things I had always imagined. But we had to get back to the business at hand.

I told her about the cryptic remark I heard in Oaxaca regarding the great stud horse.

"She does something for his stallion that keeps him in stud fees," she said, repeating what I had told her. "You can't find meaning in what she meant?"

"No. But he said she was a seamstress. I've asked myself what could a seamstress do for a horse to keep its value . . ." I shook my head. "It makes no sense to me. Carlos keeps the stallion on a ranch near the city. I'm going to wander around out there and look around."

"There's something I can do to help. I'll find the seamstress."

"How?"

"Carlos isn't likely to have come into contact with a seamstress unless it was someone his wife used. I think I know who she might be, but I'll make sure by asking his niece tomorrow when we go to the paseo."

"Ah, yes, the paseo—all those handsome caballeros in their fine clothes and proud horses. But tell me the truth, señorita, having been in the arms of a real man, as you once were with me, won't you find those paseo dandies as amusing rather than interesting?"

"Juan," she whispered the name I had revealed to her, "being with a man who is one step ahead of the viceroy's hangman is frightening. If my father knew that I was carrying on a flirtation with a bandido, he would have me put into a convent cell and locked up for life—after he had you put in a dungeon."

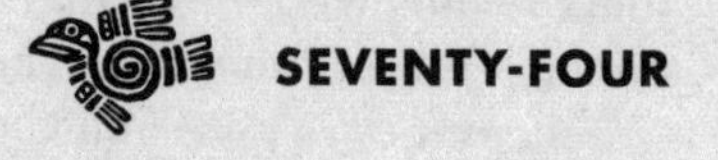

SEVENTY-FOUR

WITH LITTLE ROOM in the city to stable horses and no pasture at all, men like Carlos who raised horses and the very wealthy caballeros like the Marquis del Valle maintained small ranches outside town, bringing horses in when needed and sending them out to get exercise and mate.

These were not traditional ranchos, which were farms where food was also grown and where livestock was raised to feed a family, but small haciendas devoted exclusively to maintaining horses used for riding and for carriages in the city.

In a narrow strip of grasslands with gentle rolling hills and scattered copses of trees that began about an hour's ride from the capital were the finest horses in the colony. Most of the ranches ran along a small river that flowed down to Lake Texcoco.

As with the horse-trading area along the river in Oaxaca, here there was also a set of pastures and corrals where horse traders gathered to buy and sell.

I went by the region on my trip to the city in the carriage of the viceroy's aide, and he had pointed it out to me. My groom had been out to Carlos's ranch a number of times for Ramos and to other ranches helping Ramos's city neighbors with horses.

I told the groom that I wanted to look over the area because I was interested in buying a small ranch to raise horses. He was able to give me the lay of the land; if I kept on a low ridge that followed the river I would see most of the ranches, including Carlos's.

Carlos had invited me to his ranch to sell me a horse. I would accept his offer, but visiting at his invitation meant that I would see only what he wanted me to see. I wanted to take a look at his ranch on my own first.

I was also toying with a more daring idea. It had occurred to me that if Carlos's prize stud got stolen, it might bring about the final financial collapse he seemed to be teetering on.

Ayyo! It was a thought I had to clear from my mind because it was pure insanity.

I dressed as a vaquero once I had left the house, appearing much the same as I did when I dropped the locket into Mercedes's lap.

I first rode along the road from the city that went by the gate at the entrance to each of the ranches. The gates were symbolic only, a place to put a coat of arms or ranch name. The only fencing was around the pastures where horses were kept.

After I passed Carlos's gate, I made my way to the ridge and came back around to a point where I was above his ranch. My stableman was right: the ridge gave almost a bird's-eye view of the line of ranches below.

I sat under a tree and chewed on a piece of dried, salted beef while I studied the small ranch below. The layout was pretty much the same as the others around it, not a grand hacienda with a palatial house and a dozen other buildings, but a small house used occasionally by the owner for overnight visits, a bunkhouse, barn, corrals, and fenced pastures.

From the distance I didn't have a good view of El Rey, the champion stallion, although I was certain I had identified it for no other reason than it was a big horse, the size of Rojo, and occupied its own corral.

It wasn't only the stallion that I watched, but I tried to get as much detail as I could about the vaqueros. At a distance I had seen a man flee the murder of Antonio, but from my vantage point overlooking the ranch, none of the men stood out as familiar to me, and neither did any of the horses.

I was certain from speaking with the viceroy's aide that Carlos never let anyone near the stallion. I was sorely tempted to make my way down to the corral and get a closer look at the horse, but the chance of being caught was high because vaqueros were around.

The wranglers were about now, but what about after they had their dinner and sacked out in the bunkhouse? I silently asked Rojo.

There would be a full moon tonight that provided enough light for me to get a look at the stallion close-up.

Eh, if I got rid of Carlos and if the elderly uncle from Guadalajara died before setting his eyes on me, I could stay as Antonio for a while longer by staying out of sight on a horse ranch outside the city.

With such thoughts, I kept along the ridge with Rojo, enjoying the sight of the fine horseflesh below. Going by a corral with a pretty mare in it, I started my hum more as a habit than anything else.

The mare went over the corral fence with little effort because the third log was on the ground. She came up alongside us, neighing, exciting Rojo as the two nuzzled each other.

"You found a pretty señorita," I told Rojo. "But you aren't going to make love to her, not on this trip."

I took the mare back to the corral and put the log back up. I had time to kill so I laid back and dozed a bit. I woke up when I heard a familiar sound.

Ay, caramba! Rojo had gone over the fence to satisfy the mare. Eh, he made me jealous. Women just seemed to invite him in wherever we went.

When the mating was over and Rojo had returned in a more relaxed mood than I had seen him in for a long while, I replaced the log and moved along.

A moment later I heard the log go down as the mare kicked it as she went over it. I tried to shoo the mare off, but she stuck right with me. "You have to go home," I told her.

She got closer and rubbed her flank against my leg.

I had to admit, the mare didn't just appeal to Rojo, but to me. She was a beauty, the type I looked for in horseflesh when I was stealing horses. That life was behind me now. But there was something I could do.

"Hey, señorita, I'll tell you what, I'm going to come back tomorrow and buy you." In the meantime, I would have to get her back to her owner before she got lost.

Thinking about taking the mare back and getting her in the corral and tying a hitch on her, I was caught by surprise as four horsemen came out from a crop of trees and surrounded me with drawn pistolas.

"Hold it," I said, "I'm not armed," which was a lie, although I didn't have a pistola visible.

In the group was a gachupin and three vaqueros. The arrogant-looking Spaniard came up beside me and hit me across the shoulder with a quirt.

"You horse-thieving sonofabitch, we're going to hang you from the nearest tree."

SEVENTY-FIVE

A TRAP, THAT'S what I had walked into. The ranchers in the area had been plagued with horse thieves and had set up the sweet mare in a corral, removing the top fence timber to make it easy for her to be stolen.

Tied to a tree, listening to them talk, I knew that word had quickly gone out that they had a horse thief. It was an invitation to a hanging, not an arrest.

More of the horse ranchers had gathered until there were four gachupins and half a dozen vaqueros.

My laments that the mare had followed me on her own volition fell on deaf ears. I got another hit from a quirt from the man who hit me earlier. His name was Lopez, and he had taken charge of my hanging.

"Shut up or I'll stuff my whip down your throat," Lopez said.

I couldn't tell them that I was a respectable citizen named Antonio de los Rios, because I couldn't pass for Spanish wearing a livestock worker's clothes. I looked exactly like what I was—a mestizo horse thief.

Lopez threw a noosed rope over a thick limb and got off his horse and pulled it down over my head.

"I swear I wasn't stealing—" I started for about the tenth time.

He kicked me on the side. "Shut up or I'll strangle you myself." He jerked the coarse noose tight around my neck.

"Put him in the saddle," he told the vaqueros.

It was the first time in my life I hated being in the saddle. I had spent most of my life envying those who were able to ride a horse every day, but this was one time I wished I was on a donkey, where my feet touched the ground, rather than on a tall stallion.

Rojo was nervous, and I hummed and held my knees tight against his flank. "Steady, amigo."

"He thinks he can talk to a horse!" Lopez howled.

"Should we blindfold him?" another Spaniard asked. He appeared more nervous about lynching me.

"Hell, no. Let him look el diablo, his new master, right in the face the moment he dies."

Rojo stamped his hooves and shifted enough for me to feel the rope closing around my throat.

"Steady," I croaked, my humming getting hoarser as my wind was being shut off. He didn't like the sound of Lopez's voice. Neither did I, but this wasn't a time to be particular.

"What's that he keeps whining?" the blindfold advocate asked.

"El diablo's song," Lopez said. "He's letting him know he's on his way."

He gave me a big grin to let me know he was enjoying watching me sweat from the anticipation of dying. But not a quick death. My bandido companions and I spent many a night around the campfire talking about the difference between the slow strangulation of being hanged from a horse and the quicker, neck-breaking technique used on gallows.

"El diablo awaits you, thief!" Lopez raised his quirk to give Rojo a good swat.

"Stop!"

Everyone froze as if a shot had been fired. The whole group of us turned to the newcomer.

"Why are you hanging my vaquero?" El Mestizo asked.

Lopez stared at him for a moment before answering. I could tell he knew who El Mestizo was.

"He's a horse thief," Lopez said.

"Did you steal a horse?" El Mestizo asked me.

"No, señor, it followed me. Followed the stallion, actually. I was returning it when these men jumped me."

"He's a lying bastardo! And it's time for him to die." Lopez lifted the quirt again to swat the stallion.

"Señor," El Mestizo said quietly, "I told you he works for the Cortés family. Neither the marquis nor I will be pleased if you hang our man."

That froze the bunch of them better than if a reprieve from the viceroy had arrived. Lopez was down, but not finished. Of the bunch of them, he appeared stupid enough and eager enough for a bloodletting to defy even the heavens.

"He was caught red-handed," he insisted.

"I can prove that the mare followed me with no effort on my part," I said. "Put her back in the corral and I will show you."

"Do what he says," El Mestizo said.

"And if the mare doesn't follow him, he hangs," Lopez said.

El Mestizo pursed his lips and nodded in my direction. "Sí, he hangs."

My heart was pounding, my throat was parched and raw, my legs ached from pressing desperately onto Rojo's flank, but I know females, at least the four-legged ones.

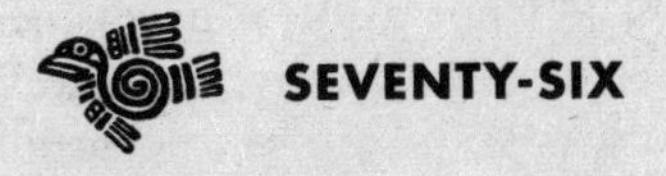

SEVENTY-SIX

I SAT IN the shade of the blacksmith shop at El Mestizo's ranch and drank cool water flavored with lemon as I watched El Mestizo correct a blacksmith's work on a horseshoe. He didn't ask my advice and didn't need it—like me, he had learned the art because he was a lover of all things about horses.

My throat still ached and my back and shoulder were raw from Lopez's quirt, but I was alive. After I demonstrated that the mare would follow me with no effort on my part, El Mestizo had put salve on Lopez's agitation by telling him the marquis would be sending him a note of thanks.

El Mestizo sent the blacksmith away so we could talk. He wanted to know what I was doing in the area dressed as a stockman, and my answer caught him by surprise.

"Looking for the murderer of Antonio and Ramos de los Rios."

He paused as he was about to give the horseshoe on the anvil a tap of a hammer. He turned slowly to face me.

"Is it not true," he said, "that Antonio was killed in a robbery on the Vera Cruz road and Ramos was struck down by a thief in the evening walking home in the city? They died far apart in time and distance, though in a manner that is sadly much too common in the colony."

He listened gravely as I laid out why I believed the attack on Antonio was an assassination and not just a robbery.

"I put aside your suspicions about Carlos when we spoke in my carriage," he said, "because there was suspicion but no proof. The most telling point of your tale is still that it comes from a seasoned bandido. But some highwaymen are more violent than others."

I shook my head. "No, it makes no sense. The coachmen were not near their weapons and Antonio wasn't armed. None of it made sense. I've seen a hundred bandidos like those two in bars from Xalapa to Vera Cruz. Every one of them knows you don't kill unless it's necessary."

"And Ramos?"

"He was hit several times on the head with a club . . . yet his purse and jewelry were left untouched. He was frail. There was no need to beat him to death."

"Another robbery turned to murder," he said. "It happens a thousand times, but I agree that, unless the robber was frightened away by other people, it appears strange that the theft would not have finished his mission. I knew Don Ramos. I'd bought a sword from him last year. He was rather feeble. Hitting him several times was unnecessary. A good punch would have sent him down, much less a beating with a club."

"So you agree with me."

"I agree that the circumstances of both incidents are strange. And I concede Carlos has a motive for both crimes. He's desperate for money, and everyone he has turned to has refused to assist. We Cortéses have our own reasons for refusing him, but it can be said that

Carlos does not stimulate sympathy toward himself from anyone."

"What do you think of Carlos?"

"Are you asking me if he would murder for a large fortune? Certainly—but so would most people I know."

El Mestizo put aside his tools and came over to me. I couldn't tell from his stoic features what he was thinking.

"Do you have any idea of the mire you are getting yourself into? You don't understand the system and how it all turns on silver and gold. If Carlos finds out you're not Antonio, nothing you say or do would save you. Even if you had absolute proof of his guilt, he would offer the viceroy part of Ramos's fortune, the archbishop another part, and your part would be your neck back in a noose."

"There are other ways to extract revenge," I said.

"You're not involved in this. You came upon Antonio by accident. Had you arrived at his coach before the other bandidos did, it would have been you who would have robbed him."

"But I would not have murdered him."

I had not mentioned my suspicions about Carlos's stallion. His deceased sister's husband being a murderer was enough for El Mestizo to deal with in one day.

"It doesn't matter. You are now involved in something beyond your ability to cope with. It is a miracle that you haven't already been unmasked. It will happen, soon, and when it does, take what you can from Ramos's house and leave the city at a gallop on that fine horse you stole from me."

"I can't do that. You told me that my destiny lies in

the city. I have to finish what I came for. If that includes a rope around my neck, so be it."

El Mestizo gave me a long look. "Perhaps," he said, "perhaps. You certainly tempted fate today."

"No, I told the truth, señor; I was humming out of habit when I attracted the mare."

"Which habit is that? Horse stealing?"

SEVENTY-SEVEN

THE SOCIETY BALL I was ordered to attend by Doña Bernaldina was another opportunity for me to expose myself, but I had been warned not to offend the marquis, that he could help get my money released, so I was fated to go for good reasons, none of which made me feel any less certain I would meet up with someone who had once looked down the barrel of my pistola.

I got the tailor out to fit me again, this time sticking with black except for dark gray stockings and a gray hat, and those only because the tailor said I looked like el diablo dressed entirely in black.

Mercedes would not be at the ball because her father, as a mere merchant, despite his wealth, was not considered colonial aristocracy. One had to be a descendant of nobility or the conquistadors; merely having money was not enough.

I found the way the gachupins ranked themselves on a social ladder less reasonable than how léperos did it on the street. A lépero's ability to fight for survival was the key to success on the streets, but the gachupins held in esteem even those who had done little but possessed much.

The palace of the Marquis del Valle was his new home. Four years earlier he sold what is now the viceroy's palace on the Zócalo to the Crown for use as the colony's seat of government. His conqueror-father had built the viceroy's palace by stealing the location and the building materials from what had been Montezuma's palace.

Cortés, of course, was the biggest bandido in history, having stolen an empire.

My entrance to the ballroom in clothes similar to all the other men created no great attention, and I quickly faded back, trying to keep away from everyone by pretending to be fascinated by the room's painted panels.

El Mestizo found me and asked in a low voice whether I was trying to hide myself in the paintings. "Or planning to come back later and steal them?"

The fact that I was once again socializing with notables seemed to mildly amuse him.

The party had no sooner started when a sensation was created as the doors to the ballroom opened and a parade of Spaniards wearing Aztec costumes marched in.

The "indio" procession was colorful, with the Montezuma character dressed as the emperor would have appeared, including a brilliant headdress that was several feet high. Behind him came twenty-four Aztec nobles, all dressed only slightly less colorfully than the emperor.

"What's this?" I asked El Mestizo.

"A joke in poor taste. Montezuma is Alonso de Avila, a friend of the marquis. His brother is the Aztec on his right. At the moment they are unhappy with the way the colony is being administered."

"Why are they displeased?"

"Like my brother, they're encomienda owners. Even though they received encomienda rights from their father, just as my brother has, the rights are not permanent. They've petitioned the king to make the right of encomienda pass to the owner's male heir, as a title or another estate would."

"Like a fiefdom," I said, repeating inn talk I'd heard over drinks.

"Yes, as if they were lords of the realm and the indios were their subjects. The king has refused. The encomienda owners believe they are entitled to the right. The Crown of Spain never financed the conquest. My father gathered adventurers around him who volunteered, and he borrowed the money for weapons and ships. The encomienda was their reward. The Avilas are just heirs, but some of the conquistadors are still living, and they also want the right to pass to their descendants as if they were feudal lords."

The sudden entrance of the Aztecs may have come as a surprise to the guests, but obviously not to the host. Even as we spoke, as if they were changing sets for a play, servants were transforming the ballroom into what a great hall would have looked like in Montezuma's palace, replacing food and furnishings, adding feathers, pottery, and blooming plants all about.

With the marquis playing the role of his father, Hernán Cortés, and Avila as Montezuma, the two Spaniards acted out a short drama in which Montezuma surrendered his empire and his crown to the conqueror.

I found the play by grown men, one of whom was the wealthiest and most prominent man in the colony, amusing and was surprised to see El Mestizo's features lined with tension, his body rigid.

Why was he disturbed by others acting out a scene from the history of the colony? One that everyone in the colony knew, although it was not completely accurate. Montezuma never handed over his crown to Cortés. Instead, the Aztec emperor died from a wound received from a stone thrown when he went to a balcony to try and calm a crowd that had gathered because it was believed the emperor was being held hostage by the Spanish. Which he was, of course. And there was the matter of whether he died from the stone or was strangled by the Spanish when he refused to cooperate.

As I stared around the room, I saw more rigid postures, more tense features that would shatter if hit by a stone. Not by all of the guests, most of whom, like me, appeared amused by the silly farce, but in a group of men who had congregated together near the marquis. And I saw something else in the faces of these men—elation, as if the interchange between Cortés and Montezuma had special meaning for them.

"Señor," I said to El Mestizo, "what is the importance of this playacting by your brother and his amigo?"

El Mestizo's features were now worried.

"That man wearing a red sash," he said, nodding toward a portly man across the room, "is the royal visitador. He was sent by the king to inspect the colony, to judge how well the viceroy is performing his duties and the temper of the people. He will not be amused by a drama in which my brother receives a royal crown."

A stir passed among the guests as Montezuma's slaves marched in, carrying a large arrangement of flowers that was presented to the marquis. The flower design spelled out a phrase that I was unable to read but heard others speak.

"Fear not," El Mestizo said to himself, repeating what I heard.

I wondered why, if there was nothing to fear, El Mestizo and some of the other guests acted as if they were sitting on a keg of gunpowder.

SEVENTY-EIGHT

WHEN I CAME out of the ballroom, instead of my open carriage, a covered coach came forward to pick me up.

"Come aboard," Mercedes said, speaking through a crack in drawn curtains.

When I was inside, seated across from her, she said, "I sent your carriage home."

"How did you get out of the house at night without your chaperone?"

"My father went to Vera Cruz to purchase goods coming off the fleet. He will not be back for days. My aunt enjoys a splash of brandy in the chocolate drink she has after dinner. I made sure she had a generous amount of my father's strongest this time."

"And the coachman you bribed to keep his mouth shut. Once again, I am amazed at how clever you gachupins are."

"Don't call me that," she snapped. "It's not a nice word. I know there are Spanish who deserve it, but I don't rake the backs of my servants. I'll give my coachman a coin for the extra work he did tonight, but he would do it for me regardless because I treat him fairly."

"I surrender!" I held up my hands.

"No, it's me that must surrender tonight."

I started to move across to the seat next to her. "Sí, we are meant for—"

She pushed me back to where I'd been.

"I was talking about the apology I owe you."

"Ah . . . but, no, it's not necessary." I touched the scar on my cheek. "It caused little pain and—"

"You deserved the cut for attacking me. But I didn't thank you for returning my locket. It's very precious to me. My mother died when I was a baby and the picture in the locket is the only one I have of her. Do you have one of your own mother?"

I stared at her gravely. She was in dangerous territory. There was a certain amount of excitement generated in a woman when she deals with a dangerous man like a highwayman. But finding out I was born in a whorehouse and raised on the streets as a dirty lépero was not going to gain me respect from a woman.

I told her anyway. I could tell it hit her hard.

"The lépero act you put on at the ball . . . ?"

She pushed back the curtain to let air in and stared out for a moment. When she turned back to me, she was solemn and sincere.

"I am very proud of you. All the young men I know have had all the opportunities in the world and accomplish nothing except what is provided for them. You have been a beggar, a thief, and now you are a gachupin. And you have succeeded at each of them."

That got us both laughing, and then she was in my arms, her warm, wet lips against mine. She smelled like a spring day and tasted like the nectar of the gods. When she pulled back, we were both breathless. We opened more curtains to let a breeze pour through.

"I actually came tonight to tell you something important," she said. "I believe your seamstress is a woman named Nina Alvarez."

"Yes!" I slapped my head. "He called her Nina."

"Who?"

"Carlos, when, uh, they were together. I forgot, but I'm sure that was the name he used."

"I learned from his niece that Nina was the seamstress for his wife when she was alive. I thought it might be her because many of the wealthiest women in the city go to her for their dresses. She wasn't always a seamstress. Her family once had money, but it was lost in speculation on a silver mine."

"Do you know her?"

"I've seen her when I've visited other women and she was there, but I haven't used her services. My father insists my clothes be made by a seamstress who buys cloth from him."

"Is she noted for any particular type of sewing? Does she do anything with horses?"

"I can't imagine her doing anything with horses. She does very fine, fancy weaving, creating intricate patterns. No one else I know of can create the designs she's capable of doing with her small fingers."

"How about fur?"

"I'm sure she trims dresses and capes sometimes with fur, but not horsehair, if that's what you're wondering. Not unless one wanted her to make a broom or a brush."

"She's doing something for that horse. I have to find out what it is. I'm certain Carlos is hiding something that could bring him down if it was exposed. I need to get this woman to tell me what it is."

"I'll help you with the woman and Carlos. His sister has set up several lunches for me to attend at her home with Carlos. To warm us to each other, she told my father, even though I'm already boiling over from the idea of marrying him."

"Excellent. Keep your ears open when you're

around him. I find him to be a pompous braggart, the type who would flap his tongue and step on it for a pretty señorita."

I couldn't bear the notion of Mercedes in the arms of another man. I kept my thoughts to myself, but I had already decided that, regardless of whether I was able to prove Carlos guilty of murder, I would kill him before I'd let Mercedes be trapped in a marriage with a man she despised.

"I must warn you, Ju—Antonio, I won't help you do anything that would harm Nina Alvarez. There are no opportunities for women, so any other woman in her position would have worked hard for a marriage proposal, but she went to work and earned her own living. Because she works for a living, she's looked down upon by women she grew up with and shared a carriage in the paseo with her before her family lost its money."

"She'll not come to any harm from me. It's more likely harm that would come from Carlos."

"He's not some sort of mad dog—"

"He's a merciless killer. What will he do to her when he no longer needs her? From what I overheard, it's obvious she knows a secret that he never wants to be repeated."

"No harm will come to her as long as he needs her."

"Sí, señorita. And tell me, what need will he have for her after he marries the rich Cruz daughter and gets a fat dowry?"

SEVENTY-NINE

AFTER ALL BUT selected guests had left the marquis's palace, the marquis; the Avila brothers, Alonso and Gil; and a group of ten others settled into comfortable chairs, drank aged brandy, and voiced their anger and grievances about the king's policies in the colony.

Carlos was among the select group that remained behind, and it was a surprise to him that he had been invited both to the ball and then into the private smoking room, the inner sanctum, of the marquis.

As he listened to talk that amounted to sedition against the king, he realized the marquis was gathering influential Spaniards in the colony around him. That was why he had gotten the invitation to the ball when he had expected to once more be treated as an outcast by the high and mighty Cortés family. He was still a man of standing in the colony, due to his famous stud if nothing else, and would be another sword in a fight. But the talk in the room had petrified even a man with dealings as nefarious as his own had been.

Sedition against the king.

As a man of few scruples, the sins and transgressions of others rarely bothered him, but a rebellion against royal authority—a coup in which the viceroy and major peninsulares were seized and many of them murdered—shocked him to the roots of his soul. Not because he had any love for king or country, but because the chances of succeeding were slim and the consequences of failure were shockingly severe.

Rebels weren't hanged—they were tortured to get confessions and then either turned over to the Inquisition to be tortured some more and finally burned at the stake or beheaded. Their property was seized and their families impoverished.

Carlos was skillful in judging others, and, as he looked around the room, he saw no one he would have risked his life for to join in a rebellion against the king.

The Marquis del Valle was not a conqueror or even a warrior. In Carlos's eyes, his brother-in-law completely lacked the abilities that the marquis's father had had in great abundance.

When Cortés's army had its back to the sea while facing tens of thousands of Aztecs and the soldiers decided to abandon the conquest and flee, Cortés had had his own ships burned to stay the men and force them to fight another day.

The present marquis, Carlos thought contemptuously, would have rowed out to the nearest ship, boarded and sailed away, leaving his men to fend for themselves.

The rest of the men in the room were cut from the same cloth as the marquis. All were about the marquis's age or younger, none had commanded in battle or even fought in a war, nor had any of them made a single mark on the world that hadn't been handed to them by family.

But he listened quietly, keeping hidden the contempt he felt as he listened to the grievances of men he considered only above paseo dandies because they were a decade or so older in age.

A major grievance of the group was that all

important governmental and military positions were held by peninsulares from Spain, most of whom had purchased from the Crown their official offices and had come to the colony only for a few years to rob the colonists blind with exorbitant taxes and official fees, then returning home with their fortune made.

Alonso de Avila said, "At our instigation, the city council of Mexico sent the king a letter two years ago asking his majesty not to send another viceroy to rule us. The letter pointed out that, no matter how presentable the viceroy appeared in Madrid, the administrator would come to the colony with an army of friends, relatives, and dependents who would assume offices that rightly belonged to the conquerors and their descendants."

Carlos had not been an administrator and didn't have an encomienda, but he knew that the resentment over the peninsulares' dominance antagonized all criollos, including him. Encomienda owners like the Avilas and Cortéses were especially incensed because the king had been whittling away at their grants, and they were certain that someday the king would nullify them.

"We remind you, your lordship," Alonso said to the marquis, "that your father—and ours—conquered the indio world without help from the king. The king provided no money, no ships, no soldiers, no weapons, not even hay for horses."

He went on to describe that while Hernan Cortés and his backers raised the money for the ships themselves, the common soldiers volunteered and provided their own arms in return for a share of whatever treasure was found.

"It is time we got what our fathers fought for," Gil

said. "And the only way we will get it is to seize the colony."

An uneasy ripple went through the crowd of men, but Carlos realized that this was not the first time the subject had been broached at a gathering between those present. Realizing he had been left out of previous meetings and had only been invited because others had no doubt refused angered him.

"Here is the plan," Alonso said. "We will take control of the colony from the administrators in Madrid. Dividing into groups of swordsmen backed up with horsemen we can trust, we'll first seize the viceroy and his top aides, killing the ones who resist, especially the military commander. He's residing in the city to be close to the social life while his army is spread around the colony, some fighting Chichimecas in the north, others fighting to the south in Zapotec and Maya territories. He also has troops protecting the Vera Cruz and Acapulco roads to the east and west.

"What he doesn't have," Alonso said, triumphantly, "are troops protecting the capital, because it is not endangered from indios or foreign enemies."

The viceroy would be seized at the same time as the military commander, followed by the visitador to keep the king's inspector from taking command.

"Once the viceroy, the visitador, and the military commander have been taken, the rest of the government officials will be confused and helpless," he assured them.

"After we have taken control by killing or capturing the officials," Gil said, "a red cloak would be waved in the Zócalo."

Ayala de Espinosa said he would be in the cathedral

waiting for the signal. "When I see it, I will strike the bells."

The ringing bells would be a signal for conspirators in other parts of the city to kill important peninsulares—wealthy merchants and mine owners who would oppose the takeover—and take their gold.

"Their money will finance the raising of a large army to fight when the king sends troops," Avila said.

Finally a mention of reality, Carlos thought, smothering the urge to make a sound of contempt. And send troops, the king would for a certainty. The Crown was not about to give up its richest colonial possession.

Alonso de Avila offered a toast to their success, and glasses of brandy were raised.

All from the Avilas and nothing from Martín the Younger, Carlos thought, barely keeping his contempt from showing. Big words, the language of braggarts, but where would they find men to fill the shoes of conquerors? he wondered. Not in this group.

"Once we've seized control of the colony, we'll strip the peninsulares of their wealth and ship them back to Spain," Gil de Avila said. "Packed in salt, if they resist."

That got chuckles and cheers.

Carlos noticed that the marquis seemed hesitant. The man loved the attention, the prospect of glory, but the specter of failure was an uninvited guest in the room.

Once the killings were done, the heads of the dead peninsulares would be displayed in the plaza to frighten the rest of the city into submission.

When the smoke—and blood—cleared, the marquis would be declared king.

King. The word made grown men quiver from both the sheer power and majesty of it. Martín the

Younger sat up straighter in his chair when the magic word was spoken. A king was an absolute source of power, answerable only to God. A look from a king can lift one to great heights or completely destroy one.

"As soon as power is in our hands," Gil de Avila said, "we will seize all of the gold and land of the peninsulares."

"And burn the viceroy's records and archives," his brother put in, "so that there will never be a written record of the presence of the peninsulares in our new nation."

"What is the most urgent thing we must do?" an encomienda owner from the Puebla region asked.

A good question, Carlos thought, and one that the silent marquis should answer.

"My brother will lead a force to take possession of Vera Cruz and the fortress at San Juan de Ulúa," Alonso said. "The fleet is anchored in the bay. Before the ships are loaded for the return to Cadiz, we will seize it. The loss of the fleet and its treasure will cripple the Crown for years and provide us with the money to arm a large enough army to fight off any attempt from Madrid to retake the colony."

"They must seize the packet boat, too," another man piped in, referring to the smaller, quicker vessel used to carry correspondence and news between the colony and Spain. "That would delay Spain from getting news of the revolt."

Avila looked around for a moment and then turned to the marquis. "I see that your brother is not present. Has he decided not to join us?"

Carlos noted the polite tone and lack of the use of the nickname El Mestizo when addressing the marquis about his brother.

"My brother is a man who loves his horses and

desires to stay out of politics and even social events. He is also one of caution. He believes the colony is difficult to rule because it is so large and spread out and he fears that the indios will rise against us if Spanish troops are no longer a threat."

"That's unfortunate," Alonso said. "We wanted him to lead a force to the north to take control of the silver mines in Zacatecas and Guanajuato. There are many mestizos in the region, and they would rally to him."

Carlos closed his eyes for a moment to keep his composure as he reflected on Alonso de Avila's remark. Did they think that just anyone could lead an army in battle? El Mestizo had neither the fighting experience nor the temperament to lead men in battle. The same was true of everyone else in the room, including Gil de Avila, who, they appeared to believe in their grand scheme, could simply ride to Vera Cruz with a host of volunteers and take charge.

Seizing the governor's palace in Vera Cruz would not be that difficult if it was done without warning, Carlos thought, but taking the fort, which had thick walls and cannons manned by professional soldiers on an island offshore, and the fleet, anchored in the bay because ships drew too much water to reach a dock at the city, would take planning and an army trained not with dueling pistolas and paseo ponies but cannons, muskets, boats, and knowledge of sea battles.

"My brother is loyal to me," the marquis said. "If I ever gave him the call, he would be there beside me."

If.

Use of the tiny word carried enormous meaning to Carlos. *The marquis was hedging,* he thought, *listening but not making an actual commitment.*

Alonso de Avila picked up on it, too. "Noble sir, your father was your age when he set forth to conquer a new world. I know how it must offend you that you are barred from achieving the greatness on the field of power and holding the reins of power you so deserve."

"The king keeps you from power and glory," Gil said, "because he knows that if he doesn't, the entire colony will raise you on their shoulders and proclaim you their ruler. The king, as we all know, also covets your vast estates."

A point that got the marquis's attention, Carlos thought. The marquis earned a kingly amount from his vast encomienda holdings, a fortune that could be wiped out by a blink from the monarch.

"You are the first man of the Americas," Alonso said, "but until you lead an army or a government, your place in history will not be etched."

"You have your father's blood," another said, "we know that, and we will not hesitate to follow your lead in battle."

"My oldest son is in Seville for schooling," the marquis said.

That brought a pause in the room.

"As soon as we seize the fleet, we will send an emissary to Seville to bring your son back from Spain."

Alonso de Avila looked around the room at the men who had been assembled and then spoke to the marquis. "Once the colony is in our hands and you wear the crown, I am certain that you would give generous grants of lands and indios to those who supported you."

"And titles of nobility," the marquis said. "Including one for you . . . Duke Avila."

Alonso de Avila giggled like a little girl.

Fools, Carlos thought. Children playing the game of giants. It occurred to him that there were thirteen people in the room.

Not an auspicious number for a revolt.

EIGHTY

MERCEDES TOLD ME during our carriage rendezvous after the ball that her father was planning to make arrangements with Carlos for the dowry as soon as he returned from conducting business in Vera Cruz.

My first instinct was to kill the bastardo rather than spend any time in what El Mestizo believed to be a useless effort, but getting him alone would be a problem. Besides, each time I casually suggested Carlos should get justice at my hands, Mercedes threatened to make the next scar she left on me run from head to foot.

That put me back to finding out the secret Carlos and the seamstress shared about his prize stallion. Nina was a popular name, and I had to make sure that the woman Mercedes believed was Carlos's lover was the woman I had seen in Oaxaca.

Mercedes came up with a ruse that would permit me to get a look at the woman.

I sat at an outside table at a tavern across the street from the woman's shop and drank good Spanish beer and smoked a twist of tobacco while I watched Mercedes get out of her carriage and go into the shop.

Half an hour later Mercedes came out of the shop with a woman to examine a piece of fabric in full daylight.

It was the woman; I was reasonably sure. I would

be positive if she would take off her clothes and let me touch her body, no?

Now that I knew who and where she was, I had to come up with a plan to get her to reveal Carlos's secret. She was a woman in love. It would take more than Mercedes and me telling her that Carlos was a bad person to get her to turn on him.

Someone even more intuitive about human nature and underhanded than I am was needed. And I had the perfect person in mind.

I was musing over how to bring my clever notion into play when I heard excited people on the street spreading shocking news.

A plot by criollos to seize power over the colony was discovered and arrests were being made.

El Mestizo had been arrested.

EIGHTY-ONE

A DARK PALL covered the city like a cover over a coffin. I didn't see this in the sky, but in the fear and darkness on people's faces and in their eyes. One report of arrest, quick torture, and confessions quickly followed another. Only days passed before the first arrest and the executioner's block was bloodied. And it remained bloody.

Rumors spread like wildfire, but I was able to gauge that talk of insurrection by brothers named Avila had been going on for months and that the royal visitador had had a secret mission of finding out whether the rumors were true. Convinced that they were, he set into motion Crown officers who had been prepared to round up the suspects. The tongues of those arrested flapped as the screws were tightened on the rack and more arrests were made.

Some of those arrested were among the largest encomienda holders in the colony. However, the Marquis del Valle was not arrested. He was briefly questioned, but not kept in custody.

I dropped by the government center to ask the viceroy's aide that my inheritance be released and to get information about El Mestizo. His retort on my money was quick and ruthless.

"All large transactions in gold, silver, and anything else of value have been forbidden by the visitador to keep rebels and their families from hiding money.

However, I will get to work on getting your money released mañana."

Mañana meant tomorrow morning . . . or some indefinite time whenever he got around to it. In other words, it would be a cold day in hell before I saw my fortune.

Riego was reluctant and nervous about discussing the arrests, but that made him an even better source of information, because things flew off his tongue that no one else but the royal visitador, the viceroy, and God in the heavens knew.

"The marquis is not cleared yet," the aide whispered. "They are torturing El Mestizo to get him to confess that his brother was involved in the plot."

"None of the plotters have named the marquis?"

"So many names have rolled off the tongues of rebels on the rack that half the city would have to be arrested. His name is too honored to be listed as a plotter unless—"

He stopped, and I finished his remark. "Unless someone with the same name states his guilt."

I already knew that El Mestizo was not involved in the plot and that he feared the stupidity of his brother and his amigos who staged the marquis being "crowned" as ruler of the colony in front of the royal visitador.

My gut twisted at the thought of him being tortured. Ultimately, he would confess, of course; not even the strongest or the bravest could resist long the hot pinchers that a torturer used to rip off flesh bit by bit.

"Such foolishness," the aide said, shaking his head. "No action was ever actually taken by any of the schemers to carry off the plot. It reminds me of schoolboys plotting against the headmaster. Personally I believe the rebellion was nothing but talk, but one must not state such an opinion. It was time to sweep some dirt out of the colony."

Riego told me that an administrator, Alonzo Muñoz, had been named special representative of the king to handle the conspiracy.

"Muñoz has been given absolute power to deal with the conspirators."

The aide spoke with an edge of apprehension in his voice, as if he might be the next one dragged out of his house in the middle of the night to find his next bed a torturer's rack. And he had good cause to worry, because no one was safe from Muñoz's tentacles, perhaps not even the viceroy.

I pretended to have heard about Munoz for the first time, but his name was spoken many times in taverns, almost always in a whisper and with fear.

I could have told the aide that if he wanted more information about what was happening in the city, he should spend a night visiting taverns and inns.

Muñoz had quickly gotten a reputation for capricious cruelty as he began a reign of terror against anyone even remotely connected to the plot.

A person of little importance one moment, Muñoz was suddenly flush with power when the investigation was turned over to him, and he proved himself to be arrogant, haughty, and cruel. Surrounding himself with toadies, and parading through the streets with his coach surrounded by heavily armed shield bearers, he acted as if he were a prince of the realm instead of an administrator.

Muñoz treated those under him with contempt and considered even the highest-ranking peninsulares in the colony beneath him—which no doubt was the source of the aide's apprehension when he spoke about the man.

People knew Muñoz's mission was not to get to the truth but to break the spirit of any possible criollo sympathy or rebellious spirit, to ensure that no criollo would ever again think of plotting against the Crown.

Even after arresting and punishing conspirators, Muñoz continued a witch hunt, filling the jails and dungeons with men who knew nothing about the plot but who might have been sympathizers or merely at some time have complained about the way the colony was administered from Madrid.

Someone had informed on the conspirators, but no one in the city was safe—innocent people were being arrested and tortured, property was seized, and word spread that most arrests were made because the Crown officers earned a percentage of everything they seized rather than the strength of the evidence against the accused.

The Avila brothers, Alonso and Gil, were arrested along with others, Riego told me. They were quickly tortured and beheaded, and their property seized.

"But for the grace of God our land would have ended up in the hands of these worthless dogs," I told the aide. "The man who revealed the treason deserves all of our gratitude. May I have his name so I might light a candle in church and ask God to reward him?"

"The name is a state secret," the aide said.

EIGHTY-TWO

"CARLOS INFORMED ON the marquis and the rest of them," Mercedes told me.

We were back at the convent, with the viceroy's carriage outside by hers and his guards eating and playing dice. At the collection box I put a gold coin in without objection this time. Then I put in another. The way things were going in the colony, I might need some divine intervention just to stay alive.

"He told you that?"

"Not in so many words, but he gloated about the arrests and said that the money woes others were having had filled his coffers."

"Filled them with blood money. I should have known; he was at the ball that night. I've heard that a group of them stayed behind and talked insurrection. He must have sat there calculating how much he could get for turning them in."

She crossed herself. "I won't go to the paseo with my friends because I don't know which one of them will next tell me that their father or brother has been seized and they will lose everything."

In truth, I had no sympathy for the criollos and didn't care what their fate was, except for Mercedes and her family.

"I have more news from my lunch with Carlos and his sister," she said. "El Mestizo has been turned over to the Inquisition because the viceroy's torturer was unable to get him to implicate his brother in the conspiracy."

She made the sign of the cross again and so did I. We both knew what it meant. I felt as if I had been kicked in the stomach.

"The Inquisitor torturers are seasoned brutes who are brought in from Spain," I said. "They never fail to break a person. Even the few that do not confess are so broken in bone and spirit they don't live long afterwards."

She touched my face with her fingers. "You frighten me. You look hurt, yet there is a savageness, as if there is a smoldering murderous rage beneath the pain."

"The pain is for El Mestizo. He saved my life—eh, he *made my life* bearable when he lifted me from the gutter. And the rage is for Carlos. He won't die quickly, I can assure you of that."

"Punishment is for God to provide."

"Exactly. I'll have my sword wetted with holy water before I chop the bastardo's nose, ears, and cojones off."

"Besides torture and murder, do you have any other plan for bringing Carlos to justice? I think we should explain to Nina Alvarez exactly what Carlos has done."

I shook my head. "She's in love. You would never convince her that he was a murderer even if you had witnessed him kill. The only way to break the spell is to make her believe he has betrayed her love."

"He's going to marry me rather than her, isn't that betrayal enough?"

"No, señorita, he's doing it for money. That's something she understands. She knows how far one falls when there's no money. The way to turn her against him is jealousy, but it can't be of you." I grinned. "However, I know a woman who might be able to help us."

"How *well* do you know this woman?"

"Not in the biblical sense, my love, but enough to know she is a better liar and actor than a practiced lépero like myself."

Mercedes held her face in her hands. I thought for a moment she was going to cry.

"Insane, that's what life in the city has become," she said. "It's as if the world was suddenly struck by a plague of madness. Murder of people I know by a man I might be forced to marry, acquaintances arrested and tortured as rebels when they knew nothing of the plot, even my own father could be arrested for no other reason than this Muñoz creature wants his money. It's unbearable to even think about what is happening."

"Eh, I, too, could be arrested for my money," I boasted.

"No, you forget—you are a peninsulare."

"I HAVE SPOKEN THE TRUTH."

El Mestizo's father had conquered the country for Spain, and the mother [Doña Marina] had been his most devoted friend and helper; and here now was the son, stretched on a bed of mortal agony, because to his grizzly judge at the trial he would divulge nothing of the secrets of his confederates, were any such secrets in his keeping.

Happy invention! that of water and cord, as administered at the hands of Pero Baca and Juan Navarro, by order of Muñoz. It does not add to the merits of the case to know that Martín was convalescing from serious illness.

"I have spoken the truth and have nothing further to add," Martín said, as they stripped him and laid him on the rack. Being again urged to speak the truth, he replied, "It is spoken."

The executioners then proceeded to bind with cords the fleshy parts of the arms, thighs, calves, and large toes, and gradually to tighten them all at once.

"Speak the truth," they said.

"It is spoken," was ever the reply.

Six times they poured a quart of water down his throat, demanding each time a truthful declaration.

—Hubert Howe Bancroft, *History of Mexico,* 1885

EIGHTY-THREE

"KILL ME IF you will; I can tell you nothing more. You already have the truth."

The priest, Fray Dominic, stared in disbelief at El Mestizo. It was not just the words that the half-caste son of Cortés spoke, but the fact that he still had the strength to speak them. He had been ill when the torture started days ago, and it was amazing that he had the strength to keep talking.

The fray did not use his hands on El Mestizo or apply any of the torture himself. As a priest, he was not permitted to personally draw blood or elicit pain from a person. But that did not prevent him from assisting in other ways.

His first duty, as a servant of God and the Inquisition, was to guide the two lay torturers, Pero Baca and Juan Navarro, by instructing them on which persuasions to apply to the person being put to the question.

His second obligation was to listen to the person being put to the question and write down the confession. And when the subject was not going to survive the abuse, his final duty was to give the last rites, often hurriedly as the tortured man's breathing became gasps, his eyes still bulging from the pain.

El Mestizo had been asked repeatedly to confess that both he and his brother, the marquis, were involved in the conspiracy with the Avila brothers and others to seize control of the colony.

His refusal to admit to the crime led the fray to instruct his two assistants to begin the persuasion with the cord.

El Mestizo had been strapped down on a wood table that was slightly tilted so that his feet were a little higher than his head. Cords were put around his arms and legs and tied to pieces of wood. The wood pieces were twisted, slowly, tighter and tighter, until they worked their way through skin and flesh and then against bone.

The pain was unbearable to most, but for the few who suffered through it and refused to confess, as El Mestizo did—no doubt empowered by their master, el diablo—water was added.

A short, hollow piece of iron cut from a musket barrel was placed in El Mestizo's mouth and stopped just short of gagging him. A little gauze was put in the pipe and water poured in. The thin fragment of cloth permitted the water to flow into El Mestizo's throat slowly, drowning him a drop at a time.

When it appeared El Mestizo was close to the edge of passing out or even dying, the water was stopped.

The fray found it interesting that the man had endured the torture so well. He attributed El Mestizo's ability to resist to the fact that the man had tainted blood, even though his father was the great conqueror. No doubt the indio blood gave him endurance and also brought el diablo to his aid.

Fray Dominic reflected on the fact that El Mestizo was the eldest son of the conqueror yet had been denied the title and inheritance because of his tainted blood. While that was just and right in the eyes of the Crown and the church, it obviously would not endear El Mestizo to his brother.

Based on his knowledge of human nature and the

baser traits of men, he changed the question: "Confess that your brother Martín the Younger, Marquis del Valle de Oaxaca, inheritor of your father's title and estates that should rightfully have gone to you as the eldest son, plotted against the grace and majesty of our beloved king."

"You have the truth and nothing more," was the reply.

Fray Dominic's favorite torture device was the most subtle. It was an iron statue of the Virgin Mary that had arms extended and sharp spikes on a chest plate.

The victim was placed just inside the jointed arms, and a crank was turned that caused the arms to close, bringing the person closer and closer to the spikes. When a victim felt the sharp points against his chest, he was put to the question.

But the fray realized El Mestizo might welcome the escape into death provided by a blade through his heart.

Mulling it over, the fray decided it was time to increase the pain even though that carried a serious risk of death. Two other procedures were available to get the man to confess to his brother's transgression: the Strappado would be applied by tying El Mestizo's wrists together behind him with a rope while he was standing on the rack. The other end of the rope was tied to a rafter above him, without enough length to permit El Mestizo to reach the floor. Pushed off the rack, his shoulders would break before he hit the floor.

Then he would be laid back on the rack and his bones manipulated to create excruciating pain until he gave the answers the fray wanted.

The fray knew from experience that at this stage answers sometimes didn't come because the pain would be so intense and mindless babble would escape from the person being tortured.

After the Strappado, it would be a while before the torturers would be able to apply the second extreme method—the Péndulo, a curved blade that swung like a pendulum at the victim. The blade was razor-sharp and would be lowered a tiny bit with every swing, slicing a little more, working its way slowly through flesh and bone over a period of hours until it reached the heart—or the question was answered to the satisfaction of the priest.

Fray Dominic did not have the authority to implement either the Strappado or the Péndulo without the express permission of the archbishop because both procedures brought death more inevitably than the cord and water methods.

Even with his tainted blood, El Mestizo was a person of importance in the colony.

That was unfortunate because Fray Dominic didn't believe that a person's position in life should interfere with God's work.

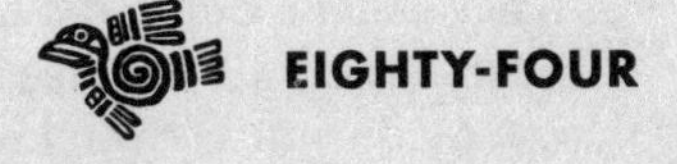

EIGHTY-FOUR

DIEGO STOPPED AT an army outpost on the Vera Cruz road east of Xalapa. He had first stopped at every pulqueria and tavern on the road and in Xalapa, asking bartenders about a bandido with an exceptional horse. As a vaquero, Diego remembered as much about the masked man's mount as the man himself. He recalled that the highwayman was lighter skinned than an indio, making him a mestizo or even Spanish.

Having no luck, he stopped at the military garrison that was the headquarters for the entire bandido-infested road from Vera Cruz to Xalapa.

He spoke to an officer as they walked down a line of eight thieves chained by the ankle to individual posts, waiting for their turn on the gallows that had been set up in back of the main building.

"Hanging 'em all today?"

"No, we do only a couple a day so we don't have to dig so many graves at one time."

"I'm looking for a mestizo or Spanish robber," Diego said, "who rides a fine horse, one you'd never expect a bandido to have."

"Never heard of him," the officer said, walking away.

"I know him."

The statement came from a prisoner boiling in the sun while waiting for the hangman.

Diego stared down at him. "You lie to me, you filthy swine, and you'll go to the gallows with your cojones stuffed in your mouth. What's your name?"

"They call me Cerdo the Lépero."

Diego fanned air with his hand. "I can understand that. Why do you say you know this man?"

"He had a big horse, bigger than any horse I'd ever seen, a chestnut but more red than brown."

That jolted Diego. "That's him. What his name?"

"Juan the Lépero."

"Where do I find him?"

"I don't know, señor, I haven't seen him in two years, three years, maybe more."

"You still hear about him on the road?"

"No, señor, nothing since he stole my money and my own fine horse. Maybe he's dead now." Cerdo made the sign of the cross. "In hell, I hope."

Diego turned to walk away, and Cerdo whined behind him.

"I helped you—buy me from the hangman!"

"*Vaya con el diablo*, you stinking swine. Hopefully you'll meet your amigo with the big horse there."

Diego set back on the road to Vera Cruz, to return to the location where he had arranged the ambush. He wasn't a particularly bright man, more doggedly determined when told to do something than inventive, but his gut was telling him something was wrong. He was trying to fit all the pieces together and so far had not been able to do so.

It took him most of the day to reach the spot along the road where he had stayed on his horse and observed the attack.

He ran it through his head again: Antonio de los Rios jumping from the coach and running toward the cliff, a masked man suddenly appearing, attacking his assassins with deadly accuracy while the gachupin went over the cliff, probably carrying a pistola ball in his body.

Diego led his horse down to the spot where he was certain that the Spaniard had gone over. There was no ledge. And it was a long, sheer drop to the rocky river below.

Could a man have survived such a fall? Yes, if he plunged feetfirst into the pool of water directly below, missing the rocks. But even if he had hit the water and survived, it raised another question.

How did he get back up to the carriage, where he was when the army patrol found him?

It wasn't possible to climb back up at the location he had fallen over because it was a cliff, though there were other places that a man could use to get back up to the road. But it would take some time.

The notion that the bandido who had intervened could be posing as Rios had not occurred to Diego; for a thief to pass himself off as a wealthy gachupin was too bizarre for Diego to conceive. He was too much a creature of a highly structured society to think that a common highwayman and a gachupin could be the same person.

He headed back up the road in the direction of the capital, with a question to ask a condemned man. He wanted to ask Cerdo the Lépero what his amigo with the chestnut stallion looked like.

As Diego headed back in the direction of Xalapa, a man crawled out of the bushes farther down the road from where Rios had originally gone over the cliff.

His clothes were filthy, ragged, and bloodied from his climb up the slope. He got himself onto his feet with a cry of pain and a branch he used as a crutch and shouted at the mounted man as loud as he could.

Diego heard the shouting behind him and turned in the saddle, glancing back, and then around, suspecting the man was a decoy in an ambush.

He didn't see anyone else but left in a full gallop, sure that it was a trap set by bandidos. Even if it wasn't, Diego wouldn't have helped the man anyway—he was obviously a filthy lépero.

Behind him, eating his dust, Antonio de los Rios fell to his knees and wept with his head hung over.

He was still on his knees when a mule train carrying goods from Vera Cruz came up the road behind him.

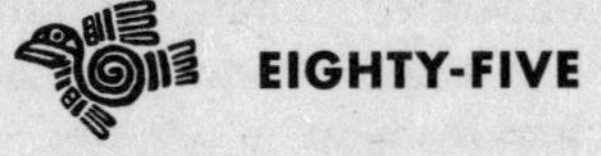

EIGHTY-FIVE

"HE WAS HANGED an hour ago," the officer at the outpost jail told Diego when he asked to see Cerdo. "The other prisoners begged us to do it because he stunk so bad."

Grumbling at his own carelessness at not having questioned the lépero, and knowing that he would taste the whip if he told Carlos of his negligence, he went looking for the officer, Capitán Lopez, who led the patrol that found Rios after the attack.

He found him at the post cantina. He bought the man a bottle of cheap wine and asked about the incident, giving the officer a piece of eight rather than an explanation as to why he was asking questions.

"Were Rios's clothes wet? Dirty from a climb up the hill? Was he injured from a fall into the river?"

All the answers were no.

"And you never saw a man with a big chestnut stallion, more red than brown?"

"Only Señor Rios."

"Señor Rios? He has a chestnut?"

"A fine animal, one of the biggest stallions I've seen. And as red a coat as I've seen. The stallion had been hitched to the carriage for the journey from Vera Cruz." Capitán Lopez stared at Diego. "Señor, you look as if you've seen a ghost."

Diego mumbled something and left the cantina, once again cursing himself for his stupidity. He remembered something Carlos had said about Antonio the day Carlos had gone to welcome the heir to the city. Carlos told Diego that Rios had not only cheated him out of the inheritance, but that he couldn't even sell him a horse because he had brought a good one with him from Spain.

He hadn't thought about it at the time, but now it struck him: there was no horse hitched to the carriage at the time his assassins attacked. And while Diego was a bit dense when it came to people, he knew horseflesh. The bandido who intervened had had a chestnut stallion—and there was no possibility that there were two outstanding chestnut stallions on the road that day.

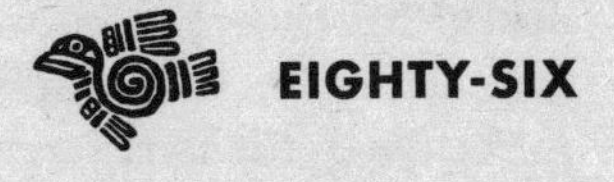

EIGHTY-SIX

WHEN THE COUNTESS Isabella opened the door to her room at the inn, she stared down the barrel of the pistola I was holding.

"Buenos días, Countess, come in, come in," I said, pulling her in and pushing the door shut behind her, "we have much to talk about."

She shook her head sadly. "You again. Frankly, you have become something of a bore. If they hanged you, my life would be so much simpler." She smiled sweetly. "Yours, too."

A blade popped out of her right sleeve and she shoved it in my gut. It stuck there. We both looked down at it.

I grabbed her wrist, twisting it, bringing the blade out, then removed the strap holding the spring weapon from where it was tied on just above the wrist.

"Strong stomach," she said.

I grunted as I looked at the deadly little blade. She certainly knew how to go for the gold. I had sold gold candlesticks and some swords of Uncle Ramos's for gold coins to use when—not if—I had to leave the city in a hurry. She had stabbed the treasure belt I had tied around my waist.

I hit her with my open palm, sending her careening to the bed. It wasn't a hard slap, just enough to sting.

"That was to get your attention."

"Bastardo!"

"Countess, did you know how mean it is to gut a man? If you cut my throat, I'd die quickly. But to die slowly from a gut wound? From a blade up your sleeve? Mi Dios, I've known bandidos twice your size who are less vicious than you are."

"Leave or I'll start screaming."

I tossed her a ruby broach I'd taken from Ramos's jewel box.

She looked at the piece of jewelry and then examined me with the eye of a cunning fox. One with sharp teeth.

"The clothes of a gentleman," she said. "Soft leather boots, the best pistola, a sword with a Toledo blade. Hmmm. Señor, you are getting more interesting all the time."

"I see you're warming to my charm."

"Truthfully, I would like to win your heart—so I can slice it into little pieces. Do you know what you cost me?"

"*What I cost you?*" I struggled to keep my composure and didn't manage it. "You robbed me of the money I had saved to buy a ranchero."

"Money you had stolen. The Vera Cruz governor took all the money I had collected on the way over and in that little miserable town, just because you beat up his nephew."

"Cousin."

"Whatever. I didn't need your help, you country bumpkin. If I hadn't convinced the governor of my innocence—"

"Convinced him while lying on your back with your legs spread."

She shook her head with regret. "You are becoming a bore. What is it you want in return for this little trinket?"

I held up an even bigger broach, this one with a ruby surrounded with pearls. It got her attention.

"Help me out, you get this one, too."

"And if I don't?"

"You get this." I held up my pistola.

"Tell me what you want. And how you got the fancy clothes and weapons."

I gave her a more or less truthful account of why I wanted to bring Carlos down because of his murderous schemes, who Nina was, and how I needed her to convince Nina to reveal Carlos's scheme.

"She needs to know her love has been betrayed."

"And how am I to do this? Order a dress from the woman and say, oh, please betray your lover to me while you're hemming my dress?"

"I leave that entirely to your devious tongue. I'm sure you have talked men out of their pants on two continents and can manage to create a betrayal by a lovesick woman."

"So, if I help you and you keep this inheritance you spoke of . . . you will be grateful to me, no?"

"Eternally."

She didn't have to tell me she would blackmail me for a piece of my inheritance the moment I was solidly in the saddle. I knew that already. And I didn't have to tell her that I wasn't planning to stick around to be blackmailed by her or hanged by the viceroy, whichever came first.

EIGHTY-SEVEN

"I'M DOOMED," I told Mercedes when I met her the morning after enlisting the countess. "This came last night."

I gave her the letter I'd received. It was a message that the uncle from Guadalajara was coming for a visit. I didn't tell her that I had the majordomo read it to me.

"The message is two weeks old," she said. "Our ridiculous royal post works so well, people arrive before their missives. He could already be in the city."

"I don't even know what he looks like, or I'd waylay him and cut his throat."

Mercedes crossed herself. She had been doing that a lot since I came into her life.

"I don't like it when you talk that way. You must give up your old ways and learn to live in civilized society."

"Civilized society? Have you looked around lately? Innocent people are being grabbed off the streets and tortured—and this is how a civilized society acts?"

She brushed away my question with a wave of her hand. "The message says he's going to stay with Carlos."

"He could be there by now, Carlos and him talking to the constables or on the way to my house with that Muñoz demon."

"You must leave the city."

I shook my head. "Not until El Mestizo is released. I went to the bishop in charge of the Inquisition here in the colony this morning. I let him know I would be very generous with the church if El Mestizo was released."

"What did he say?"

"That only a higher authority could grant such a request. And he didn't mean God. That leaves Muñoz, who would rip off his mother's fingernails if it would get him praise, and the viceroy, who would have to justify the release to the king. The Inquisitor looked at me as if I was next on the rack and told me that I should show my faith with the donation anyway."

"What are you going to do? And I hesitate to ask you that question because whatever your plan is, I'm sure it will violate the laws of God and the king."

El diablo, too. It was a good question, although I needed more than a plan—I needed a miracle.

"The countess and I are paying a visit to Nina Alvarez this morning," I said. "Even if I find out Carlos's secret, I'll be on the run from now on because I won't be able to fool the uncle unless he is blind and deaf." Or dead, I added silently to myself. I didn't mention that I had packed a few things from the house and had two mules loaded and ready to go at a stable on the other side of the causeway.

"On the run," she repeated.

"I'll head north. That's where men go who have the kind of problems I have. There's new territory being opened up and settled, and a person can breathe without some royal administrator or encomienda owner breathing down his neck. No one looks at your pedigree, because they need every man and woman they can get. And they need horses, ones I'll provide."

"I'm going with you."

"Never. You cannot become a fugitive. Even if no one bothered pursuing me because they had Carlos's crimes to deal with, it's a rough life, not one for a woman whose hands have never been dirtied."

"My hands are as strong as any other woman's, and I can stick them in mud just fine. Let me tell you something, Antonio, Juan, or whatever name you are using at the moment: I am utterly disgusted with the life I have here, where, even if Carlos is no longer a threat, I will be married off to a man I don't love and spend the rest of my life wavering between utter boredom and quiet desperation."

I couldn't see Mercedes in "quiet" desperation.

"I want to go to a place where I can read a book without shocking everyone around me, where I can ride a horse and do other things that men find pleasure in but are forbidden to women."

Ayyo! I had a female rebel on my hands.

I gave her a hug, pulling her close to me to feel her warmth and strength. "Two things I must do before I leave. Get El Mestizo free. And I have to see that Carlos has a rope placed around his neck. I may not survive either task."

"I'll help you. I'm having lunch at Carlos's again today with his sister. I'll find out what I can."

EIGHTY-EIGHT

I PRETENDED TO be Countess Isabella's bored, arrogant dandy of a brother, sitting in a chair and smoking a tobacco twist while she selected the fabric and talked about the style of the dress . . . "One to be worn during my pregnancy," she told Nina Alvarez.

The seamstress had been curious about Isabella Ramirez—she left off the countess title, of course. In the chatter that went on during the selection of materials and fitting, the countess made her moves against the other woman like a master swordsman, using her words and gestures to slowly cut and then widen the wounds.

Isabella began by getting Nina's sympathy, revealing that her family had once been wealthy, "Really Puebla aristocrats, financially at least, but I felt abandoned by my own friends when my father lost his fortune."

I could see that Nina was sucking it in, barely restraining herself from telling her own life story.

The countess went on to tell her that after the fortune was lost, she ended up being promised in marriage to a very old man who bailed her father out of debtor's prison.

"Fortunately, he died—my betrothed," she said, "unfortunately, before the wedding vows had been uttered."

The two women got a laugh out of that one, and I smiled and continued to look around, hoping to appear to be a worthless brother who had been unable to renew the family fortunes while my sister sold her body to an old man.

Nina finally shared with Isabella her own background as a privileged girl who turned to sewing for the rich after her family fortune was lost. "But it's been a good life," she said, "and an honest one, but lonely."

"I was lonely, too, but a wonderful man who became my lover changed everything," Isabella said.

Isabella went on to describe how her lover had been in terrible financial straits and that she had helped him.

"I did a terrible thing," Isabella said, pretending to be embarrassed. "I flirted with a silver-mine manager who was deep into his cups and got him to reveal that a new discovery had been made. My lover was able to buy a share, and now he is financially secure again." The countess blinked her eyes demurely. "You think I'm terrible, don't you?"

"Not at all, how marvelous of you," Nina said. "And you must not be embarrassed by what you did. I will confess to you and to God that I have done even worse and feel that I have not committed a mortal sin because I did it for love of a good man."

I choked on my tobacco twist at hearing her call Carlos a good man.

Isabella pretended to feel faint and had to sit down while Nina got her cool water. Isabella gave me a small smile, full of menace. "Your gold chain—give it to me or I'll walk out now."

What a scheming, greedy bitch! She strips me of my hard-earned wealth even as she plays another woman for the fool.

I quickly slipped off the chain and gave it to her.

I bit hard on the tobacco, getting bitter juice. If I had had the countess as a bandido partner, I'd own a hacienda by now. But wait—no, I was wrong. More likely I would be buried in an unmarked grave and *she* would own the hacienda.

Isabella now had Nina's complete sympathy. They sat together and whispered while I pretended I didn't hear what was being said.

"I'm worried about you," Nina told the countess. "You carry your lover's baby, but he may not honor his commitments to you now that he has used you to get the information he wanted."

"No, Carlos would never do that."

The name gave Nina a little start, just a blink, but the name was a common one.

"In fact, Carlos had been pursuing the dowry of a rich young woman here in the city because he was so desperate for money, but he will no longer go through with that plan. Just today he arranged for my father's release from prison so our wedding can be announced. I do feel sorry for the young woman being rejected, but I'm sure Mercedes de la Cruz will find another to wed."

My stomach wrenched as I saw Nina Alvarez first appear stunned and then begin to unravel as Isabella slashed her with lies about how Carlos treated her with respect and reverence despite their difference in social class.

"He'll marry me even though I'm the daughter of a failed merchant and without a dowry because he truly loves me. He says I am the only woman he has ever loved, that he never loved his wife or a merchant woman who had done small favors for him over the years."

"No!" Nina was shaking, ready to collapse.

"Is something the matter?" Isabella asked with sickening sweetness.

I sat, mortified, my head turned away, unable to watch, fighting the urge to jump up and stop the torture. I reconciled my conscience thinking about El Mestizo being tortured in the Inquisition dungeon and how much murder and betrayal had come from Carlos because, with Nina's help, he had been able to maintain a fraud for years.

"I'm the one!" Nina said, "I'm the merchant woman he's casting off."

It was my turn, and I jumped into it without enthusiasm.

"Carlos is an unequaled caballero," I said. "Why, the man owns the finest stallion in all the world, in the bloodline of the conqueror's warhorse itself, said to be the fastest horse in the colony. He sold me—"

"A fraud!" she shouted, almost in hysteria. "The great stud died years ago, and I have sewn a chest patch for the stallion that looks like the true one."

She grew quiet for a moment, looking at me, then at Isabella, realizing from our cold countenances that neither of us was any longer caught up in emotion about Carlos.

"Why are you doing this?" she asked, quietly.

"You owe us a favor, Nina," I said. "You've been played for a fool. It's time you started looking for a man who would truly love you, instead of one who just wants to use you."

EIGHTY-NINE

MERCEDES SMILED POLITELY and sipped her chocolate drink made with ground cacao beans and peppers as Tía Beatriz and Carlos's older sister smoked stinking tobacco twists and gossiped about other women in the colony.

She hated every moment of these chatty gossip events. She even found going to balls a bore. The closest she had come to enjoying the city's social life were carriage rides in the paseo, and that was mostly because they got her out of the house and into nature.

If she could, she would have spent all of her free time outdoors—around exciting people like Juan rather than people who take delight in picking apart the character or woes of others or spend their lives concerned with what they should wear to the next ball.

With the two older women engrossed in their petty gossip, she slipped away to walk in the garden.

Juan was never far from her thoughts, and he dominated her mind now. Love was not supposed to be part of the equation for a young woman of her class. That was a fact of life that her father had recently been reminding her of. For those of her class, a marriage was arranged based upon financial considerations.

After marriage, a woman would bear children and take care of the home, while her husband dominated every aspect of their lives. Because wedlock was not based upon love, it was considered permissible for a man to have affairs and even to have children outside the marriage, as long as he did not legally "recognize" them as his, thus making them heirs.

A woman having an affair was considered a great sin both to the husband and to God.

When Mercedes mentioned such inequalities to her paseo girlfriends, they howled with laughter at her ridiculous notions that there should be more opportunities for a woman in life other than being chained to the house in marriage or a convent.

Expressing these thoughts to her father and aunt had caused both of them to turn red and appear ready to suffer apoplexy.

Juan, though, seemed to lack any preconceived notion that a woman wasn't permitted to enjoy life outside the strict confines of the house. She wondered if it was because he had not been raised in a home with a family and a set of social rules.

Whatever the reason, his attitude was attractive to her—as was everything else about him, from the top of his head down to his feet.

Mercedes had been admiring a bougainvillea plant clinging to a wall next to the open doors of Carlos's smoking room when she heard excited voices inside.

"This is not Antonio—the portrait looks nothing like him," Carlos said.

"Nonsense, I had the portrait of him and his family commissioned when I was in Madrid. Señor, I certainly know my own nephew."

"But—but uncle—"

She heard Carlos gasp.

"*We have been duped!*" Carlos shouted.

* * *

A few minutes later Mercedes's aunt and Carlos's sister looked up from their revelry of rumor and innuendo as Carlos stormed up to them, red in the face and shaking with excitement.

"Where's Mercedes?"

"Why . . . I don't know, dear," his sister said, "she was here a moment ago."

"She left in her carriage, señor," a servant said.

THE HORSE WAS EVERYTHING

The horse was an essential element of colonial life in New Spain. Its blood lines were always traced back to the fourteen famous horses in the Conquest . . .

To go about on the same level with the commoners, to court the ladies on foot, or even to affirm his lineage were all equally thinkable . . .

The horse was everything. Mounted on one, a gentleman could take part in jousting and catching the ring, he could find his rank in the cavalcades and in the retinue of the powerful, he could travel and pay visits . . .

—Fernando Benítez, *The Century After Cortés*

NINETY

THOUGHTS ABOUT THE magnitude of the fraud Carlos pulled off for years crowded my thoughts as the countess and I left the seamstress shop. A small white patch on a horse's chest and keeping the horse from close observation had kept Carlos in rich stud fees—and brought into question the royal bloodline of thousands of horses throughout the colony, with the scandal even reaching to Europe.

Meticulous records of the bloodline of a colonial family's valuable horses were as carefully maintained as the lineage of the family. For many families, even wealthy ones, horses ranked among their most prized and valuable assets. The colony was a land of caballeros, and horses were the pride and joy of them all.

The viceroy would have to answer not only to the king, whose own stables included horses of the conquest bloodline, but also to the thousands of caballeros in the colony who bought, sold, and mated horses based on the fraud.

The countess interrupted my thoughts with a cold splash of greed and avarice.

"I'll have my things sent over from the inn as soon as I get back there," she said.

I knew exactly what she was talking about, but I pretended to be dense about it, which was not difficult for me. "Sent over?"

"To our house, of course."

"*Our* house? Are we going to be married, countess?"

"Not yet." She got close, within kissing distance. "We'll have to wait to see how things turn out with you as Antonio first before we make a decision like that. In the meantime, we will take everything of value from the house and even sell it while we wait for the viceroy to release your inheritance."

"I must concede to a wiser and more clever plan than anything I could have come up with. You have everything planned out."

"It was foolish of you to have thought otherwise," she said.

The carriage stopped at her inn, and I assisted her down. Still smiling, I waved as the carriage rolled away to take me back home.

Actually, I had not thought "otherwise" about the countess's capacity for greed but had figured that she would quickly make a move to take over "my inheritance" completely. As soon as she cleaned out the house, I would find myself in that unmarked grave I always see when I look deep into the woman's eyes. If el diablo had a daughter, she would be it.

About now an unsigned message composed for me by Mercedes was being delivered to the viceroy's aide, informing him that staying at the inn was a notorious actress and temptress who was recently incarcerated in Vera Cruz and now has been fleecing local men.

Cries for assistance from me would come from her cell in the viceroy's jail, to which I would promptly reply that I was making arrangements to buy her freedom. It would take a few days before she realized that I was the one behind her woes. She would then try to use my own criminal background to get her out of jail, but by then I would have headed north, leaving the city in my dust. I hoped.

It was a cold, cruel world we lived and died in, with some of us handling the cruelties better than others. If I had not turned her in to the viceroy for what she did to me, I would have done it for what she did to Nina Alvarez.

The countess was a vicious bitch, and I could see that she enjoyed destroying the other woman, going beyond mere revelations about Carlos's scheme to slicing her up emotionally.

Back at the shop, I had finally grabbed the countess by the arm and pulled her from the shop, leaving Nina sobbing behind us. There wasn't an ounce of pity in the countess, a fact I knew well; it was a miracle I had survived our first meeting.

I had no great sympathy for the seamstress because she had lost Carlos; he would discard her as soon as he didn't need her. But Mercedes said she had worked hard and fought to make a living as a woman, so she didn't deserve to be ground into the dirt.

I put aside thoughts of women except Mercedes, because now I had to get El Mestizo released before he was tortured to death and get myself too far from the hangman for his noose to reach.

NINETY-ONE

"CARLOS IS CONVINCED that you're a bandido," Mercedes said.

Smart man. We were in her carriage on the way to the convent at Chapultepec.

"The uncle from Guadalajara hasn't seen Antonio since he was a boy," she said, "but he has a family portrait that he showed Carlos and—"

"And Carlos said I don't look like Antonio."

"I also heard him tell the uncle that he had received a message from a man he sent to Xalapa to get information. Something about the bandido having a chestnut stallion and Antonio didn't have one."

We had met outside the city, and I hitched Rojo to the carriage for the ride to Chapultepec. Before we reached the convent, I was going to leave the carriage and Mercedes was to turn around and return to the city. It was the viceroy's day to tend his rose garden at the convent, and I was going to pay him a visit—one that most likely would turn out to be a battle for my life as I fled his wrath and guards.

"You must tell the viceroy the complete truth," Mercedes said. "He is a good man; he will do the Christian thing."

I merely nodded.

Eh, "the Christian thing" would also include hanging me as quickly as possible. And the "complete truth"? Mercedes was too young and had been too sheltered to realize that even the most indisputable facts were subject to interpretation—the greatest minds in the world could not even agree upon whether the sun flew around the earth, as the church claimed, or the earth around the sun. Truth was what the man with the biggest gun said it was, and it only lasted until another bigger gun rewrote it.

El Mestizo had already warned me that, no matter what evidence was presented to the viceroy, Carlos—as the true heir to a big fortune—could buy his way out. Mere murder had a price, but what Carlos had done to the bloodlines of horses was a worse crime to the gachupins because it would cost so many so much.

The viceroy was also hardly going to listen to the truth from me. Once I revealed to him that I was a mestizo bandido, it wasn't likely that the viceroy would let me get much farther. He would have me silenced quickly and permanently because I was a threat to the colony and his tenure as its lord and master.

But I had to get across to the viceroy that if he acted expeditiously against Carlos with a permanent solution—summary execution after taking El Mestizo's place for a bit of torture—it would keep a flame away from the powder keg Carlos had created.

"As soon as El Mestizo is released, I am going to disappear," I told Mercedes.

"I'm going with you—"

"No, I told you, there are too many hardships."

"You can't tell me what to do."

That was probably true. Her father had tried it and failed. Carlos, too. But she had never spent days in the saddle or worked with her hands until they were raw and her back ached.

I didn't say anything because I knew it would do no good. I would go north and make a suitable life and come back and get her even if she had married in my absence.

"Ah, señorita, living like a gachupin has been a burden on my shoulders. Life was so much simpler for me when all I had to worry about was begging for food."

I dropped some gold coins into the collection box again as I entered, hoping I would be able to buy my way into heaven.

The viceroy was on his knees with his back to me trimming a rosebush when I came up behind him. I pulled my bandana up to cover most of my face as I approached him in the deserted garden.

He started to turn as he heard me approach.

"Sister, I'm glad you're—"

The cold feel of steel against his ear shut his mouth.

"Don't turn your head, señor, or speak, because my finger is very nervous on the trigger. You have never seen me and will never see me again, but listen carefully because you must right a wrong and avoid a scandal that would ignite the wrath of the king . . ."

NINETY-TWO

CARLOS INTERCEPTED THE viceroy's aide coming out of the government center as he pulled up in his carriage with his Guadalajara uncle.

"He's an imposter!" he told Riego.

"Who's an imposter?" the surprised aide countered.

"Antonio de los Rios—only he's not Antonio; he's the bandido who shot the other highwaymen."

Riego gaped at Carlos. "What madness are you shouting?"

"Look." Carlos grabbed the painting of the Rios family that the uncle had brought. "This is Antonio."

Frowning, Riego peered closely at the boy Carlos pointed at in the background of the painting of the Rios family.

"It's a child," Riego said.

"But—but you can see he's not Antonio." Carlos was so angry and excited, he stuttered.

"Señor Rueda, you are being offensive. It appears that you are so overwrought about your personal problems and not getting the inheritance that it has affected your mind."

"Can't you see that he doesn't have the mannerism of a gentleman? Did you know he shoes horses?"

"I understand El Mestizo also has learned the art to protect his valuable mounts from incompetent shoers," the aide said.

Carlos was ready to explode. He knew Riego didn't like him and would find reasons not to rule in his favor.

"Everything about him is slightly askew," Carlos said. "I learned from his servants that he doesn't use his fork and knife as they are accustomed to seeing people of quality use the utensils. He even sometimes addresses them as if they were equals instead of servants."

"I don't know what to say about Señor Rios's table manners or the way he talks to servants," the aide said, haughtily, "but he carries papers that give him ownership of the Rios estates. Frankly, señor, I would be careful with my opinions about the young man who has become heir to an estate that you also desired. I would hate to meet him on a field of honor. Don't forget, he killed two bandidos while defending himself."

"You don't understand—there's the red horse."

"Red horse?"

"The chestnut with red coloring, you fool. My man Diego said the bandido who came to Antonio's aid had the chestnut horse, but that the carriage didn't have a horse hitched to—"

Carlos abruptly shut up. Saliva from his mouth ran down the corner of his mouth. He had called the second most powerful administrator a fool and just intimated that Diego had been at the scene of the attack.

Don Domingo stared at Carlos, his own mouth agape.

The attention of the men was suddenly diverted to a guardsman of the viceroy who had galloped up to the palace.

"Señor Riego! An urgent message from the viceroy! An order for arrest and seizure of a stallion."

"The arrest of Don Carlos de Rueda and seizure of

his stallion, El Rey, is ordered forthwith," the aide read aloud.

When the aide turned back to speak to Carlos, the man was gone.

"Where'd he go?" he asked the uncle.

The elderly man shook his head. "I don't know." He pointed at the line of horses hitched at the posts in front of the palace. "He took one of the horses."

Riego shouted orders at the palace guards to find Carlos, sending them to Carlos's city house.

The uncle stared dumbfounded at Riego. "How does Carlos's man know so much about the horses of Antonio and this bandido?"

Riego ignored him and stared at the viceroy's message again, trying to make sense of what had happened. As he gathered his wits, a wagon piled high with maize pulled up and a thin young man with a bad leg crawled down from it.

Still in shock by the sudden events, Riego merely stared at what appeared to be a filthy beggar approaching him with a bad limp.

Pulling himself up straight, the emaciated beggar said, in an upper-class voice, "Señor, I am Antonio de los Rios of Madrid, here before you by the grace of God and his majesty the king."

NINETY-THREE

RETURNING TO THE city in her carriage, Mercedes had just reached the causeway when she told her driver to turn around.

"Do you know how to find the ranch of El Mestizo?" she asked her driver, who was also the house stableman.

"Sí, señorita."

"Take me there."

She wasn't going back to the city. Not now—probably not ever.

She had been struggling with the decision to leave and go with Juan because she had a good concept of what being on the run with him would be like—all she had to do was look at the hardships of people around her to comprehend that life would be hard and harsh if she left the safe cocoon where she had been born and raised.

But it was her one chance at happiness and to experience infinitely more of the world than she would be able to locked and stuck away in an arranged marriage.

She would not miss her father, although she loved him as a daughter should. But there was not a great deal of warmth in their relationship, and sometimes she felt as if she were an item on his ledger of goods, but she knew he cared for her and she cared for him.

What she felt for Juan she couldn't express or even

understand. Although her feelings for Juan were in her heart, he stirred her desires, too. He was also different than other men in a way that was important to her—he respected her, not because she was a woman, but as a person.

Raised in a society in which women were rarely taught to read and didn't know the breed of one horse from another, Juan excited her because he was interested in her opinions and ideas.

That he was a wanted horse thief and bandido who might end up with his neck stretched at the end of a rope was intimidating, but if they traveled north and started fresh in a land where questions weren't asked . . . she could help Juan build his dream of a horse ranch . . . maybe even start a family . . .

She was knocked out of her musing when her carriage came to an abrupt halt as they entered the long road that led to most of the horse ranches of the wealthy outside of the city.

Carlos raced his horse up to the open carriage. His expression scared her—he was grim and wild-eyed.

"Where is he?"

"Who?" she asked.

"The bandido posing as Antonio."

"I don't know what—"

"Shut up! You're lying!"

She gaped at him, mortified. He had never spoken to her before with such venom in his voice.

"I know you've seen him. Your aunt saw you sneaking out. They're coming for me, but I'm going to kill him first before they find me."

"Drive on!" she shouted to her groom.

Carlos shot the groom in the head.

"I'll make sure he comes looking for you," he said.

NINETY-FOUR

I WAS RUBBING down Rojo in front of El Mestizo's stable when my benefactor arrived, and I watched him step out of his carriage. I resisted the urge to run over and give him a hand and instead pretended I didn't see what an effort it was for him to move his pained body.

He supported himself with a cane, and I didn't look over to him until he was seated on a bench, with his back to the stable wall. His head was tilted up to catch the sun. His skin had a gray pallor, the color of flesh attacked by maladies that eat body and soul, only in this case it had been the hand of man and not of God that had sucked his lifeblood.

He was lucky to be alive, but his body would never recover, and I wondered how long he would live.

"I wish I had a good woman who would give me a rubdown as often as this horse gets one," I said.

He said nothing, just sat still, soaking up the sun, and I went back to rubbing the stallion's coat. I was saddling Rojo when he spoke.

"I felt from the first moment I saw you that fate had placed you before me, but I had always thought that you were on a collision course with my brother. It is a great surprise—and a pleasure—for me to discover that God's intent was to save my life."

"Señor, I don't know anything about God's

intentions, but I know I would have died begging while crawling on all fours if not for you."

"What I did took a few coins I didn't earn. Anyone could have done the same thing with little effort. But you are the kind of man that my father would have wanted holding a sword beside him. There are few such men left—neither my brother nor I are among them."

That wasn't true, at least in the case of El Mestizo, who had survived the tortures of the damned and had not given up his brother's folly.

I told him that as we drank brandy and I smoked tobacco.

This was the last time I would see my benefactor, and we both knew it. I was sure that by now there would be posses in all directions from the city searching for me.

I stayed awhile longer and talked to him, getting him to laugh as I described my adventures with the countess in Vera Cruz and Mexico City.

"The woman has more tricks than an indio conjuror," I told him.

We barely spoke of Carlos, though he admitted that the man's refusal to show the stallion in public had raised a few eyebrows over the years, but no one wanted to delve too closely—Carlos was part of the Cortés family by marriage, and the horse was of the bloodline of Cortés's own warhorse, so it would have been sacrilege to have questioned either.

"Besides, nobody wanted to probe any deeper," he said.

When I got up to leave, he didn't ask me where I was heading and I didn't volunteer it. It didn't matter—we both knew I would never be back to the city or anywhere else my face was known.

I had a question that had been on my mind since the day I woke up in the stable and saw him staring down at me.

"Why? Why me? You speak of fate, of your brother. What is it? Why did you help me?"

"You're my nephew. More than that, the two greatest bloodlines in all the Americas run in your veins."

The words didn't mean anything.

If he had told me I was the king of Spain I would have found it no more dumbfounding than for him to tell me I was his nephew—*a Cortés*.

"I knew it when I saw you. Your mother was a granddaughter of Montezuma and a Toltec princess he married before the conquest. Because she was both Toltec and Aztec royalty, she grew up as a ward of my father on his hacienda in the Oaxaca area."

"More likely a prisoner of your father," I said, "to keep her from rallying indios against the invaders."

"Perhaps, but my father did not have the same disrespect and contempt for indios that many others who had not fought them have. He witnessed their courage. But that aside, your mother was a beautiful young woman. So lovely that my brother . . . impregnated her."

My blood rose. "You mean he raped her."

El Mestizo turned away for a moment before coming back to meet my eye. "I don't know what happened. A pretty young india girl, a young caballero who had too much to drink—whatever took place, understand that the marquis is not a bad person. I was raised in the shadow of my father, and no one expected anything from me. He was still a boy when our father died and he was pushed out front, with everyone in the colony expecting him to be the warrior-conqueror that our father was."

"Eh, my heart bleeds for the rich bastard," I joked, but my guts were wrenching and my heart was choking in my throat. I realized I had a tight grip on my pistola. "How did my mother end up in a whorehouse?"

"My brother's Spanish mother, Juana, was responsible for that. My father had already recognized one offspring of an india—me—as a son. Juana, the Spanish aristocrat he married after the conquest, wanted to make sure there were no more claims against what she wanted for her own children. My father was already dead, or he would never have permitted it."

"Your father stole an empire, abandoned your mother, and gave what should have been your inheritance to your younger brother."

El Mestizo smiled. It caught me by surprise.

"My father *won* an empire, the same way the Aztec and every other indio empire ever did, through force of arms. He married a Spanish woman instead of my mother, and left his title and estate to his Spanish son because that was the only way they could be kept in the family. If he had left it to me, the king would have forfeited it."

"Your brother—does he know?"

He nodded. "Doña Bernaldina suspected it when she saw you at the viceroy's ball."

"Ah . . . so I got the invitation to their party so she could get a look at me without soot on my face."

My head was swirling, and I could see that El Mestizo was tiring badly, barely able to sit up straight.

"I'll help you into the house."

He waved me off. "No, leave me here to enjoy the sun. I can feel its warmth healing my broken soul." He smiled up at me. "Go on, Don Juan Cortés y Montezuma. Take the fine horse you stole from me and go far enough away so the viceroy forgets you ever existed. When we meet again, we will both be in hell."

"No, amigo, I have felt el diablo's grip on my ankles many times, and I know he is getting impatient waiting for me, but you will sing with the angels and drink fine brandy while I sup on worms at the Dark One's table."

Martín Cortés, the second Marquis del Valle de Oaxaca, was coming up the road to the house as I was leaving it.

He stopped his horse and stared at me, keeping his features blank, his thoughts a secret.

I stopped the stallion abreast with him.

"How is my brother?"

"As well as any man whose bones and flesh have been broken for a crime he didn't commit can be."

"Those who did this to him will pay."

"No, they won't," I said. "Because you are not the man to do it. You'll sulk back to Madrid or wherever the king decides you'll go and keep your mouth shut because you have the cojones of a mouse."

He reacted as if I had slapped him in the face—which I had—jerking out his quirt and raising it.

"Do you know who I am?"

"No, señor, I do not know you."

I rode on, not looking back. I did not want to ever see his face again.

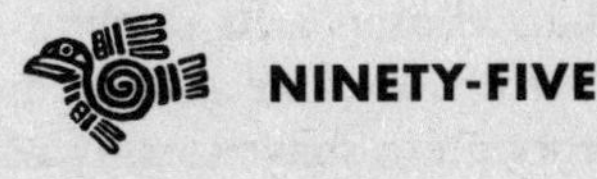

NINETY-FIVE

THE MAN WAS waiting for me as I came through the ranch gate and onto the road. He was sitting on his horse a hundred feet from the gate—just sitting there, smoking a tobacco twist, no gun in hand.

I didn't know his name but we had met before, in a manner of speaking. He was the one I had observed on the ledge watching murderers attack and kill Rios and his coachmen.

Seeing him again made my flesh crawl.

I had had a premonition that something would go wrong with my plan to head north and leave my problems in the dust Rojo kicked up. Things had been going too well. I knew it was time for something to go wrong.

I settled Rojo into a slow walk as I sized up the situation and looked around to see if any more surprises could be waiting for me.

I had a pistola in a holster strapped under the right side of my jacket that I could pull with my left hand and one attached to the saddle I could pull with my other hand.

Not seeing anyone else lurking around, I kept a steady eye on the man as Rojo slowly took me to him. I didn't see a weapon in his hand, but I knew he had to have one in easy reach.

If this was going to be a shoot-out, my biggest advantage lay in having it occur before we got into a range where pistolas were reasonably accurate because the guns I had were a little unusual.

From Uncle Ramos's fine collection of weapons, I had chosen two dueling pistolas; a sword with a hard, Toledo steel blade; and a dagger that was sharp enough to shave cleanly with. Examining the dueling pistolas, I had learned that Uncle Ramos had been both clever and devious because one of the barrels was rifled.

Rifling involved making a spiral cut into the inside of a barrel so that when the ball fired, it would spin and go straighter as it fired out. It was a very expensive process and would be considered ill-mannered to have the spiral grooves done to dueling pistols. Eh, the last thing anyone wants on the field of honor is to have the pistolas accurate. Most duels end up as draws because the shots go wild.

There were interesting things about the dueling pistolas. Ramos had three made—even an ignorant lépero like me knew only two are used in a duel. Two pistolas were exposed in the wood case, but the weight of the box had not felt right to me after I removed them. I found the third one, the gun with the rifled barrel, in a secret compartment.

When I confronted the majordomo with the hidden pistola, he confessed that, over twenty years earlier, Ramos had had the rifled gun made and concealed in a way so that after his opponent had chosen one of the two exposed weapons for the duel, Ramos could take the rifled one himself without anyone noticing.

But his opponent had backed off to the challenge, so the gun was still a virgin. I carried it now in the holster concealed beneath my jacket.

Sitting on his horse, the man still had not touched a weapon as I slowly moseyed up to him. His lips were twisted in a sardonic grin, his face full of malicious amusement.

"Don Carlos has your woman," he chuckled. "He says he wants to talk to you."

"Keep grinning at me like that and I'm going to cut your lips off."

That didn't sit well with him.

I tensed as I saw his hand brush his pistola, but he wasn't ready yet. He just kept his grin.

He was a coward—that was why he had stayed back and let the two men he had hired do the killings. He would shoot me only when I had my back turned to him. I knew that because the man and his master were different from street trash only in the clothes they wore, which meant Carlos wasn't waiting to talk to me.

Once we got to Carlos's ranch and he stepped out to confront me, this man would shoot me in the back. I knew Carlos' way of thinking.

The more I thought about it, the more sense it made. Carlos took no chances, and neither did his assassin.

I didn't muse over my conclusion but reacted out of pure instinct.

I grabbed my Toledo blade by the hilt and pulled it out, swinging it in one fluid motion. As it came across in the air, the blade caught a beam of sunlight and reflected like a diamond. The cutting edge of the blade caught him across the throat.

The man went off his horse backward, and I didn't bother looking to see if he still had his head—he deserved to die. I was his executioner, not his murderer, but I still didn't enjoy killing. I wiped the blade on my bandana and threw the bandana away.

I planned to take a roundabout way to get to Carlos's ranch, hopefully one he would not be watching.

Not wanting the executed man's horse to return to Carlos before I got there, I tied its reins to a tree.

"We have more business to take care of," I told Rojo.

My gut twisted thinking about Mercedes—if Carlos had harmed her, he would not die quickly.

NINETY-SIX

FROM A HILLOCK near the heart of his hacienda, I scouted out the main buildings of Carlos's ranch. I saw no vaqueros working, no movement at all, and that surprised me.

Witnesses, I thought—Carlos sent them packing because he didn't want anyone around who could talk about the murders.

Mercedes would also be a witness. He would have to kill her, too. And he would have killed his hired assassin, as well, because he knew too much.

Ayyo . . . gachupins created such bloody complications as they competed with each other for *more things*—more gold, more prestige, or whatever else they lusted after.

In my mind I placed Carlos on the second floor of the main house watching for me and his man to approach from the direction of the road.

I descended from the hill in the back, pistola in hand, having Rojo jump one corral fence to keep my approach mostly blocked by outbuildings and then over another fence.

As he came off the second jump, Rojo turned his head left. I followed his gaze and saw the barrel of a musket poking out of a window.

The musket went off, and I felt the stallion jerk under me. My feet were already kicking out of the reins as he went down on his right side. I couldn't clear him fast enough, and I hit the ground with my left leg under Rojo's flank, my pistola flying out of my hand.

The stallion let out a screeching cry of pain and kicked, but he couldn't get up.

I reached for the backup pistola on the left side of the saddle, my leg still pinned under Rojo, when a shadow fell across me and something slammed into my head, knocking the senses out of me for a moment.

Like a snake still thrashing even after its head's been cut off, my hand went back up to grab for the pistola but another hand beat me to it.

Carlos glared down at me, his face a mask of hate and rage.

He stomped me in the stomach. "You are a filthy bug, a disgusting lépero. You have ruined everything I have worked for!" He cocked my pistola. "Now it's my turn."

He grunted and stumbled, his knees buckling until he knelt beside me. Mercedes was behind him, a fire log in her hand.

He still had the pistola in his hand, and as he brought it around to shoot me in the face, I punched him in the abdomen, not with my fist but with the spring blade I had taken from the countess and attached to my own wrist.

His eyes bulged and he gaped at me as I pulled the blade out and swung up, sticking it in the soft flesh under his chin.

NINETY-SEVEN

I KNELT BESIDE Rojo and gave him one last rub-down, tears freely flowing down my face as I took my pistola and ended his suffering.

I felt like I had just lost a good friend.

Mercedes refused to let me take her to El Mestizo.

"I'm not leaving you," she said. "I'm going with you to help you build that new life you've been talking about."

"That's insane. You know nothing except instructing servants and flirting with caballeros."

"You can teach me. If you can learn how to be a gachupin, I can learn how to be a mestizo."

We rode out of the ranch together, with her mounted behind me on the best stallion I could find from Carlos's herd of horses. I didn't take El Rey, but left it for the viceroy to find and deal with.

"I can ride a horse myself," she said, but I told her to wait because we would get hers on the way.

"Why can't we take one of these?"

"We're going north to raise horses, and I want to do it with a horse that has the bloodline of the conquest—one that carries the bloodline of the finest stallion in New Spain—like Rojo."

"Where are you going to find such a horse?"

"In its mother's womb not far from here. Ayyo! I almost got hanged because I let Rojo make love to her."

"Will the owner sell the mare to you?"

"Sell it?" I howled with laughter. "Woman, mestizos don't pay for horses."

"We steal them!" she shouted.